To Donna

D1528155

Along the Way

By

Michael J.Morris

Thank you
for your purchase
and I hope this
brings back Memories
of Manchester
M J Morris

Forward

I have always felt that the Forward to most books is either very helpful in setting up the story I am about to read or just a chance for the author to provide discourse that they felt compelled to write, many times unrelated to the story itself.

In this case I just want to thank you for choosing this little story of mine and helping you to understand the structure. Each chapter is titled after a song that I have found especially poignant in my life at some point. At the end of the book, I have included an appendix that lists the songs and the performers. I suggest that if you haven't heard one or more of these songs to find a source and give them a listen.

One final word - these characters are fictional, but many are based on some people that passed my way. Manchester College is very real, and I believe, one of the finest places in the country to get an education. My daughter was the fourth generation in our family to graduate a Spartan. And obviously, Fort Wayne is my hometown. I can't think of anywhere I would have loved more to spend my life.

This book is dedicated to my wife, Michele, my children - Kristin and Stephen, my sister and brothers, and my parents. And of course, I want to thank Manchester College for the backdrop to most of the story and the commitment the school has to its students, including me.

Finally, I would like to thank the National Writing Project, and specifically the Appleseed Writing Project in Fort Wayne for inspiring me to complete this book.

Chapter One
<u>I'd Like to Get to Know You</u>

I don't know where it went. I don't know if I threw it away a long time ago, or if I just misplaced it. It really doesn't seem that important anyway. But it has always been filed away, at least in my mind. Not because I yearn for that girl or because it was a missed opportunity. But, it was a defining moment for me. And that picture and a letter are all that I have left of her.

Over the years, I have noticed that there is a small section of my brain maintained for the express purpose of filing these experiences that have molded me as I am now. I have no delusions that I am more than I have ever thought that I am, but I do pride myself on the fact that I am a decent, caring person, and that I am good to my family and have deserved the respect of my peers. Yet, I know what I have gone through and what is in that tiny section of my brain. Whenever a so-called crisis evolves in my present life and sometimes for no reason at all,

4

this data center churns up and sends me to the appropriate flashback in my past. It is through these messages that I have been able to put my life in its proper perspective and keep it constantly balanced. It was on a normal day though that the past surfaced from its tiny section in my brain, and it was that picture and letter that my mind was reaching for.

In the picture, she was walking away from the camera. Her head slightly turned to see if the picture was being taken. Of course, it was. I don't even know who took the picture. The only thing that I remember is that slight smile, knowing that she was teasing me, hundreds of miles away. Oh, and I had never even met her.

My brain chose to take me back on a routine day. The traffic around me allowed my thoughts to wander. Suddenly, my mind was triggered back by a song on the radio. It is really amusing and amazing how our culture became so music based in the 60's and 70's. Observing the students in my classes, it has carried on today. No matter the age, the race, the gender, the social standing - there is some form of music that stimulates our emotions. I am a firm believer in music and its effects. Daily I see these effects on my students.

That day on one of those "oldies" stations on the radio, I heard "I'd Like to Get to Know You" by Spanky and Our Gang. Driving home in the car on the way home from school, the radio is usually no more than a background sedative after a long day. Admittedly, I didn't listen to the song immediately, at that time in the day I seldom do. With traffic backed up and getting slower and my son David's birthday party only minutes away, I just wasn't ready for memory lane. Those lines though - "I'd like to get to know you, yes I would", they grabbed my attention and propelled me beyond the traffic and my present day thoughts. The present was a blur, and gradually I was transported back; images of late 1967 and 1968 took over.

Ray Osborne was the first face to appear; that song took me directly to my memories of him in that year, the late summer day when I was headed off to college. Ray and I went back to fourth grade together, so it was by no means unnatural that when I went off to college that he would be my only friend sending me off and corresponding with me on a regular basis. I have always sensed that he wished he were me, leaving Fort Wayne for new horizons and adventure.

Ray was there when I first attempted to ask Mary Syminski as my first date in my sophomore year in high school. He was also there when I spilled a malt all over Mary at the Dairy Freeze the next night on the date. He is a gangly sort I guess. Medium tall, skinny, light brown hair. Yet, he had a way with girls. He could talk to them without breaking into hives and sweating through a t-shirt and shirt. I was in awe of him.

I don't think he ever really believed that I actually envied him. He had worked hard to put away a tidy little sum for his future, and he was sure it was going to happen. He left high school and immediately into the work-a-day world. The factory where he worked gave him satisfaction; and he had a fiancé, Diane Fisher, waiting for him over four hundred miles away. They wanted to be married on their own terms in the time period they selected. I wanted that too, but an education was also important for more than the usual reasons.

I began my studies at Manchester College immediately after high school. Fears of the Vietnam War made me irrational at the time. I had been an uninformed teenager in the area of government and foreign affairs throughout my high school years. Manchester was always a part of my plans, although I had toyed with the idea of going to Ball State or Hillsdale. But as summer approached, my awareness of Vietnam and what it was doing to the young people of America heightened my need to be in college. Then I heard about Terry Jones, a high school dropout who used to be a friend in my freshman year. Terry had joined the Army to prove to his family that he wasn't stupid and worthless. He was in the jungles of Vietnam when he was accidentally shot by one of his own men. Terry died a long way from home, and I was pretty sure without making his point.

Without any school assignment attached, I began to research this war. No high school history class motivated me to learn better. I then knew the warmth and safety of college was better than fighting a war no one seemed to want. To this day, I still maintain the Vietnam War increased the education of more people than any other event. At the very least, a large number of young men attempted education beyond high school.

Manchester College is a small private college located less than an hour from Fort Wayne in northern Indiana. Here, I could be away from home and able to "do my own thing", yet I would still be able to get home quickly if it became necessary. By no stretch of the imagination was I even attempting to break from my family, as evidenced by my almost weekly trips home once I started at Manchester.

If this gives you the impression that I was an insecure teenager tied to his family and friends at home, you are probably right. It took me at least five to six weeks to realize that my life as an individual had started. Dirk Thomas, Don Bates, and Wayne Renfroe had a lot to do with my initiation to the burgeoning new world. Oh, yes, that world opened up because of Linda Warner, Julie York, and Alicia Williams, especially Alicia. And, as always, Ray Osborne.

That day in late August of 1967 was sunny and hot. I had driven my '60 Ford Fairlane from my grandparents' cottage at Lake Webster, just a half hour north of Manchester. The last words of parents, grandparents, and siblings were soaring in my mind. Grandpa was the most eloquent, "My eldest grandchild, Mr. Mark Logan, set to test the waters of academia.

Better yet, at my alma mater. We're all proud of you son." He stopped for a second then and put his hand on my shoulder. He turned me away from everyone else and confided only to me, "We will always be here for you. You know that don't you Mark?" With that my grandfather hugged me for the first time in - I still can't remember another time. That always seemed strange to me since he was minister.

Each one of the family had their say; I choked back the intense feelings. I felt at that time the crossroads that were approaching. I knew what it meant, and it was obvious to them as well. Before my mother could say another word, I gave her a peck on the cheek and jumped into the car. Ray came over, reached in, and slugged me in the arm. "Get back in town as soon as you can. I'll take care of everything till then." I wasn't quite sure what he meant, but there were many times that I wondered what Ray was getting at.

Then I took a long last look; as if I would never see them again. Actually, I never saw them with the same eyes again. As I accelerated away from them and as they faded farther into the distance in the rear view mirror, I remembered when I would stay there at the cottage and go home with my family after a last fling at the lake before the school year began. That never happened again.

Since the drive was a short one, I was in Manchester in no time. Manchester is not only the name of the college, it is also in the name of the town, North Manchester. There is no South Manchester, or any other Manchester for that matter. Probably one of the biggest draws for the town was the college, still is. It is ironic that the college was also despised by most of the townspeople who were a combination of itinerant workers, farmers, store owners, and factory workers. A number worked at the college, but many of them disliked the atmosphere of the campus and its students.

I had attended freshman orientation in July, and I had checked out the campus once football was done the previous fall. I still loved the stereotypical nature of the school. The campus at Manchester is green and almost parklike. When I visited the campus in the fall of '66, I fell in love with the quaint old dormitories and classroom buildings, many of which were built at the turn of the century. Calvin Ulrey Hall, the dorm that I had chosen, was one of these. There

were a couple of dorms that were much newer,
but they had much less intrigue and character.
The class buildings were situated within the vast
city block that was the main campus. Except for
the student union and a girl's dorm, all of the
other buildings were contained in that city block.
There was a fine arts building next to the science
building. Across the commons area were the
library and communications building. The social sciences and business classes met in the
administration building north of the other buildings and directly opposite was the auditorium
and lecture hall. Behind these buildings, on the
perimeter, were the dorms. Men's dorms on the
west side; women's on the east. Supposedly this
would keep the men from "disturbing" the wom-
en. After all, it is a Christian college!

What I hadn't noticed on the two previous trips to Manchester was the students and
faculty. They were people I passed and gave me
information. Sure, I did remember a female face
or two, but for the most part, they were all new
to me. Paradoxes were abundant here. It was
truly a microcosm of what the world was like at
the time.

Getting out of the car behind Calvin Ul-rey, I only noticed the building. What happened next started my education, before any class had convened. I entered the structure with my arms full and my legs shaking. The halls were empty and dark. Quickly, I turned around and looked at the parking lot outside the dorm. There were a few cars, but there was no evidence of life inside.

Then I saw him coming toward me. A more unimposing figure, I had never met. He was five feet ten, probably two hundred and forty pounds. He wore thick Coke bottletop type glasses that were solidly black rimmed. His clothes were well worn and severely covered with holes and dirt. His eating habits were up front on his sleeve, the front of his shirt, and the corners of his mouth. When I left home, I saw this same person in my slob little brother Wade. His name was Don Bates. That is what he told me as he approached me; he also told me that he was a senior. The fact that Don was a senior escaped reason. Later, I would realize that Don compounded this jaded image with his inability to get to class. He was, I learned afterward, the epitome of the "professional student."

He informed me that he had been assigned to assist me and all other new students in learning the ropes of college life and become acclimated to my new living environment. A beer (one of many no no's at Manchester) looked very much at home in Don's left hand. A huge sandwich was loading down the right hand. As he led me into deep into the murky second floor of Calvin Ulrey Hall, he turned and without any remorse belched to the point I was sure it was his normal way of exhaling. "This is home, I love it and it loves me. You might say we are one and the same." Peering past Don to the faint hall in front of me, I could see what he meant. There were various forms of filth dripping from places that didn't look as if they could hold anything. I could swear that I saw a furry creature the size of a small dog scurry from one mass of slime to another.

Bates went on, "I'm resident director on your floor because no one else can control me. They gave the job to me thinking I would be the best influence on me. They were right; look at the improvements." I didn't have the faintest clue as to where these supposed improvements might be. "If you do anything worse than what I

14

do, I'll have to shit all over you, literally." He then looked me over and concluded, "Brown hair, green eyes, about six foot I would guess. Naive as hell! The only time you'll get in trouble is during 'rhine' week." He laughed a sinister laugh and slapped me on the back.

That word rhine was new to me at the time. I didn't find out until a few days later it was a contortion of the word "rind" like that of a watermelon. It was in reference to the color of that particular part of the fruit - green - and made the analogous transition to that of a freshman in college. It was, of course, a derogatory term embellishing all the bad connotations thereof. I was oblivious to all of this, primarily because of my trust in my fellow man, others would call it stupidity.

I eventually found my room. The door wasn't locked, so I entered. To my surprise the room was clean and well organized, a complete departure from the hallway. Had it not been for the noises in the lower bunk, my first impression of this room would have been by far my best experience at Manchester. Keep in mind that I was inexperienced to the sounds of lovemaking due to my lack of experience in the activity. This was not by choice, but was more indicative of my lack of self-confidence and Christian up-bringing.

The noise was coming from my first roommate, Wayne Renfroe, who was with one of his many conquests. At the time I was under the impression they would be getting married soon, probably had something to do with my ethics and values of the time.

Wayne rolled toward the outside of the bed and looked over to me. "Hi! I'm Wayne Renfroe. You must be my new roommate. If that is true, learn now that I will be on occasion using this room for in depth investigations. That means you will have to excuse us until I can finish the probing of this young lady." I stood there astonished and not moving at all.

As I was walking down the hall, I was sure that the resonance of the young girl's wails were only in my ears, but I began to notice that most of the doors were open, and in them were fellow Calvin Ulrey men laughing and com-menting on the sounds.

I spent most of my first day in the lounge waiting for my room to be free. I learned there that no one ever goes to the lounge except those wishing to be in transition from one place

16

to another. There were girls coming in looking for their boyfriends, parents leaving suitcases for their sons, and fellow Calvin Ulrey men heading for the vast interests of the campus. I was thinking of Ray and wishing he were in my place, and I was home. College hadn't even started and I was behind.

Chapter 2
<u>Shapes of Things</u>

The first days of college were difficult.
They included freshman orientation and lectures
from the dean and various professors. Peppered
throughout all of this were rude comments and
actions from Don Bates and the increasing num-
bers of upperclassmen as the week went along.

I went home the first weekend, risking
the wrath of Don and his cohorts. The warmth
and familiarity of my family and friends overwhelmed me, and I needed to get some clothes
washed. I called to let my parents know that I
was coming home. Mom answered. She asked
how it was going, and I had little to say. She
had gone to Manchester, as had my father. She
knew about the first week, I am sure, but said
nothing except "What would you like to have for
supper?" I don't remember what I said. Mom's
home cooking! That was good enough for me.
So, I jumped in the car, and I was on my way.

The trip to Fort Wayne took less that fifty minutes. One farm passes by, and then
another. It was endless. As I came to the south
end of Fort Wayne, I debated on stopping by

18

Ray's house before I went home, but it was near supper time. Wouldn't want to be late.

My family's home was in one of those areas that was built up after World War II after the GI's came home. Prefab homes were everywhere. Ours was pretty much the same, although I thought that it was the best in the neighborhood then Going by it now, with adult eyes, I know that it was actually just like all the rest. Mom and Dad kept it up very well. Just by looking at it, you knew that a close knit family lived there.

Mom met me at the door. "Why did you wait until today to call? I could have fixed something a little more special for you." I was after all the first of my siblings to go away to school, being the oldest, so I am sure that Mom was just as happy to see me home.

I shrugged; I couldn't tell her that I had tried, but found that "rhines" didn't have phone privileges and that it was sheer luck that I got through when I did. Each time I was near a phone to call home or Ray, there was one of the upperclassmen leering at me. For my mother I laid it on thick, "I really wasn't sure, until the last minute, that I was coming home. I had planned on staying on campus to get ready for my first classes on Monday, but everyone else went home, so I did too." Since she had gone to Manchester, she knew the lack of things to do there, so I knew that she would buy that story.

"Your father called just before you pulled up. He will be home in about 15 minutes. Your brother is playing with friends, and your sister is down the street with Margaret." My sister is only two years younger than me. She and Margaret were the bane to my existence the last two years. Since neither of them could drive, I drove them to and from school. That meant that I couldn't stay and hang with my friends. More importantly, I couldn't spend time with Julie.

Julie York and I had been friends since elementary school. At church, we were the only high school students who came regularly, other than my sister. It wasn't until March of my senior year that I realized that I saw Julie as more than the cute girl who went everywhere that I did. She lived a block away, and I guess that the proximity of our homes kept me from realizing that she had become a beautiful young lady. At least until March. At the time, I wasn't sure that I wanted to go to the prom. The previous year had been a disaster. The girl that I took was a last minute idea of my sister. It wasn't really a disaster, but my date spent more time in the bathroom with her friends than with me. I never called her again.

It took me bribing myself to make the phone call to Julie. I didn't want to have her laugh at me when I asked her to the prom. We had spent so much time in the last few years debating who the other should date. I imagined while I stared at the phone how she would debate me on this one. The bribe – well, The Monkees were on TV and brand new. I loved to watch it; so I told myself that I couldn't watch it again unless I made the call. So, eventually, I did.

She didn't laugh. In fact, she answered quickly, "It sure took you long enough. I almost had to go with Jim Randle." From that point and for the rest of the year and the summer, we were dating.

I missed her, so I excused myself to my mother and moved to my room to call Julie. It rang a couple of times. Her mother answered, "Mark, I didn't know that you were going to be home this weekend. Did Julie know? I know that if she did, she wouldn't have taken off with

Ray." Ray?

Did she just say Ray? I had to ask her, "It sounded like you said she left with Ray. Do you mean my Ray?" She hesitated; finally, she said. " They went to Ray's house. You could probably find her there."

I don't remember telling Mrs. York goodbye or dialing Ray's number. But Ray answered immediately. "Hi Mark!"

I didn't give him a chance to go any further, "After supper I will be over."

"What the hell are you doing home? In your letter you didn't say anything about coming home." His tone was more surprised than what I would expect. There was silence, and then more silence. I began to wonder if Ray was still there.

I broke the silence, "I decided that I couldn't stay away too long knowing you were here in Fort Wayne and so is Julie. You know I don't trust you." In this area and only this area, I truly couldn't trust Ray. His reputation was known everywhere. When there is an opening, Ray sweeps in and takes the girl from other guys. It was always other guys, not me.

"Uh, about Julie..." He was struggling with what he obviously had done. Quickly he came back, "She's here, do you want to talk to her?"

I didn't give him the chance, "Ray, I was gone less than a week. Why do you need to do this kind of thing, especially to me?"

He was truly astonished, "How did you know?"

There was no sense in explaining. Ray never got it anyway. I understood that it was just the way that he was. To this day, I don't know why it never really bothered me, especially this time. He was appropriately apologetic and explained it away with his usual logic, "You really didn't tell anyone that you were coming home, and I thought Julie and I could keep each other company." He stopped for a second and continued, "Hey, why don't you come along?" It seemed ludicrous; it seemed like the last thing that I should do, but I said that I would.

We talked for a few more minutes and eventually decided that Ray and Julie would pick me up in about an hour. The alma mater, South Side High School, was playing their first game of the year at home. As I laid down the phone, I sat back and imagined what this night would be like. Ray and Julie would be there together. What was my role? I settled on the fact that I was there to keep us all friends, and that is one of the things that I am good at.

Dad had come home in the time that I was on the phone. Jane, my sister, was back from Margaret's house, and by the time I got to the table, Billy, the younger brother came in the back door. "Perfect timing!" He yelled it, so that the whole block could hear.

Before he sat down, Mom put her hand in front of him, "At least one layer of that dirt must come off before you can sit down at this table young man." In the time that we waited for Billy, Dad and Jane peppered me with questions about college. Dad's were tinged with envy. He never finished college and regretted it the rest of his life. In a way, I was living out his dream. Jane's questions were slanted toward discovering a new world. After all, she was only a year away herself.

After Mom said the prayer, we sat down to spaghetti and   meatballs. There was the usual table talk about each person's day. I learned that my brother had made the junior high football

24

team and that he would be playing defensive back. I had played at the same school a few years before. Jane had decided to try acting in her senior year. And Dad, well Dad had the day that he always did. He managed a service station. I worked there myself for about five years. He was great at meeting and greeting people, but we would have been broke if hadn't been for my mother's business sense.

Most of the time, I was listening, but I did drift to the upcoming situation with Ray and Julie. I'll admit that I was less than pleased with the arrangement, but there was little else to do except stay home with the family. As much as I loved them, I wanted more to be out with my friends no matter how awkward I felt. Besides, I had no hold on Julie. We had fun together, but I had never felt that we would be together forever. But that wasn't even the real problem here, Ray was the one that stumped me. He always got himself involved with girls with whom he had little or no interest. And what about Diane? He and Diane had been engaged less than a year now.

The horn from Ray's '56 Ford jarred me from these thought. He followed up with loud yelling, "College creeps allowed in this car for the next 30 seconds only!" He was around six foot tall and wore his long brown hair as the Beatles had in 1964. He looked awkward, but he was a very deft athlete and was honorable mention all conference the year before in tennis. The one characteristic of his that never quite fit was his constant need for companionship.

As I reached the front door of our house, Dad came up behind me. "Isn't that Julie in Ray's car? I thought that you two were still see-ing each other." This changed my perspective on the situation drastically as I looked out at Ray's car. Julie was sitting close to him, and they were acting more friendly than she and I had ever done. I know that I had to say some-thing. Gradually I said, "Naw, I figured that at Manchester there were going to be plenty of op-portunities for dates, and it wouldn't be fair to Julie if I kept stringing her on." For some reason I quickly added, "I guess that it doesn't matter to Ray though." I then realized that in those few words I had given myself away to my father, and told the truth to myself.

Dad had gone to his favorite chair. Jane and Billy had turned on the television and were watching the evening news. Finally, Dad said,

"You know Mark, you probably are right. Ray could use some of your common sense." With that he started to read his newspaper, and I stopped for a second to notice that the man with whom I had a running battle about every subject was on my side. He knew a lot, but he wouldn't fully realize it until his later years.

There was no turning back now. I left the door with a spring to my step. Masking disappointment was not usually part of my repertoire, but I had evaluated the situation and settled on the fact that I must play the part of "Joe College" and to not let the present situation get me down. I opened the passenger car door and acknowledged Julie. "Good to see you Julie! How have you been?" It was an honest question, not necessarily looking for an in depth answer.

Julie looked at me; I know what was coming, and I hated it. "I really meant to write, but, well, Ray came over one day and I, I, guess I just found out that we got along so well. I really..."

I had enough. I stopped her midsentence. "Look, we are friends, all three of us. There is no cause for explanations."

I think that I was convincing. Ray put his foot to the gas, and we were gone. Thankfully, his muffler was in such awful shape that we couldn't hear each other if anyone had wanted to talk. No one talked, until we arrived at the game.

In your senior year, you want out of school so bad. The irony seems to be that once you have graduated from a school, it has a pull left to bring you back. This is especially true for freshman in college. Everyone whom we saw that night at the game was from our graduating class the year before, as if we were required to return. But the game was uneventful, and the three of us felt out of place as our friends left the game early. I suggested that we get out of there too. Neither Ray nor Julie felt that there was any good reason to linger.

Ray suggested that we cruise Hall's, a local drive in restaurant. At this point, he and Julie gave each other a look. Almost immediately, Julie said to Ray, "Take me home first. I think that you two need to talk..

Without any explanation, Ray agreed, and we were heading to Julie's house. Ray pulled up in front and let her out. No walk to the

door. No good night kiss. Just a wave goodbye.
Ray pulled away, and I sensed that he was very
uneasy. He turned on the radio. We listened to
the Trogg's "Love is All Around" as loud as his
speakers could stand it.

Chapter 3
How Can I Be Sure

   Hall's was one of two major hangouts for students on the south side of Fort Wayne. Hall's still stands today, in fact on the same site that I used to "cruise." They have reestablished a drive-up where the old drive-in used to be. In the years between some of the land had been used to build a sit down restaurant, usually frequented by the retired set. "All my life's a circle," as Harry Chapin would say a few years later.

   Cruising was everything to a teenager in the late 60's. It was a holdover from the previous generation. There was a status that came from your car as it passed others in the hangouts like Hall's. When I was in a car, it told everyone who I was. It was a Ford Fairlane! In retrospect, it didn't quite say what I thought it said. But we were in Ray's car. His car was status for me as well, but his car was better. Because he had a job, he could afford the newest technology in his car. That's right, he had a four track player! Never mind the eight track that would be out in few years, Ray had what everyone else wanted – music that he controlled in his own car. He didn't have to listen to what the radio told him to play. He had tapes that played what he wanted. Granted, he only had two tapes: The Spencer Davis Group and The Rolling Stones. But we played the hell out of them. Imagine, Stevie Winwood blasting "Gimme Some Lovin'" at full volume! It was teenage heaven!

As Ray pulled in slowly to speaker 12, an eerie feeling crept over me. Why had Julie wanted to leave us? I had to get to the bottom of this. Ray had been so serious, and I had detected that he and Julie were holding back something from me. If they were so close why hadn't they stayed together tonight, and why hadn't they been more like a couple? Ray isn't, and never was, one to hide his feelings very well. Ray just sat there and said nothing, but he did let out a large sigh. A long pause followed and then Ray sighed again.

This was getting weird. I have sat in driveways talking before, mostly with girls, sometimes with Ray. But he was being really strange.

Finally, he just blurted out, "You know that Diane and I are engaged and that I will be going up to see her next summer right?" I nodded and wasn't sure why that was so hard to say and was about to tell him so. "Just listen to what I have to say and don't say anything until I'm finished, okay?" Again I shook my head, and he continued. "I called Diane this past Tuesday, and we talked for a long time."

That was no revelation, so I interrupted him, "You do that all the time, get to the point. What's wrong?" I'm not sure why I was so impatient, maybe I was just out of sorts because of the night and Julie not being there for me when I came home.

The words were coming hard to Ray, but eventually he put it all together. "Diane wants you to come too." He guessed that was about to speak, and I was, "Just hear me all the way first."

It was apparent now that he was extremely serious and didn't wish any more breaks in his concentration. "Julie knows all about this and, in fact, and you need to know this, I'm not sure about this marriage thing and Julie is helping me right now. I mean I love Diane and all, but she is so far away, and with you at Manchester, I got no one to talk to. Even if long distance didn't cost too much..." and here he became shaky, "I love Diane so, but Julie is here. Is that wrong, Mark?"

In a way I felt sorry for him. But in another, I didn't want to let him get off cheap. "Ray, you're still a teenager, this is the way I feel to. The difference is that I haven't made a commitment to Diane or Julie or anyone else. You have. Sooner or later, you'll either have to tell Diane or get over this idea of being so far apart." I really wanted to tell him to grow up, but he wasn't and neither was I, so that seemed stupid.

I decided that it would be more to the point to get back to the idea he had brought up, "What is this about me going with you? Wasn't it bad enough for me to be with you and Julie tonight? Do you want me to spend your whole time with Diane hanging around the backseat, or more probably the case, the front seat."

Ray continued and then I found out that his predicament was not the reason we were sitting here talking, "Diane has a close friend in LaCrosse named Alicia Williams. When Diane and I were on the phone, we talked about Alicia, and then about you. Diane is afraid of what will happen to Alicia; you see, her boyfriend was drafted and went to Vietnam. Sunday, they found out that he was missing in action. Alicia has taken it very hard and has mentioned how life isn't worth living without him."

For some reason the story intrigued me, and I caught myself looking out the car window at the stars. It was a cool September night, not a cloud in the sky. A girl named Alicia. The name sounded beautiful. Her story was sad. I broke out of it though, "What does this have to do with me? I mean I feel bad for her, but..."

Getting back to business, Ray asked me, "Are, or were you in love with Julie?" I had never really considered the point at all, at least not until at this time, since Ray had taken her away from me.

I thought for a second, "I don't know. I do know that I like being with her."

Ray just smiled, "Diane and Julie both knew that you would say that, I guess I did too." After a second he came back with another question, "How do you feel about blind dates?"

A little light bulb went on, I could smell the story now. "Alicia and I together in La-Crosse next summer, that is really a long distance blind date?" A brilliant supposition, even at my lowly undergraduate status.

"Diane is sure, and so are Julie and I, that you are what Alicia needs." The pause Ray made here was for effect. "We all feel it would be good for you too." That shook me; what the hell does that mean! I felt like a charity case or something. Ray must have sensed this and explained further, "Alicia is extremely intelligent and, you can take my word for this, beautiful. She is the person you've been waiting for, and don't tell me you haven't been waiting because I have heard enough about what you want in a wife and the fact that you don't want to do anything wrong until you meet that special girl comes along." My virtuous stand on the future was coming back to haunt me. I sat there flabbergasted.

When I had finally digested what was said. I asked Ray, "Let's assume I say I'll go with you to LaCrosse, even though I will have no money since all my money will be going to college, why would Alicia want to meet me or even know who I am. She just lost a boyfriend, maybe, and replacing one this way is not exactly what psychologists would consider wise." I was proud of the fact that I could use an education that hadn't even started yet.

"That's up to you. Diane says she knows you and how you can get people to open up to you. She figures the worst that will happen is that you will be able to put things in perspective for Alicia." Diane had lived in Fort Wayne until her family moved to LaCrosse three years ago. She knew me as well as anyone because we were next door neighbors for ten years. I had introduced her to Ray. They both meant a lot to me. They both knew me inside out.

"Wait just one minute!" I was not the sharpest knife in the drawer. "The three of you have conspired behind my back and probably behind Alicia's, without taking into consideration whether either of us want to do this. That's taking a lot for granted!" Julie was in on it too!

"That isn't all my friend!" He was looser now. He thought he had me. You know, he always did get me. "In my shirt pocket is Alicia's address. We want you to write her a letter."

I was at a loss for words. "What? I... You...I...What could I possibly write? I don't know her; from what you have told me, I am sure she doesn't know me. What could I possibly say?"

He pulled the slip of paper out of his pocket and handed it to me. I unfolded it as he started the car. There was the name - Alicia Williams, 468 Kirkwood Terrace, La Crosse, Wisconsin. I remember distinctly thinking how stupid the whole thing was and, paradoxically, how excited I felt about writing the letter.

Ray and I talked over the logistics of the coming summer and what the plans were. I heard less than half of it. I just kept staring at the name on the slip of paper. What would I be getting myself into? Would there even be a person on the other side of these letters that cared? I knew that I would do it, but I wasn't sure why.

I snapped myself back to the present. I realized that the drive home was even longer now. A road crew had torn up one whole side of State Street and traffic was stacked up for blocks. I took out my cell phone and called my wife to let her know that I would be late. As I stuffed the phone in my pocket, I wondered whatever happened to that slip of paper.

Chapter 4
The Letter

That weekend went by too quickly, but I have seldom been involved with a weekend that went on seemingly forever. Over and over that weekend, Ray and I talked about this letter writing situation. And as I discussed it with him, I became more and more intrigued with the idea. In fact on Sunday afternoon, just before I climbed into the car to go back to Manchester, I gave Ray a call. "Listen, this still sounds crazy, but you tell Diane I'll write Alicia sometime this week." I had thought out the next part all day Sunday. "There is one hitch for both of you though - neither of you can tell Alicia that I am going to write her. She will hear about this first from me, okay?" Ray had no trouble with that. More than likely this made it easy for him anyway, because he wouldn't have to get involved in the procedure again until next summer at the very least, and it takes him off the hook for this whole idea with Diane.

The whole family was there to send me off again. Mom and dad were on the glider on the porch. Billy was playing fetch with Curly our dachshund; my sister, Jane, was begging for her own car behind the glider. Grandma and Grandpa Logan were sitting at the folding table under the tree in the front yard, waiting for their weekly game of canasta with mom and dad.

The car started right up. Even though it didn't look like much, that old '60 Ford was worth every penny of the $100 that dad had paid for it. It was mine though, the symbol of my independence and, in that aspect, I was proud of it. But on the drive back to Manchester, I didn't pay much attention to the car. The turns in the road that, later in my trips back and forth to college would be intuitive, were only minor distractions. In my mind I was writing the letter. Each time it got better, and once I even entertained the idea of pulling off the road and writing it down.

The parking lot outside Calvin Ulrey was adequate for all of the residents of our hall as well as those of Ikenberry Hall. So when I pulled into the lot and saw spots on the front row, I was surprised. Either I wasn't the only person to head home for that first weekend or there was something going on in town. As I became more aware of the town and campus, I knew better than to think it could be the latter.

Even in the one week experience that I had, I was aware that serenity is not usual at any time for Calvin Ulrey. Threateningly, quiet halls greeted me as I walked to my room suitcases in hand. A sense of panic swept over me, they all knew I went home for the weekend! Surely that is punishable by some form of dastardly deed. I wasn't wrong.

I traveled to my room unencumbered. I put the key in the lock; I was home free! The key did not unlock the door because it was already unlocked. My stomach turned even though it seemed to be empty. The door swung open; I was framed in its opening. Don, Wayne, Dirk Thomas, and a few other CU men were on my bed and Wayne's. Whether they had been here very long was not one of my worries at the time. I decided to act like they were dogs about to attack. I remembered my father said, "Act casual. They sense fear." I hoped it worked for human animals as well.

I put my clothes in my closet and strolled over to my desk. Acting calm, but crumbling inside, I sat and spoke, "How are you guys? Did you have a nice weekend?" If my voice hadn't quivered with each word, I probably would have at least fooled myself.

Dirk Thomas, a senior all-conference basketball player for Manchester, rose from the bed first. My dresser stood between us as a barricade. He was six foot seven and, as he peered across the dresser, I anticipated the impending doom. But when he spoke, he spoke in a deliberate paced manner, "CU is proud of its many accomplishments. We work together and play together." He stopped, strolled around the room for at least a full minute. Then he turned sharply and put his nose directly in front of mine. "We don't go running home to mommy." I sensed hot beer laced breath.

I looked around the room in a quick survey of attitudes. No friendly faces anywhere. Dirk hadn't moved, in fact it seemed that he was trying to obstruct my view. Don was up and moving. He reached for objects under the bed that I could barely see. He picked them up one by one and passed them out to the assembled group. Periodically, I caught glimpses of some of the items - shaving cream, Ben Gay, and shaving lotions.

They began to circle around me. I had no idea what was about to happen. So when they did attack, I was unprepared. My assumption was that one of them would hold me while the others would beat me up. Nothing could be further from what really happened. Wayne, Dirk, and two guys I didn't even know each grabbed one of my arms and legs, pinning me with my limbs spread to the four compass points. Then Dirk started to unzip my pants.

In retrospect, I probably overreacted a touch, but I started to thrash and kick. At the same time, yelling at the top of my lungs, "I'm straight! I'm not gay! Leave me alone." Their response was uncontrolled laughter, and if I hadn't been shaken by their reactions, I could have freed myself. When I did realize that I had the opportunity to get away, they were back at work on me. Not too well though; I got a good kick off at Don's stomach, an easy target. He immediately focused the pain and anger on the offending leg, pulling it as if to dislodge it from its socket.

The pain of the leg distracted me from seeing that my pants were at my ankles along with my underwear. It was then that I noticed Dirk had gathered around him all of the substances. He opened each slowly. His words had a ring of retribution, "Rhines learn quickly here at CU that you do as we say, or you get burnt." He laughed a sinister laugh and began to pour the sweet smelling after shave between my legs.

Burnt was right! Almost immediately my eyes started to water, but they weren't finished yet. A progression of the substances were placed in the area of my groin; and, as I struggled to get free, I found the intensity of the heat grew. After the Ben Gay was placed strategically, my underwear and pants were replaced. Surely that was the end, I had been fool enough to think.

Don struggled to his feet, obviously still reeling from my kick. Coughing and hacking he screamed to the others, "He's not done. He deserves more for kicking me." They moved in unison. Dirk called to Wayne, "Open his closet door. He'll spend the night with his odor and clothes."

I guess it wasn't enough that they may have snuffed out my potential to father children. Once in the closet, I found that one can be jailed without escape once pennies are wedged into the lock side of the door frame. I almost lost three fingers as Dirk closed the door. The last words said as the lynch mob left the room were directed to me by Dirk, "In about two hours we'll check back to see if you are CU material yet."

Even though I have always been a little claustrophobic, my biggest concern was the aching burn between my legs. I really anticipated that they would return after a couple of minutes, but when an hour passed and no one came, I resolved myself to the fact that Dirk wasn't kidding.

I sat there in the closet trying to keep my mind off my desperate condition. Then I remembered the letter. My mind went back to it, and once again as I had done in the car, I wrote the letter in my mind. By the time that Wayne returned and released me, I had to write the letter down.

I sprinted past Wayne to my desk, grabbed a sheet of paper, and began to write. Wayne started to ask what I was doing, but thought better about it. The words just started to flow.

Dear Alicia,

Life has been unbearable without you, please come home! Hello! My name is Mark

Logan, and I have been chosen by a select group to bring you some words that you can hear nowhere else. I am one of millions of persecuted teenagers in college who, without regard to his own life, writes total strangers. Many times, shocking as it may seem, the people that we poor wayfarers write do not want to correspond with us.

After much consideration, the panel of expert (yes, expert) has decided that you, Alicia Williams, the caring and fine example of person that you are, will be allowed to take part in this once in a lifetime experience. Should you determine that you do not want to hear from or write to me, just tear this note up, or better yet, give it to another cute girl that you know, whichever you deem to be the most appropriate.

Seriously, and I can be at times. I know that things are rough for you right now. Diane Fisher explained it, and her fiancée Ray Osborne told me. They both think that I can help you, and for some strange reason that is unknown to me, that you can help me.

I don't see that I have any problems, do you? I had planned on telling you all about me. But that seems more presumptuous than I have already been. Maybe next time, whether in this lifetime or another.

Well, I guess I better go. By the way I like to write, if you couldn't tell. But I don't see this being anything like what Diane and Ray think. I think you need a friend, and I listen (or in your case read) pretty good.

Sincerely,

Mark Logan

The letter was finished in seconds. Wayne had returned during the process and was looking over my shoulder. He sat back on his bed and shook his head. "You are really weird. What in the hell are you doing? You don't even know this girl. You don't seem to want to meet her all that badly, but you are going to write to her. Lifting you is not a good idea."

I sat there pondering the word "lifting." That must have been what I just went through. Then it hit me, the burning was still there. I hurtled down the hall to the bathroom. Wayne yelled after me, "Be sure to use hot water it is

46

more effective. I ought to know, I was lifted while you were gone this weekend."

With the shower on, hot water hitting my back, I turned and the full force of the hot water hit the affected area. My shrieks caused an avalanche of laughter up and down the hall.

What a Sunday afternoon! As I managed to get my body to an even temperature again, and the catcalls had subsided some, I reflected on the situation. Wayne said he had been through this. It seemed that the others were rather adept at what they were doing. So, it was safe to assume that this was not a vendetta solely against me. Just as that thought solidified in me, another freshman ran past me in much the same state as I was in not fifteen minutes before. I debated about telling him about hot water, but realized the learning process was best in the traditional manner.

Maybe this was a form of initiation. If so, I thought I could handle it. If not, how much worse could it get. Still, no one included me in their groups, and Wayne spent his time hanging around with Dirk and Don. I held out hope that I could make it through to the next weekend and become a part of the group when stayed this time.

That evening a meeting was held by the dorm officers. Because it was an official meeting, I was less apprehensive about attending. After all, Mrs. Harrington, our dorm mother would be there. She was a diminutive white-haired widow who was supplementing her social security check by supervising this motley outfit. Her room was positioned across from the lounge on the main floor. It was virtually the middle most room in the hall. She had such a beautiful smile and seemed so genuinely helpful to all of us. Surely, nothing would happen with her at the meeting.

Don chaired the meeting with all of Calvin Ulrey's residents reclining, sitting, or standing in various positions around the basement recreation room. Don walked slowly to the make-shift podium consisting of a table with a cardboard box set upside down on top of it. He smiled over at Dirk and the rest of the officers, put his fists in the air, and screamed at the top of his lungs, "Let the games begin!"

Waves of cheers flooded the room. I felt panic setting in and, as I gazed around the room, I could see the same feeling on only about a quarter of the faces. Not a freshman was smiling. We were even less excited when Dirk brought out a board with names all over it. I saw my name and, as my eyes surveyed the rest of the names, it became clear that the only names on the board were freshmen. It was a chart, and at the top of it was the caption "Rhine Bowl - 68." The Christians and the lions - why did that image appear just then? More importantly, why was I debating inside myself, which I would be?

Don bellowed for everyone to shut up. He then delivered his litany, "It has been tradition at Manchester College, and especially at CU, that the upperclassmen welcome the incoming naive, stupid," Dirk came to him and whispered in his ear. Don laughed and corrected himself while looking directly at Mrs. Harrington, "I mean these impressionable young men we call rhines, I mean freshmen. Yes, we will be celebrating your attendance here. You might call it a 'rite of fall.' Each of you new rhines, you don't mind me calling you that do you?" He paused for response that could not possibly come due to the fear among those whom he had addressed. He continued. "I didn't think that you would mind. Anyway, this is the time to test rhines' abilities in a plethora of athletic, intellectual, and other meaningless endeavors." I was impressed with Don's vocabulary, to this point I had heard no better than two syllable words from him. Even if he had someone write this speech for him, he still pronounced the words pretty well.

Mrs. Harrington stood at this point, there was a sour look on her face. Don must have realized he overstepped an invisible boundary, so he sat down and let her have the floor. "Now Donald, and all you other boys too, this got out of hand last year, so I am going to have to put my foot down and ask you to limit your activities to those prescribed by the college." She waved a paper in the air and placed on the table in front of Don.

She looked him in the eye, "Donald, do not lead these young boys astray. If you do, it could finally be your undoing at Manchester." She put her hand on the college memo again, pointed her withered first finger at Don's nose and walked out of the room.

Donald picked up the paper. Looked it over for two, maybe three seconds and promptly wadded it up and threw it towards Dirk who ceremoniously did a hook shot into the trash can.

Still, I was impressed with the fact that as Mrs. Harrington left, there was no disrespect for her directly through gestures or any words spoken.

Dirk went to Don again and whispered into his ear. Don fell off his chair laughing. Dirk was composed though. He looked right at me, "Mark Logan, to the front." I was there before Dirk had finished my last name. "Mark, you will be our representative to the Rhine Counsel. This is the highest honor that any rhine could get. Actually, it is the only honor that a rhine deserves. The Counsel is having its first meeting in library room 122 in two minutes."

I was in shock. I knew where the library was, but I hadn't been in there. Dirk didn't give me a chance to think, "Why are you still here. Are you trying to disgrace CU? Get going!" I was at the door when a question came to mind, so I stopped and blurted it out over Dirk's messages to those remaining. "What am I to do when I get there, sirs." The sirs part sounded too formal, but somehow I felt that being too formal at this time would be better than showing any disrespect.

Dirk moved through the crowd to me and grabbed me by the shirt, "You're going there not to screw up, because if you do, you could always spend more time in your closet."

Enough said! I was moving faster than what I ever thought I could. The library was less than a block away, so I arrived with seconds to spare. I burst in breathing very hard. In the room there were eight people sitting around a huge table. I took a seat and waited. Not a minute later, the only door into the room opened again and there stood Dirk. He walked to the other end of the room and sat at the chair at the end. He immediately took over, "Most of you are unaware of what is going to happen to you in the next week, but it is probably better that way. If at any time though, any upperclassman goes beyond the realm of decency, which is almost impossible, report the incident to Dean Jenkins. Those of you assembled in this room are the monitors of Rhine Week."

All of us were staring at him. What did this all mean? What could we do about it? As if he knew our thoughts, Dirk continued, "From this moment on, you will be like slaves. This will go on until 3 PM on Friday. Each of your dorms are having meetings right now; they are being told why you each were asked to attend

52

this meeting. By the way, they are being told
that you are getting special privileges, so it is
possible that your fellow rhines may not be talking to you when you return."

With that he left and a few other people
left as well. Those of us stunned and sitting there
were obviously the freshmen. We were frozen
with fear. We looked at each other, wanting to
compare notes to find out what to do. In a stupor gradually we all left.

Eventually, I did get back to CU. I
climbed the stairs slowly and reached my room
just as Wayne was leaving. "You get off easy
don't you? I have to wash all of Dirk's clothes
by midnight. Great deal you must have made!"
It hurt to have him say that. I mean, we hadn't
been roommates long, but I had hoped that we
could get along. So I decided to tell him what
happened.

As I reached the door, Dirk called for
me down the hall. "Mark, do you play euchre?
We've got a game going, and we need a fourth."

I had to weigh my values very quickly at
that moment. Whether it was gutsy on my part
or sheer foolishness, I yelled out to Wayne,
"Wayne, I know what they told you, but this is
my form of initiation as well. They want you all

to hate me. That way they get their laughs on
you and me at the same time." I wanted to go
on, but Wayne's eyes had gone past me to the
other end of the hall. Dirk and Don were standing shoulder to shoulder. Other upperclassmen
were coming into the hall. They were all coming to me. Wayne came to me and whispered in
my ear quickly, "Good choice, eventually they
will probably agree." With that he was down the
stairs and out of the building.

    After they were finished with me, and I
had taken a cool shower, I was assigned to be
the slave of Don, clearly the worst master of the
bunch. My insolence supposedly was the reason
for the severity with which I was being treated.
I noticed that it really wasn't that much different
from the way that Dirk treated Wayne. That was
until Thursday. Until then my most disgusting
role was of cleaning man; I cleaned the room
that had never been cleaned before. I also
washed and dried the clothes that had never been
washed and dried before. That probably wasn't
true; after all Rhine Week happened each year,
so Don's room was cleaned once a year.

    Thursday, everything changed. I
thought that I was home free; I had lived through

the week and was no more humiliated by my fellow CU men than I had done to myself through the years. We were gathered together again that evening in the rec room of CU's basement. Again Don stood before us with that look he saved for his deepest moments of plea-sure-filled torture. I had come to know the look well in just four days. He strolled in front of us as he spoke, "Literary agents will be flocking to this place within weeks. Why, many of you will probably become famous and thank me for this moment." He stopped when one of the other upperclassman corrected the term "famous." He felt that it would be better stated as "infamous."

Don chuckled and bowed to the correc-tion. He turned once again to us. "What the hell! Infamous, famous - doesn't make much difference; I just know that each and every one of you will be known by every girl on campus." A few freshman smiled; I knew better. "It's not what you think boys. You will be lepers. They won't want to come near you."

In great detail, Don proceeded to tell us about the grand finale to Rhine week. We were to write a poem; not just any poem, but one that contained as much filth and pornographic ma-terial as we could muster. Even though I had written poetry in the past, I felt embarrassed in writing this type of poem. Don finished the meeting with a warning. "If your poem doesn't match my rigorous standards for poetry, you'll have to use one of my poems." We weren't sure how the poems would be used, but as we left the room, the freshmen all seemed to agree using a Don Bates poem for any occasion would be worse than coming up with a new one.

      The meeting had been just before we all went to lunch. That gave us the rest of the day to prepare our poems. Since my classes on Thursday ended at eleven, I had the rest of the day for my masterpiece. I found myself on my walk to the student union to pick up my mail thinking of rhyming words like truck, ditch, and sick. My face flushed to the realization that I probably would be writing down the words that rhymed with the words in my head. Eventually, I brushed off all of it and decided that I could be creative and not have to use any of this at all. The real world - do it or a royal flush was ahead! You know - inverted freshman, strategically placed, head in the proximity of the water in the toilet bowl, and the ceremonial flush. Options for the royal flush - empty, full but wet, or full, but solid.

My mailbox was relegated, as were all freshman mailboxes, to the far end of the student union. Seldom was there much there. Ray hadn't written all week, and mom's letter was yesterday. This time though my mailbox was full. The usual junk mail found its way to the trash: ROTC pamphlets, magazine advertisements, and a monthly bill for my schooling. In the back of the box, crowded out by the other mail for front position was a pink envelope. It stuck out like a sore thumb. I didn't want to appear eager, but I grabbed for it and turned it to the side that was written upon. It was from Alicia. By that time in my life, the mail had no special meaning for me. That all changed with a small pink envelope.

Chapter 5
<u>Ain't Too Proud to Beg</u>

I couldn't open the letter. I walked, as in a daze, out of the building and down the sidewalks to my room. She wrote back! I guess I didn't really believe that she would. I began to wonder - What did she say? The logical response would be - Open the letter, stupid, and find out!

I did open the letter after I had verified over and over that it did come from LaCrosse. I was back in my room alone when I ran my fingers under the wax stamped flap. I thought to myself - classy, and that is when I smelled the perfume. I loved the seconds that it took to open the letter. I didn't even know this person, and yet I found myself anticipating her every word. Slowly, I unfolded the trifold letter as if it were a fragile thing. Flowing female script filled two sheets. I stared at the style of her writing and the effect on me was hypnotic. Through my reverie, I finally began to read:

Dear Crazy Person!

What is really on your mind? I know, sex! Well, you have to be one of those guys who gets vicarious thrills by reading the written words of vivacious young women through the mail. I'm not that kind of girl; you'll have to get your word thrills somewhere else with someone looser with her language than me.

That is the best that I can do. Does that prove to you that I don't need cheering up? I hope so. After I received your letter, I went to Diane and asked her what was going on. All she would tell me was that you are special and that we need each other.   I know I don't know what all of that means, but I will tell you right now, you can save yourself a lot of time. I am alright, and you don't have to cheer me up. No offense, but I do have friends here, and they are con-cerned about me for the right reasons.

I haven't meant any of this to hurt you, and I hope I haven't. Just get things straight, Ray and Diane's intentions were good, but let me assure you, they were unnecessary. Thank you for the attempt.

Sincerely,

Alicia

P.S. You sound like a really nice guy.

I was stunned. Her response was totally
contrary to what I had expected. I had been
charming, hadn't I? I really had seemed sincere,
hadn't I? It was the joking around, that put her
off. No matter what, I just went back to her last
words, "...a really nice guy." She didn't need to
throw that in at the last second. Why did she?
That was what I clung to as I began the letter
back to her.

Dear Alicia,

You can't get rid of me that easily. I
write to you expressing a deep need for a pen
pal, and you turn me down. Have you ever
heard of that happening? Some pretty pitiful
people around the world spend considerable
time each year writing letters that don't take
them very much time at all, just to put a smile on
someone's face somewhere else in the world.
And you want to take this experience away from
me. You should be ashamed! I'm deeply hurt!

In your letter you never get to the crucial matter, in fact you ignore it! Maybe I need someone to write to! I need your thoughts, your jokes, your opinions. Don't you see? This is safe for you and me. We never have to see each other, so we can step around all the games that friends and, more importantly, young people in love have to play. How many times can that happen between a boy and a girl?

Let me give you a perfect example of why I need you, and maybe you'll find something that I could do for you. Right now I am supposed to be writing a poem that is as disgusting and crude as I can get it to be. This is part of my initiation to college. From what I understand, the females of this campus will consider me as dating material sometime before Ho Chi Minh strolls through Central Park after this is over. I could use someone who is detached from the situation, someone who could look at what I have myself into and give me some advice. I need you. Have you ever heard the song by Spanky and Our Gang, "I'd Like to Get to Know You"? The words fit what could be our relationship. I don't lose anything by writing to you except time. I really would like to get to know you, not for any other reason than to have a friend without conditions or strings.

Think about it, please. At least answer this letter. I promise only eyes to read your heart.

Your friend,

Mark

No sooner had I finished the letter, than I realized that I had shed some tears in the process. Why? What was I doing anyway? This is a stranger I am begging to write to me! For some reason this had become important, and I wouldn't let it go. As I sealed the envelope and placed it in the dorm mail container, reality hit me - I didn't have a poem yet! Alicia was forgotten for the moment, but not for long.

Chapter 6
A Man Has to Go Back to the Crossroads

That night I was in rare form. My poem was the highlight of the evening, filled with innuendo. Thus, I bypassed the requirements of the upperclassmen including Don. He was particularly impressed with the rhyme I used with the phrases "tender sighs" and "throbbing thighs." Thus I was chosen to lead the CU men in the annual trip to Oakwood Hall, where all the freshmen girls were cloistered. (Times had changed a little by 1968. The girls were allowed to stay out until eleven during the week, and one on the weekends).

CU rhines were smartly attired in bathrobes and umbrellas. That was it. In one hand an umbrella; in the other the poem. There was nothing else!!! It was then that we were told that we were to read our poem to an Oakwood girl who was chosen by our master. Remember my master was Don. Standing there, almost naked, I looked down at the poem that I had written. I was embarrassed and hadn't even read it yet.

Don took great pleasure when we arrived ambling through the possible victims. He spent considerable time in announcing that I would be reading my poem to the freshman representative to the homecoming court, and that I would be the first to read.

Her name was Jennifer Lawson, and I can tell you now that I didn't become a leper to her. By our senior year, she could actually say hello to me without laughing out loud. Both our "sponsors" led us to the stage, which consisted of a chair on a platform. Jennifer was to sit on the chair, her hand extended to me. I was to go to one knee, hold her hand with my one hand and the umbrella and poem in the other. Needless to say, in that position Jennifer could possibly see all that I had to offer. That is if she was looking. She made every effort to look anywhere else, but her sponsor adjusted her head to the right angle.

I played it pretty well. Concentrating on the poem, I barely heard the catcalls and rude comments all around me. I do remember looking into Jennifer's eyes once, but that just threw me off, so I finished what I started. When I finished, Jennifer ran back to her friends, and I got up and looked for the rest of the freshmen. Not a one of them was in a bathrobe anymore. They had joined in with the upperclassmen in the fun.

Mixed within me were the incongruous feelings of hate, anger, and shame. I looked for Don, not sure what I wanted to do. He was gone. Dirk called for order, "Well, it's time to leave. Gentlemen, let's show our respects to the ladies." He bowed at the waist to the girls, and quickly added, "Except you Logan. I think the girls know how you feel." With that everyone was leaving. I weighed my possibilities. I could stay, but that would continue my embarrass-ment. I could run out and get away from Manchester. I could suck it up and head back to Calvin Ulrey with the rest. I went back.

The march back to the dorm was filled with deriding calls that I barely heard. I wanted to get back to my room, pack my bags, and nev-er return to Manchester. It wasn't to be. Instead, we were ushered back to the rec room where the freshmen were herded to the front. Our instruc-tions were to sit on the floor. I did what they said, but had reached the point that this was the end. Anything else that would further embarrass me would be the final straw.

Don came in with a large paddle, the type that all college campuses are known for, especially for fraternities. It was ominous in his hand, but I was no longer devastated by anything or anyone, including Don Bates. He addressed us, "It's over. Right now you rhines are the lowest you will ever be here at Manchester. Some of you are hurt, others are humiliated. Still others are considering leaving Manchester. You won't. You are now a part of us and have given us entertainment that I and other upperclassmen of the past have given other upperclassmen." At this point he stopped and motioned to me, "Mark Logan, come forward."

I really didn't feel like it, but my new found strength made me bold. As I walked forward, I couldn't put my finger on it, but things seemed to have changed. As I neared the front, the freshmen began to clap. Dirk and Don were clapping too. In fact when I turned around, everyone was clapping. Don put his arm around my shoulders and spoke to me loud enough for all to hear, "Mark, you never knew it, but you were our 'target rhine.' You did more than the other freshmen, not because you told them about the secret, they knew that. We told them while you were at the rhine counsel. From that moment we were on your case, and you never complained."

The pause was deafening. Dirk brought me the paddle. "Congratulations, Mark. You,

66

like me, and others in this room, were tested.
You made it, but we knew that you would. This
paddle is yours until next year. Then you chose
the target rhine."

I had been had. Not only the upperclassmen, but my fellow freshmen. It didn't feel
like betrayal though. In fact, I felt like I had
come out the hero. Following the meeting in the
basement, everyone wanted to tell me their part
in the deception. I felt a part of this group.
They wanted me to be there.

The night was momentous. I reveled in
my notoriety and was warmed with my acceptance. When I went to bed that night, my mind
was clear, except for an image of a girl that I had
never met. I wanted to tell someone off campus
of my week. It couldn't be my family; this was
something a guy faced and kept separate from
his upbringing. I couldn't tell Ray; this wasn't
his world, and he would just blow it off. He
would use the situation and put into his perspective, and doing so would minimize it for me.
Julie was no longer in the picture.

As ludicrous as it sounds, Alicia was my
best choice. And so I got out of bed and began
the letter, this one much different from the one
before.

Dear Alicia,

     I am sitting here tonight very much alone. As strange as what I am about to tell you sounds, it is true. I could only think of you. My head started to hurt with the thoughts that had accumulated there. So I wrote this poem. It is yours for being the name that I put to the feeling. Don't read anything into it. I wrote it for my imaginary friend.

     The evening is screaming for me to an-swer,

     I choose to sit and think.
     I don't know you,
     But the mysteries of distance and time
     Bring me closer,
     To find the understanding,
     The caring,
     Of a friend.
     Help me to fight the night
     Which wants me to be alone.
     Give me your words
     You will be with them.

     That's all. Sorry for writing back (not really).

Throw this away if you want to.

Mark

      I really hadn't planned anything that went into that letter beforehand, and the poem was the first I would ever let anyone else see, other than the one that I had read earlier that day. I signed more quickly than I should have. My name was blurred, and it looked kind of sloppy, but I decided that it was better to be spontaneous than neat. Just as quickly, I had the letter in an envelope. In no time, I was dressed and headed for the postal box outside the dorm. The letter was in the box before the euphoric feeling was gone.

      I made my way back to the room, alternately feeling fantastic and terrible. Some have said that those go well together when you feel deep emotions. No way! How can you have strong emotions for someone you have never met? How can you have feelings for someone who has none for you? Empty questions with no answers flooded my brain.

      I settled into my bed to attempt sleep, wondering how the events of the day had all put

me into such a mood. The next day was Friday;
I fell asleep with the decision on going home for
the weekend undecided.

Chapter 7
I Had Too Much to Dream Last Night

The decision to go home was made for me. There was a message for me at the lobby desk Friday morning. My mother had wanted me to come home at least Saturday afternoon for Billy's birthday. It seemed like a reasonable request, and I made it clear to my dorm mates that I would be back as soon as possible. No one cared. In fact, that afternoon by the time that I packed the car, I saw only one other car in the lot.

Those two days at home were not significant. As a matter of fact, I found myself thinking often about what I would be doing on campus. Ray and I spent Friday night cruising like we had the previous week and so many weeks before. We talked about Alicia and the letters I had written so far, but what we said to each other was little more than small talk. Ray had done his duty on this front and wanted little else to do with it. What we didn't talk about was what was really on our minds.

Ray had a date with Julie on Saturday. He again asked if I would want to go along, half-heartedly this time. I begged off with the logical excuse of my brother's birthday party. That is where I began to play the part of friend to Ray. It was that part of maturation that I couldn't notice at the time, but Ray wouldn't notice for a long time. It wasn't his fault or mine; our paths were already taking diverging directions. Sad, but true.

Billy's birthday party was like all of the Logan birthday parties. All of the relatives, including aunts, uncles, and cousins, who could muster the time, would be in attendance. Being the oldest of the new generation, the usual games and activities seemed childish.

It was on this occasion that I was first asked about my views on Vietnam. Uncle George who had served in Italy in World War II came to me placing his hands on my shoulders. He looked deep into my eyes before he gave me his speech, "Mark, college students everywhere are questioning this war. I hear Manchester is no different, in fact, it sounds like those hippy radicals run the place. Son, don't let those traitors get to you. Our country doesn't make the kind of mistakes these hippies are flapping their big mouths about."

I didn't know how to reply. I knew that George had been awarded the Purple Heart, and I had always respected him for that. Seldom did he mention what happened in war, and I never asked. I wanted to know then though, but with his words I couldn't frame a question that wouldn't seem to be like the hippies he disliked so much. So I offered all I could with full sincerity, "Sure, Uncle George."

He smiled at me and tousled my hair, just as he had done all my life. I was still just his little nephew, even though I was an inch taller than him. That brief discussion prompted me to analyze how I felt about this war. My father, though a veteran himself, had not offered an opinion himself, so all I had to go on was what I heard so far on campus and my high school history class. A birthday party didn't seem to be the appropriate place for such a discussion, so I made a mental note to approach my father later.

One thing led to another, and I never had that discussion. By the time I knew it, I needed to head back to Manchester. I left before noon on Sunday. My weekend sent me back to Manchester more aware of my need for independence. The trip back was short because my mind was a blur of my newfound friends at

Manchester, my old friends in Fort Wayne, Alicia seven hundred miles away, and Uncle George. It was quite a mix of thoughts and emotions, with no conclusions to any of them.

The parking lot behind Calvin Ulrey was empty when I arrived. In fact, so was the dorm and most of the campus. I was virtually alone. Yet, it wasn't as depressing as it sounds. I went to my room and found it as empty as the rest of the campus. Wayne had gone home for the weekend. This was the first time that I had the room, the dorm, and the campus all to myself. I decided to discover them all now in a new perspective, alone.

Looking around the room and taking it all in, I accepted that this was now home and felt very comfortable with that. My stuff was there, and it resembled my values at the time. There was my stereo (actually my parents old hi-fi), posters of the Beatles against the wall near my bed, a stack of long play records with the books on my bookshelf near the window, and a myriad of endless odds and ends scattered everywhere. After my visual inventory, I realized very little in the room reflected Wayne. He had no posters and used my stereo. His desk area was devoid of anything except his books and papers, which were neatly arranged.

I left the room and CU to begin a stroll around campus. It was late afternoon by then and the campus was starting to come back to life. My first stop was a return to Oakwood Hall, the freshmen girls' dorm. Soon, I would want to date one of these people, it would be only prudent to scout out the possibilities.

Oakwood is on the opposite end of the campus, but very near the new Student Union Building, so it was at least on my way to get a bite to eat. Of course, there were few students in the dorm and those that were there were actively engaged in various forms of lovemaking on the front steps. The building was brick and foreboding. For many years in mind, Oakwood was the dictionary picture of what Victorian must be. Looking through the faces, I couldn't see any that I knew, though I really didn't try all that hard. Disappointed, I made my way to the Student Union.

The building was the newest on the campus. It offered a cafeteria, lounge, and snack bar on the upper level; a bookstore, post office, a recreation area with pool tables, and rooms that were designed to house student government and the school newspaper were on the lower level. As I entered the usually bustling building, the lack of human encounters made the building seem barren and unwelcoming. I climbed the steps to the snack bar to buy my evening meal. The cafeteria was not open on Sunday nights.

The snack bar was named , The Oaks, after the hangout previous students at Manchester had frequented on the basement level of Oakwood Hall for years. Since Oakwood was solely used for its cafeteria and housing of freshmen girls, the new facility was added into the new building. It had the atmosphere of a soda shop, complete with jukebox and the culinary trappings as well: hamburgers, fries, milkshakes, and all the rest.

The Oaks was not deserted in the least, but not knowing anyone there, I felt very isolated as I made my order and later looked for a seat. Stumbling around the round red and white checkered table clothed tables, I toyed with the notion of just taking the hamburger, fries, and cherry Coke out to the front lawn and be alone by myself instead of with all these strangers. But there was one table near the jukebox with no occupants. Knowing I had nowhere to go, I ate at a leisurely pace, uncommon for the average college student and me especially. I spent the time perusing the people around me, taking in their nuances, an activity that I carry through till today.

It was while I was surveying the crowd and paying special attention to a table with four girls that she must have come up behind me. She was about five foot-seven and just over a hundred pounds. Her attire was not unusual for the times: bell bottom jeans, tight at the hips; leather sandals with no socks; what was once a white t-shirt, tie-died into sunbursts of orange, yellow, and blue; and very obviously no bra. She was standing in front of me now, smiling, her long straight blond hair flowing across her t-shirt. She was saying something to me, but for some reason the words weren't getting through to me. Nor could I speak to ask her what she had said; my mouth was open wide, and I couldn't retract it to make it functional again.

"I said, is this seat taken?" She was being kind at my obviously impenetrable gaze. No words would form no matter how hard I tried, so I motioned for her to take the seat. I did a quick inventory of the room. There were now a few empty tables available in the room, she could have chosen any of them. As that thought entered my mind, it was as if she knew she answered the question that was forming in my mind, "I really do hate to eat alone don't you? I saw you over here and thought that we could be company for each other. I hope you don't mind."

"I..." Well, the words were coming now, okay word. Eventually, I managed some more, "I'm glad to have some company. My name is Mark Logan." I reached across the table to shake hands and pulled it back quickly, remembering the etiquette of the girl offering her hand first.

Just as quickly, she offered her hand and laughed, "Pleased to know you, Mark. My name is Linda, Linda Warner. I do know you though. I was there when you read your poem; you are a bit of a celebrity. You put on quite a performance." Her emphasis was on the word "quite."

Despite my obvious embarrassment, Linda put me at ease with her laugh. We talked nothing but small talk from that point on and were just beginning to delve into our backgrounds when I heard some words coming from the jukebox, "But I'd like to get to know you, yes I would." My mind drifted away from the present conversation. I felt a twinge like I was in the wrong place and time. Alicia was in my mind. I had a real live beautiful girl right here with me, and I start thinking about another girl whom I don't even know.

When I returned from the world I created, I heard Linda saying "Hey, Mark, where are you? I must be one lousy conversationalist if you need to get that far into a daydream." She was laughing, but she was also getting up to leave. I fell over myself with words trying to explain what happened, but she just smiled back as she went out the door, waving the peace sign as she left. I sensed the ludicrousness of this scene: drifting into a dream world for a girl whom I had never seen, when just that moment a dream was sitting next to me, and I virtually ignored her.

Chapter 8
It's Raining

Glenn Yarborough and Rod McKuen were staples of lovesick young people in the late 60's, especially at Manchester. Relaxing on my bed, I listened to all of the lonely songs that I could find. I have always found it paradoxical in myself, as well as others, that the very thing that causes pain is what we, or in this case, I turn to. Music is so universal; I guess it just verifies for us that we share our pain and sadness with others.

Wayne came in happier than I had ever seen him, and that is saying something since happiness was a chronic condition with him. Wayne looked like a surfer with his flowing blond hair, a Midwestern surfer. His lean features came from his high school activities in all sports, yet in college he chose to do none of them. His new sport was women. He excelled in this competition better than any sport he had ever participated in.

He threw his jacket across the room, and it almost made the chair. He then went over to the stereo hi-fi, lifted the needle from the record, and turned to me his demeanor changed. "What the hell is this stuff? A Sunday night is depressing enough without you introducing sloppy sentimental crap like this to it." With his pronouncement completed, he jumped to his bunk above me and started to whistle. Then he searched through my collection and pulled out Jan and Dean.

He went on whistling to "Drag City" until he felt the urge to share his pleasure with me. "I have met the girl of my dreams." Over the course of the next three years, I would hear these exact words on a regular basis. In fact, until Wayne met Angel, his wife, I don't think he ever really knew what love was. But he certainly professed to know, on a regular basis. "Her name is Linda, and I met her Friday after you left."

It was pure coincidence, I thought to myself. I meet a girl named Linda, and so does Wayne. Linda, after all, is a very common name. It never really worked out as coincidence with Wayne though. If a girl was a point of contention, Wayne had or would be involved with her sooner or later, and seldom did his interest last very long. Except for Angel, of course.

"Would her last name be Warner?" I decided that it was better to test the water quickly if I were ever going to pursue Linda at a later date. Still, I held back hope that we were talking about two different people.

"Yeh! Do you know her?" His question hinted at the fact that he was not surprised that I would know her as a friend, but never as anything else. "I just met her in the Student Union. She sat and ate supper with me. Place was really crowded. Seems real nice." Just the essentials. Laid out matter-of-factly.

Wayne was up and off the bed. Combing his hair in the mirror, he related his excitement. "Great, that means she's back from her trip home. See you later." Without any further discussion, he was out the door.

I looked over at the hi-fi, saw that the record I had been listening to was laying next to it, so I got up and started it over again. The first words came out, "Like the tears of angels down the windows, It's raining." As if on cue, outside the rain started to fall. I sat and stared out the window, viewing couples who were caught in the shower scurrying for shelter. I was safe and warm in my dorm room. Wayne was right about

one thing, Sunday nights are extremely depressing, when you are facing them alone.

Chapter 9
<u>Why Do Fools Fall in Love</u>

Lit class on Monday was extremely exciting. An English major challenged the professor on the professor's constant references to the sexual preferences of each author that we had studied so far. The class progressed no further from this argument and, as a result, ran the gamut from modern sensibilities regarding homosexuality to the stereotyping of the artistic community to homosexual tendencies. There seemed to be more students arguing against the professor than those who were backing him. This was truly the difference between high school and college: I, and all other students, were treated as if we had fully functional brains, even if we didn't deserve it..

This class was held in one of the oldest buildings on campus, the Administration Building. Its name is kind of a misnomer since most of the rooms are classrooms and only a few of the rooms on first floor are offices for the administration.

I chose that day to leave through the front steps which look out onto the homes of

84

students and faculty. I was greeted with a beautiful fall morning. Multi-colored leaves stood stark against the sky, both in the wind and dangling from the limbs of the trees. My mind wandered to days when I was younger and built small hills of the leaves, enticing my friends to join me in the aromatic swimming in the leaves.

While daydreaming, I had covered the whole course from the Ad Building to the Student Union. Now less than a minute from my mailbox, I was desperately hoping that there was something there to lift my spirits. There had to be; it was such a perfect day.

Since my mailbox was at the furthest end of the boxes, I had to make my way through students who were reading, talking, or just struggling to get their boxes open. My box was clear at the bottom, and I often wondered if those students who could look directly into their boxes had the same anticipation that I did. I had to stoop down to mine, and even then I couldn't see what was in it. I had to grope to get what was there.

Even though I was unable to see inside and, on occasion, would reach in tentatively when I thought of the tricks that my dorm mates were capable of. There were no tricks on this day, and, actually, I found the small box jam packed with mail.

Taking all of the mail from the box, I headed to an empty chair by the pool tables. There was a letter from my mother, just fat enough to have a check. I put it aside, believe it or not. Even the money that was inevitably there did not supersede the desire in my heart for another letter. There was junk mail from record companies, magazine publishers, and insurance companies, all looking to the future profession- als for their potentiality as consumers. A note from the Registrar's Office indicated that they had received my last payment and asked for the next. Mom's check came just in time.

Stuck in the middle of the mail came the edges of a pink envelope. As I pulled it from the rest, a scent subtly wafted to me. The envelope, the writing, the scent - the letter was most defi- nitely from Alicia. I had no more hope than a letter much the same as the first she had sent. In fact, I had almost resigned myself to the fact that Alicia would probably never write again. I tore the envelope open with great anticipation of what I was to read. I was tingling with the ex- citement and hope of her words; the words of a

86

stranger, who for some reason had become a sort of obsession in the matter of two weeks. My need for her was something that even I couldn't define.

As the pages unfolded in my hands, I saw that this was not a letter of goodbye. By its mere length, it was evident that Alicia had found a reason to need me as much as I needed her.

Dear Mark,

I received both of the letters that you wrote. I've read them over and over. You are about the sweetest or craziest person I have ever known. I don't know why, but you can touch me like no other person can. At least no one anymore. Forgive me for not fully understanding your intentions before. My parents and friends have been trying to make me feel better. No one has made me smile, but you. I want to be your friend. I hope that you still want to be mine.

The next few paragraphs were filled with deep emotional sentiments about her fiance, how he came up missing in Vietnam, and his death. I didn't remember that Ray said anything about the fact that he had been declared officially dead yet. I was surprised about her willingness to go into great depth about their last few days together. His name was Nick, and I had to admit from her words, he did sound like a great guy. I read all of this, feeling a deep sense of loss for her and yet a warmth that comes when someone actually cares enough to let you see into their heart.

The final page was all for me. She talked about herself. She wanted me to know her, that was clear; I have to admit I was hungry for the information. She said that she was five feet five inches tall and a little on the pudgy side. This seems to be the same self-deprecating comment of most women. Her eyes were brown, and so was her hair. She also felt that her nose was too big for her face. It went on; she told about those things that are important to know another person like favorite foods and music and pet peeves. This all seems so trivial, but at the time nothing seemed trivial; quite the contrary, it was the most important information in the world.

In her final paragraph, Alicia brought her attention to me:

88

Mark, thank you for being so persistent. just in writing this letter, I feel like I have lifted a huge weight off my shoulders. All I really ask of you from now on is that you let me know a little about you, and don't forget to write. Maybe we really can help each other.

Love,

Alicia

If it hasn't already become really obvious before this, but I was much less worldly then, so when I read the word "love" before her name, I was transported beyond my little space near the pool tables in the Student Union. It wasn't love that I was feeling, at least I didn't think so then. But I had no idea what the feeling was.

The trance must have held me for quite a while because Wayne and Linda were standing in front of me and staring at me. I thought to myself, "Linda, you've caught me in a daydream again." I wanted to hit my forehead with my palm, but I figured that would add another mystifying aspect to Linda's view of me.

"What world were you off to?" It appeared that the question had been asked more than once of me, judging by the irritation in Wayne's voice. Linda was smiling, but plainly amazed at me.

Realizing the silliness of the moment and that it would be impossible to explain the situation with Alicia, I simply responded over my shoulder as I got up and left, "Existential thoughts hit me in the strangest environments. Excuse me, I must be off to my philosophy class."

I bounded up the steps of the Student Union and headed toward the Communications Building that sat directly behind the Ad Building. It was even sunnier, warmer, and everyone was smiling as I passed them. I let myself believe that it was my glow that made them smile. It didn't occur to me until many years later that maybe they were laughing at a fool. "Why do fools fall in love?" Not exactly lyrics that should be drifting through one's mind in philosophy class. After all it wasn't love, and I wasn't a fool, yet.

Chapter 10
I Just Wasn't Made for These Times

That first term in college went by much quicker in retrospect than I had thought. It was the scheduled events that were planned by the student government that gave us targets to shoot for. Homecoming was first. When we arrived at that magical weekend, the campus had settled in and we all felt that we were pretty much a family. Making floats, electing a homecoming queen, watching the big game against Taylor, our biggest rival – they all made this a special time, never to be duplicated again. At least, not until next year.

I sent a letter back to Alicia just before homecoming week, thinking that the activities of the week would keep me busy enough. The letter was more autobiographical this time. I knew a little about her; it just figured that she should know more about me. I almost thought about lying about myself, rationalizing that there was a good chance that we would probably never meet. Then it hit me, had she lied to me?

I didn't lie; in fact I was ruthless on myself. If I had a fault (and I have many), I brought it out in fullest detail. "I'm an overweight wimp. Incapable of showing my deepest feelings to anyone. I tend to allow people to manipulate me and I can't say no." I went on further, but more importantly I let her know about my loves. "Music, the words, are important to me. I like sports. I like people." Those words told more about me than any physical description; I hoped they made sense.

I finished the letter and mailed it in the lounge. Immediately, I was collared by Don. "Mr. Logan, for your creative abilities - that poem Rhine week was really good - you have been nominated to design this year's homecoming float representing Calvin Ulrey Hall. You will be chairman and may choose anyone else in the dorm to help you, except me, of course. Also, you will find very few upperclassmen who are very interested. Your budget is ..." His voice trailed off as he looked at a sheet of paper. I think it had more to do with the fact that he had trouble reading than searching for the right answer that took so long. He looked up quickly, "You don't have a budget, but we do have chicken wire, a trailer, and access to a tractor. The rest is up to you." Don stopped and thought.

"Get lots of toilet paper or tissues, and oh yes, paint." He walked away then.

As I looked out the front door of the dorm, I wondered how Don equated writing a poem to designing a float. I wasn't particularly artsy, and I surely was not good at coming up with ideas extemporaneously. Puzzled and desperate, I headed to Don's room, an act a person at CU never did consciously, to get more information.

My knock on the door was greeted with a grunt and, "go away or come in, but stop beating on the damned door." I assumed that meant I could enter, so I did. Bates saw me and acted disgusted, "What the hell do you want?" He was drunk and I wondered how I had missed it in the hall.

I got right to the point. "Is there a theme I will follow? When does the float need to be finished?" The words were timid, but they were important for my success in the endeavor. The thunderous laughter shook me. "You want to do this right, don't you?" He continued the raucous display for at least three minutes. When he brought himself around to my questions, he spoke to each succinctly. "'Education as a Stepping Stone.' Friday." Then he began laughing again and said, "Don't go winning any awards now. CU has a tradition of coming in last in these types of events. Don't foul us up." Don indicated the door as if a monarch had dispatched me to the battlefield.

Most of my committee ended up being freshmen because they were the ones that had no knowledge of what had been done before. From asking around the campus, this process usually took at least three days to complete and what Don had said about Calvin Ulrey was legendary. Wayne and I decided to try anyway, and so we did.

"Prime the Pump of Knowledge" was the theme for our float. It was hokey, but it followed the overall theme, and we had an excellent concept for the float: Get one of the old hand water pumps from one of the old wells and put it on the float with books surrounding its base. Tissue paper would be used to give color to the float and would be stuck strategically around the chicken wire. It was ingenious!

However, there was a flaw. Wednesday, as my committee was gathering materials in the late afternoon, Brad Tanner, a fellow rhine and pre-med student deduced what I had failed to -

we had no pump. Each of us went on our own private scavenger hunt to find a farm or anyplace that still had a pump that we could borrow. Heading out to the town and the areas that encircled the college, we all knew that we would be hard pressed to find anyone who would cooperate. That evening, tired and depressed, I returned with nothing and gathered the rest to check their findings.

Brad was the one who found our pump. No one else had anything. It didn't matter, we had a pump! Brad had bad news too. "The caretaker won't let us have it, even for the weekend."

"What do you mean, caretaker? Does this guy run the farm for somebody else?"

Brad smiled, "This is no farm. It's a cemetery." That took us all by surprise. He continued, "But nobody has used that pump for years, definitely not the residents." He did get sick laughs from all of us.

I was thinking with him, and I can't really attribute to whom or how the actual idea was born. But the question was out of my mouth before I could realize what it meant to my future, "Is it possible to get this pump without him knowing it?" The words trespassing and theft never came to mind until later.

This future doctor smiled even broader now. "Oh, wow, that is perfect . I have a plan. Tomorrow night is a full moon. If we head out to the cemetery at about midnight with tools, we could probably free the pump and be out of there within an hour. There's a road that runs behind the cemetery; we could park the car there while we sneak through to the pump."

Alternately around the room, there were comments like "sounds like fun" and "sounds just plain stupid to me." I, being the leader of this group and needing to voice sanity into this insane idea, shouted, "We have no choice, let's do it!"

Psychology class the next day was dealing with deviant conduct. It seemed fitting. To top it off, Alicia's letter was in my mailbox. She responded to my self-loathing comments with kind words of how Diane saw me and that she could put my observations of myself with Diane's and felt she had a pretty good picture of the real me. But it was the last line of the letter that hit home. "You are most definitely mature for a guy your age. I am feeling better, and I have noticed that my spirits are highest when I see a letter from you in the mailbox."

I wondered if she would feel the same about a person who was about to spend an hour in a graveyard at midnight stealing a pump.

Chapter 11
<u>The Joker Went Wild</u>

It was a beautiful fall night for driving in the country; crisp cool air and the moon was as bright as it could possibly be. It might have even been romantic had there been a member of the opposite sex in the car. But what we had was the six of us crammed into my car. Ironically, I had no trouble getting anyone to volunteer for the mission, evidently stealing for the float is not the same as working on the float. Don Bates was the first to join us (deviant conduct seemed to be his forte). Even Dirk was excited with the prospects for the evening. He was the only other person in the car who had a car besides me, but he declined when he realized that he had a reputation in that car, and it had nothing to do with males. Beyond that, being an All-American basketball player the previous year, and a shoo-in for being All-American again, it would be best that his car not be involved. He didn't seem to mind that he, himself, could get in trouble.

Personally, I tried to keep my thoughts on Alicia, probably to keep from laughing hysterically. The other sojourners included Brad and Wayne and Denny, a big lovable farm boy, also a freshman. Dirk called us the "rookies" on their first "run." Fear was all over our faces, but Dirk and Don were having a great time making jokes at our expense.

Brad verbally guided me to the dirt road behind the cemetery. It was less than five miles from the campus, but far enough away that we could be disassociated with the campus. I turned off the lights and pulled over towards a shallow ditch bordering a cornfield. Fall was everywhere: the smells of burning leaves (long before burning statutes outlawed the practice), the withered brown stalks of the corn, and the nippy night air. It all felt so good. Boy, did I feel terrible! This was my idea, and there was no doubt that what we were about to do was illegal, not to mention pretty damned scary. Paranoia ran rampant. I saw myself in jail. Worse, I saw myself in Vietnam after being kicked out of school.

We gingerly walked through the cemetery, spying headstones easily with the bright light of the moon. The pump was easy to find and easier to get to even than we had hoped. The caretaker's home was only about three hundred feet away though, so we had to be careful. That detail was lost on none of us.

It was decided by Dirk that he and Don would go into the well to free it while Wayne and I held the flashlights. Denny and Brad were stationed as lookouts. For nearly half an hour we were at our posts uninterrupted, save the few expletives from the mouths of Don and Dirk. It was around half past twelve that the caretaker came out of his house. We could see that he was carrying a gun, and he was coming toward us. Dirk and Don had us lower the cover of the well over them and told us to hide. We did.

I found myself behind a headstone, lying on the damp ground over it. Then it hit me in the stomach, over a dead body, I was lying on the ground over a dead body. I looked at the headstone and saw the name Metzger. I apologized to him. His name was Edgar; he had died in 1955. I had time to read since the caretaker was staring into the depths of the cemetery and yelling. At times his words were actually audible to me at the back of the cemetery. "I know you are there. You always do this to me. Leave me alone." He punctuated the last choppy sentence with a shot into the air.

I wanted to move so badly. I didn't. I couldn't. No one else moved either. Eventually, the caretaker went back to the house and we, one by one, went back to the pump. Opening the cover to the pump carefully, I heard stifled laughter. I shone the flashlight down to see Dirk rolling on the surface of the pumps standard. "That guy is really Looney Tunes. Did you hear what he said?" Dirk directed the question to me. Since I hadn't really heard all the caretaker had said, I indicated that I hadn't. "A caretaker of a cemetery and he's afraid of ghosts! He thought the noises we were making were the ghosts he has been hearing!" For a second I was smiling, but intelligence, or the lack thereof, took over. Maybe there were ghosts!

Dirk and Don hadn't even considered what was going through my mind, that was obvious. Howling sounds and screams came from the hole. Wayne tried to quiet them, I think he had the same fears that I had. But Don made an obscene gesture with one of his fingers and went back to screaming and freeing the pump.

The caretaker's door never opened again. I figured the noises coming from the pump platform were more than he could stand; I know they were not helping me any. No more than ten minutes later, the pump was free and the six of us were hauling the pump to my car. It didn't fit in the trunk, so Brad and Denny climbed into the trunk and held it in as I was driving.

We considered going through downtown North Manchester, but that was a problem since the police station and everything else was right on the main stretch. We didn't risk this and took the long way around through residential neighborhoods, so that no one would be suspicious.

Once we arrived back at the dorm, there was another dilemma. Where were we going to store the stupid thing? Don's room was the obvious choice of everyone, except Don. After very little thought, Don had us load the pump back into my car, and he gave me instructions on where to drive.

About two miles from the campus, an old empty farmhouse and its barn were to be the home of our pump and the site of our float building. We unloaded the pump into the barn and covered it with a brown material that is hard to describe in any other way due to the darkness in the barn. The odor of the object would lead one to believe that it had been used on an animal who had relieved himself.

With our pump secured, we were on our way back to the dorm. Everyone unloaded happily, even cocky over the conquest of the night. It was my first college prank, and it was successful. I was one of the guys. Dirk and Don were even treating me that way.

A habit that all college students eventually developed was to check to see if there are messages left for them. Today, with cell phones, I am sure that this no longer is necessary. At the lobby desk there was a bulletin board. Its primary purpose was for the conveying of messages that had come into the dorm while its inhabitants were out. I never really checked the board that often, but this night I was feeling good and just thought I was owed a message from someone.

My name was there! Mark Logan! Right there on the traditional yellow note. But the name of the caller was the real surprise! Alicia Williams. How did she know how to get hold... Diane! I answered my own unstated question. Her phone number was after her name. The call was taken at 12:34 A.M., about the time I was reclining in a graveyard. If I had just been in my room! I looked at my watch. It was 1:21 now. I began to tear myself apart - should I call? Is it too late? I reached a decision quickly; I had to call. It might be really important.

I then became aware of a fact about Calvin Ulrey Hall that I had not needed to be aware of before. There was only one pay phone, and it was almost always busy. Even at 1:30 in the morning! After waiting for another five minutes, I finally had access to the phone. I didn't dial it right away. In fact, I almost chickened out altogether (phones have never really been a working part of my repertoire, especially when I am calling a girl). I did call though.

The phone on the other end rang once before there was an answer. A quiet, muffled sound came through the line. It was crying. A brief wave of foreboding ran through me. Something was wrong!

Chapter 12
Cry Baby

I had never met her. I barely knew anything about her. Still, I was standing in this phone booth, tears welling in my eyes, and she hadn't even said a word. In my mind I was thinking dreadful thoughts ranging from the ridiculous; she doesn't want to write to me anymore: to the truly hideous; she is contemplating suicide. I couldn't go on this way so I spoke. "Alicia, this is Mark. Is there something wrong?" To the point is good, but somewhat crass when it is blurted out like I did.

There was obviously an attempt on her part to bring herself together. A gasp, then a sigh, and then words, "I am sorry to have bothered you so late." How could her voice have been like I had imagined. It was eerie. "I just, well I get the feeling from your letters that you are a good listener. And I need to tell someone." Her voice trailed off into a breathless whisper. The quality in her voice that came through most was the whisper even when she wasn't trying. Her tears came through to me in that whisper.

"Just talk, I'll listen." The truth was that no matter what she was about to say, I knew I just wanted to hear that voice.

"Nick has been found." There was a pause. "Oh, my God, I never have told you his name." Embarrassed silence followed and I didn't know what to say. She started again, "My boyfriend who was lost in Vietnam, his name is Nick Hartman. Word has come to his family that he was captured and is being held in a POW camp." She stopped, obviously crying. I felt the urge to say something, but there were no adequate words. I just waited. And waited.

"I don't know why I called you. It just seemed like the only thing that I could do." She sounded desperate and alone. "You were kind to call back, but this is costing you a lot, and it's so late. Thank you for listening to me."

Afraid she would hang up, I blurted out, "Don't hang up!" Then I composed myself. "You began writing to me because I filled a need. You called me because that need was urgent. I think that if you don't talk to me, you'll never write to me again, and that would be a loss for both of us." I am absolutely sure I had never been more serious in my life.

Softly, she spoke, "I want someone to talk to in the dark. Tonight I'm scared of everything and I, well, I feel guilty. You know, writing you and enjoying it. It just doesn't seem fair to Nick. This has nothing to do with you, but I wish I hadn't started writing to you."

Lost in her words, I didn't come back to her right away. I spent considerable time on the words that I used when I began. "You haven't done anything wrong. Put it into perspective. You have been writing to a guy you don't even know for no other purpose than to have someone to bounce ideas off and occasionally to share a tear. I don't know Nick, and I don't know how he would feel, but I do know that most guys are not threatened or jealous of a few words on paper that are only between friends. You are my friend and, even though you probably don't think that this is possible, I really care and want to help."

When you are on the phone, have you ever noticed that you can feel the expression on the caller's face? I felt a smile on the other end. It didn't feel like a broad, boisterous smile, but it was warm. So was her voice, "Thank you. You are good with words aren't you?"

"Only when it's important." I remained serious though I was tempted to degrade myself.

"Your phone bill will be enormous. I'll let you go and write to you tomorrow." She was calmer, but I sensed that there was something else. There was. "If we are friends, would you do something for me?"

"Sure." I responded without doubt.

"You know Diane and Ray have scheduled for you and Ray to come up to Lacrosse next August? Would you help me to get them to back off for now. It's not that I don't want to see you; I just have to get this all digested, and this summer might be too soon."

I had started to entertain the thought of a week next summer in Wisconsin and visualize how fun it would be with Alicia. Her request would be hard to grant. "Sure, if that will help, then that's what I want to do."

The smile that I couldn't see was bigger. "I was so glad you didn't say 'we're just friends', because we are more than that. I lied before, there's another thing I want you to do. Actually, both of us. Let's write as often as possible, but talk on the phone only very seldom. You're going to laugh when I tell you why I ask such a

108

strange thing." I had to admit it seemed odd.
"You say so many things that I need to hear, but
your words, the written ones, they are there for
me whenever I need them."

I hoped my smile went through the lines
like hers did. "You obviously have never taught
a creative writing class. These words I send you
are ridiculed by scholars, which makes you less
than scholarly."

There wasn't a smile on the other end.
"You have caused me to lie again. Swear to me
that you won't put yourself down to me again, on
the phone or in a letter. You write so well, from
the heart. Don't you see, that is what is really
important?"

I was stuck. I couldn't joke my way out
of this. I didn't know how to respond, but I
knew that I couldn't let this relationship with her
go. "Okay. But can I at least make fun of my
physical appearance can't I?"

"Yes, but I think you exaggerate or
downright lie about that too."

I knew the conversation was over. So
did she. We put it off for a while until Alicia
said, "Your special. Thank you for being there
for me."

"Anytime, and I mean that." With those words we said goodbye. It's funny, I don't even remember saying hello.

Homecoming and Alicia were running through my dreams all night long. I was priming the pump, and she was there with me; her back turned to me the whole time. It stayed that way until a young man bloody and dirty came along. He held out his hand to her. She grabbed for it and was gone.

Homecoming Day came and I was exhausted. The float committee had been up the whole night before, constructing the float. Though I was in charge, I learned quickly I had no authority. Don and Dirk would come by from time to time and, in their drunken states, change whatever I had done. Finally, around four in the morning, they passed out, and I was left with my committee to complete the work.

If I was pressed to assess our work, I would say that it was pretty good. We hooked up the tractor and headed for campus. The plan was to park it behind CU and pull it around just before the parade started. None of us wanted the pump to be seen too soon. As it was, we had to station guards around it for an hour.

110

College homecoming meant nothing to me then. It was just another day that the campus was filled with people who had either gone to Manchester at one time, or those that will be coming in the future. Mom and dad both graduated from Manchester and said they would be on campus in time to see the annual parade. Ten minutes before the parade, they were standing outside my door.

Dad spoke first, "Well, it looks as though the college man is doing just fine. Ready for the parade?"

Pulling on my shoes, I replied sleepily, "With a little sleep, I could be better."

"Aren't you sleeping well?" Mom had concern written all over her face.

"We were up all night preparing the float. Did you see it out back?"

"The one with the pump and the armed guards?" Dad was amused at my condition, probably confusing it with a condition I would in later days really be under.

"That's it, and I better get going because I'm to be the one pumping the pump the whole length of the parade. Are you staying for all the festivities?"

Mom quickly responded to neutralize what my father was thinking, "We don't want to take up too much of your time, but we were thinking about going to the football game and would like to take you out to lunch."

"Sounds good to me. After the parade I've nothing to do. Just a dance tonight." I jumped up to get going. "Got to get to the float. I'll see you at the Student Union at the end of the parade route."

I couldn't wait for response. My consti-tuents were screaming for me and the parade was forming. We had no problem getting the float moving, and it looked better than ever in the fall sunlight. It was a great experience for me. We were cheered all along and by the time we reached the Student Union, I felt confidant that we would easily win the best float award.

I hopped down off of the float and searched for my parents. Dad was six-five and towered over most of the crowd. He wasn't very hard to find.

There was a temporary platform built outside the front doors to the Student Union. The queen and her court were on the platform as well as the coach of the football team. After their speeches were over. The awards began. First came the award for the dorm that was best adorned for the occasion. Don was adamant about the fact that, and I quote, "Putting that crap all over the place and make it look like fags live here. CU will not be decorated!" So we defaulted on this award. Next came the spirit awards. The seniors won as usual. Finally, came the awarding of the best float trophy.

Annie Sprague, chairperson of the parade committee, made some opening comments about how she was pleased with the participation of everyone concerned. After many degrading comments from the crowd, she started the presentation. "Third place trophy goes to the Chemistry Club float 'Bubbling Minds.' Second place goes to the Thespian Club for their float 'Learning to Act.'"

I swallowed hard. I honestly expected to win a place, but I thought it would be second or third. Annie continued, "And in first place, winning a trophy and a gift certificate for $100 in the bookstore for the winners, 'Priming the Pump of Knowledge' Calvin Ulrey Hall.'"

I was frozen. Dad shoved me to the stage, but when I saw Don and Dirk there already with none of my crew in sight, I stayed back. Don made an eloquent speech, at least for him, and thanked all of us that helped him.

As he and Dirk descended from the stage, Dr. Grace, Dean of the College, took them each by an arm. At the same time a campus security cop took the trophy and check from Don's hand. The stern look on Dr. Grace's face told me that the caretaker at the cemetery had made a call. It was hard to explain to my parents what had happened, but once I did, my father laughed out loud. "Good, very good! But I did better." Before he could elaborate, my mother instituted that glare she held only for my father when he was out of line. I missed a good story that day. Years after I graduated, my father told me about his adventure at stocking the dean's office with farm livestock.

We had to give up our trophy and certificate. Don and Dirk never implicated anyone else in the dorm. The dorm was put on probation, yet it didn't seem too bad. I was treated royally by Don. I had won and gotten us all into trouble; to Don that was heaven.

Mom and dad went back home after the game. With a care package of cookies, I went back to my room. I reviewed the last few days and realized that I was no longer the same naive young man I was just a few weeks ago. I fell asleep secure and happy and dreaming of a girl with long brown hair.

Chapter 13
<u>Last Night I Didn't Get to Sleep at All</u>

My father called a month later asking if I had made a credit call to LaCrosse, Wisconsin. I guess I had neglected to say anything to him about it. It was hard to explain, but somehow he at least accepted it and advised me that if I were to make that type of call again, that the time I chose for the first call was fine due to the lower rates.

In that month's time, Alicia and I wrote over twenty letters back and forth. Most of them dealt with her feelings for Nick and her college classes. But, gradually, I was noticing that we were spending more time on my social life. It seemed that Alicia was taking an active interest in who I was dating and how each date went. The truth was that there weren't all that many dates, and she actually kept pushing me to try harder. She didn't have to, but still it was great to have someone to keep track of me.

"Breakaway Weekend" was the last weekend of October each school year at Manchester. It was the age old idea of Sadie Hawkins Day - the girls ask out the guys. From

Friday night through Sunday night, the college had scheduled activities so that the girls could have many opportunities to ask out their favorite guys. I had told Alicia about this custom, and she wrote back that I would be having to turn the girls away. The girls at Manchester evidently knew more than she did, because going into Wednesday before the big weekend, I was dateless.

After dinner that evening, I saw a message for me in the lobby. I hoped that it was Alicia wanting to talk; we hadn't spoken by phone since that pre-homecoming night. It was from Linda Warner. I was stumped, but interested in finding out what was going on. Immediately, I went to the desk and asked if the message wasn't actually intended for my roommate. "She asked for you." The reply was gruff, but it intrigued me anyway.

I was at the campus phone before I even had time to think through my usual reasons for not calling a girl. I rationalized that she was needing to ask something about Wayne. When she answered, I wasn't in the least apprehensive about talking to her. "Hi Linda, this is Mark."

"Hi Mark! How are you?"

"I'm doing pretty good." I always did like small talk. It takes up time, and you really don't have to get involved in it very deeply.

"Are you doing anything Saturday night?"

There was earthquake that registered barely on the Richter scale the next year at Manchester. It didn't shake me as much as this beautiful girl asking me for a date. "I, uh, no. No, I don't have any plans."

"Would you go with me to the dance?"

Successive earthquakes! "Uh, yeh, sure." Great conversationalist, huh!

"I know you probably have other plans, but could I take you to dinner before the dance?"

Obviously, she had no idea how meager my weekend was before this call. "Yeh, but what about Wayne?"

"Don't you two ever talk? Your creep roommate broke up with me last week."

I smelled a rat. He broke up with her, and she wants to go out with me. No Rhodes Scholar was needed here. I asked, "But why me? There are plenty of better looking..."

She didn't let me finish. "Don't get the wrong idea. I am not asking you to go with me

118

to spite your roommate." There was a defini-
tiveness in her tone. "I want to go with you
because of you. But if you doubt that, I understand, and I'll try to get someone else to go with
me."

I couldn't keep up the righteous indignation, after all this was a beautiful girl. There
were guys on campus who would pay good
money to take my place. "I want to go with you,
no matter the reason. Okay?"

With that I set up my first turn-around
date. Later, Wayne would ask why I went out
with Linda knowing that they were so close. I
simply told him that sometimes I can get lucky
too. He took it for what it was worth, which I
know was no more than deep B.S. I shot off a
letter to Alicia too. She seemed interested in
my relationships or lack thereof, so I wanted her
to be happy for me.

The next two days I did get calls from
two other girls; one to take me to the football
game on Saturday and the other to the movie on
Friday. I agreed to both, yet the Saturday night
dates were the ones that I thought of through
each of my classes. Looking back at this now, I
probably would have had better grades in the
first two years if I had just spent a little time

concentrating on what was going on in the classes, and less on women. Ah, but what fun would there have been in that.

Chapter 14
<u>Bend Me, Shape Me</u>

What a Saturday morning! The sun was shining bright even if the day was on the cold side; it was still a beautiful day. I was to have what I anticipated to be a great day. All of it opened with a flag football game. I had played football in high school and had hoped to play on the varsity level at Manchester, but a knee injury in the last game my senior year in high school didn't respond, and I gave up on the idea.

Calvin Ulrey was filled with former athletes like me, and Dirk was in charge of sports participation. When he found out that I had played football in high school, he recruited me for the dorm team. I was apprehensive for two reasons actually: the leg might not make it, and CU had a tradition of being the winners of the flag football tournament each year. This year was no different. And I feel that I played admirably, if I do say so. The difference this year was that the champions, CU, were to play the champions of Taylor University's flag football tournament. The game was scheduled to be played before the varsity game on the regulation football field the Saturday morning of Breaka-way Weekend.

I was up early that morning to get ready for the game. My parents told me that they would be there, and Linda had made a point to tell me that she would be among the crowd root-ing for CU and me. It felt good that this was all happening in one day, and somehow it made me feel more mature. I was doing all this because I wanted to. Not for my mother or father - just me.

Walking to the field with Dirk and Wayne, I sensed some respect from the people around us. We were the champions off to battle. No matter that this battle was small scale, or that no one outside of Manchester would care less. It was still something for that day anyway.

Game time came so quickly. I saw mom and dad in the stands. It wasn't hard. There were probably no more than fifty fans on both sides of the field. Ironically, just before the game began, I looked up and saw Linda sitting in the row behind my parents. I wanted despe-rately to introduce them to each other, but realized there were more pressing matters.

I played both defense and offense and all of the special teams as well, so I was on the field most of the time. As a blocking back, I caught three passes in the first half. On one of the passes, I scored a touchdown. On defense I made two "tackles" (grabbed flags). At the half we were ahead of the Taylor's team by a touchdown. I was tired, but riding a high that can't be explained to anyone who has never competed in athletics. Moreover, I hadn't embarrassed myself or my parents, and Linda was still there cheering.

It was the second half that made this gorgeous day turn around. Humbled by the first half score, Taylor came out the second half with blood in their hearts and revenge in their souls. It was a bloodletting. This "flag" football game became a wrestling match in motion. Wayne went out with a concussion almost a minute into the third quarter, and Denny broke his arm near the end of the third quarter. I was starting to find myself driven by hate each time the ball was snapped, whether I was on defense or offense. These people were out to hurt my friends and me. They had already partially succeeded.

I was at the blocking back position when it happened. Dirk, our quarterback, called an end sweep with me carrying the ball. This was not a common occurrence for our team, but with the injury list we had, I was the next best ball carrier. The snap came to Dirk who wheeled towards me and pitched the ball. It came to my right perfectly ahead of me. I had no idea how open I was at the time, nor did I care. I ran as fast as I could with the weight differential that I had from college snacking. The end zone was within sight, and I was going to make it. A rush of excitement hit me, and I so much wanted to look over my shoulder to see if Linda and my parents were pleased, but my high school coach's words, "don't look back, someone could be gaining on you," prevented any such luxury. With one more step I was in the end zone, Touchdown! I made it... That's when the lights went out.

Chapter 15
<u>Love Is Here, and Now You're Gone</u>

The weekend was a total waste for me, and I imagine it was for Linda too. My shoulder had been dislocated, but the concussion I had suffered at the same time put off the feeling of discomfort that I later found there. The doctor at the campus clinic never needed to put me under to replace the shoulder.

I came out of the stupor that evening. It was around seven. When I was semi-lucid again, I was able to see Linda at the foot of my bed with my parents. I felt ridiculous until I realized that the left side of my body was immobilized in what seemed like a straight jacket. My left arm was strapped across my chest at almost a forty-five degree angle. The harness encompassed my shoulder and went all the way to just below my chest.

My mother came to me when she saw that I was awake. "You were out for a long time, Mark. How do you feel?"

No response to that question would have been adequate, so I just struggled with, "Okay, I guess." It hit me then that they had not gone home. "You didn't have to wait. You really should be getting home shouldn't you?"

Dad circled the bed and laughed. "That's gratitude for you. We wait all this time, and all you want to do is get rid of us." I knew that he was kidding, but there was a look of concern, so I didn't kid in return. He went on, "We planned to spend the night at the motel off campus, but Linda says that she'll watch out for you and call us tomorrow. Now that you're among the living again, maybe that is just what we should do. Your aunt is taking care of your brother and sister, and you know how much she hates kids. So if you don't mind, we'll get going."

Of course, I was glad that they had stayed with me, but I wanted to be alone with Linda, so I bid them go. It didn't take much convincing before they both gave me a hug and turned to the door. Linda went to them and embraced them. They had gotten to know each other while I was out, which turned out to be around eight hours. The pain went away a little as I watched them smiling and laughing about the whole set of circumstances that they met.

Finally, Linda and I were alone. Actually, Linda was alone with me. She took care of me. At some point, I remember that she got a pizza for me and that she fed me. But the pain killers took effect just after I took them, and I dozed off.

Virtually the next thing that I comprehended was late into the day on Sunday. Dirk was sitting next to the bed, and Don was looking out the window towards the football field. The clinic was perfectly placed mere blocks from all of the athletic facilities.

Dirk spoke first, "Mark, that girl that was in here with you all night is gone, so stop asking for her, will you? Besides, I thought her name was Linda. You keep calling her Alicia." I was stunned. Dirk had no way of knowing about Alicia, and he certainly had no reason to be making this story up. "We've been suspended from school for the rest of the term." Dirk was looking down at his hands. I had noticed until then that neither he or Don was acting up. They were worried.

Dirk continued, "That's why we're here. When I say that we have been suspended, I mean Don and I. You are still okay. You didn't get in on the good stuff that happened after you left the game."

Even with the pain killer, I was feeling pain for Dirk and Don, but Dirk especially. This was the captain and leading scorer of Manchester's basketball team. He had a chance to be All-American again. Yet as my eyes went to Don at the window, I saw something that I never would have dreamed. After all of the time that Don spent trying to get out of school, Don seemed to care about staying in school, and it didn't seem to have much to do with being drafted.

I was at a loss for words, but I had to offer something, "Is there something that I can do?"

Dirk stood up and went to the window with Don. He whispered to Don and turned to me. "Our only hope is the Student Court. It convenes tomorrow morning at nine. The doctor says that you'll not be allowed out of here until at least Wednesday." Dirk paused and swallowed hard. "We were pretty mad about what happened to you. It was the last straw, so we went after those bastards." This was the first I had seen Dirk speaking from a part of his body that didn't excrete something.

128

I volunteered, "I can guess what happened, and I sure know what happened before I was hurt. I can't be in such bad shape that I can't help you guys out." I made this statement without any knowledge whatsoever on my condition. "If you can find a way to get me out of here tomorrow, I'll be there." Looking into their eyes, I knew that this was already thought out. All they needed was for me to volunteer.

Don enumerated the deception that we were going to use. Anytime he had a plan like this one, Don salivated, and that was not a pretty sight. In my condition it hastened my approval of the plan. The pain and salivating of Don were a potent mixture for an already upset stomach. After I agreed to participate, Don and Dirk were gone.

I was drowsy. I had been through a lot in the past forty-eight hours. Yet I couldn't help but reflect on Linda. It might have been a coincidence that Linda had left, and I may have hallucinated the Alicia part of all of this. All that I was absolutely sure about was that I was in no condition to do anything about it at the time. In fact, mister sandman smashed me pretty hard. I was deep into sleep when I saw the faint frame

of a girl in the doorway. Maybe it was Linda.
In my dreams it was Alicia who took care of me.

Chapter 16
<u>Don't You Care</u>

The clinic on Monday mornings must not have been the social center of Manchester. It wasn't hard at all for Dirk and Don to sneak me out and get me into my car. They had obtained custodian uniforms and acted as if they needed to clean my room when they opened their cleaning kits and brought forth my clothes. It took a little time to get my clothes on around the harness, but eventually we succeeded. They had found a wheelchair down the hall and borrowed it. The plan was for me to wait outside the hearing room and then appear when it looked the worst for Dirk and Don. I instructed them not to give me a pain killer until this was accomplished.

The hearing was convened in the administration building in the president's conference room. One by one members of the Student Court filed in and bringing up the rear was Dean Grace, the Dean of Students. He was a rolly-polly man extremely short in stature and intestinal fortitude. I know that I towered over him and most of the girls on campus laughed out loud as they peered down at him. His brow was

in constant deep furrow mode, lacking any sem-
blance of cheer. Looking at this administrative
post in other areas of education, it seems this is a
prerequisite for the job.

I was alone in a side hall, yet I had perfect view of the proceedings. Dirk had propped
open the door under the guise of needing more
air. Kent Hauser, a senior from Schwalm Hall
was the presiding officer of the court and was
asking questions of not only Dirk and Don, but
also Dean Grace. It was ever so clear from the
outset that this group was a puppet organization
of Grace. It was getting bad. Grace said that
Dirk and Don had pulled this type of stunt before and were left unpunished but warned, and
he felt there need be no more discussion. No
one asked for proof; no one even cared to listen
to a sober and ingratiating response from Don.

It was my time; Don gave me the signal.
I didn't have to pretend to be hurting, even
though the plan called for me to wince and
writhe in pain as often as I deemed necessary.
In fact each step to the room was wrought with
stabbing shots in my shoulder. This would not
have to be much of a performance. As I entered
the room, I looked at the assembled group and

gazed into the eyes of Dean Grace. With great convictions my first words were said directly to him, "This is what the Taylor team did to me. I wonder how many of them look like this?" Since Dirk and Don had told me that none of the Taylor players had any major injuries, I felt on safe ground with the question, so I came back, "These are my friends and teammates. They were only doing what I couldn't do because of what the Taylor players had done to me." A natural wince set in to my face. I bent for a chair. "I think that Don and Dirk did only what they felt they had to do for a friend, and I don't think that has anything to do with their school work. I am not supposed to be here, but I couldn't let these guys be suspended from Manchester without the true story coming out."

I nearly passed out, and in retrospect I figure I could have, and it may have helped even more. The group asked me questions about what had happened, who was involved, who had been hurt, etc. After about ten minutes of this, I was asked to leave, and then they shut the door. I waited for a while, but the pain was too much, so I headed for my dorm room. One of the nurses from the center was at the desk, so I avoided my room and went to Don's; nobody searched for anyone there. I took a pain killer and was asleep on the couch within minutes.

I remember dreaming about the game and scoring the touchdown. The exhilaration was there, and I was able to look around and see the response on Linda and my parents' faces. I could easily see my parents, and they were beaming from ear to ear, but Linda was blocked the whole time by a mysterious face. A beautiful face. I had never seen her before. Her eyes were deep brown and her long flowing dark brown hair fanned across a smile that was unlike any I had ever seen. She was smiling at me. I looked for Linda, but she had gone. The mystery girl smiled even more.

"You did it!" The words brought me around from the dream. Don was hovering over me with a beer in his left hand and his right stretched out to me. "You're one of us for sure now. Dean Grace vowed to get all of us the next time, and he mentioned you by name." What had I done! I was now lumped together with Don, panic set in. I jumped up and grabbed my shoulder instantly. The couch was not designed for rehabilitating a shoulder dislocation. I looked to Dirk for more news, and he was more than agreeable. "You are quickly becoming a status symbol for the future. Don and I were worried that we may graduate and have no one to pass the reigns of CU over to. You have proved that we have no fears of that anymore." He turned to Don and raised his beer, "Kinda makes you want to graduate doesn't it?" Both said, "Naw!" without hesitation.

Dirk came over to me and put his arm around my good shoulder. "This Alicia is going to get you in trouble though. You were talking about her again as we came in. Linda is one of the best looking girls on this campus; you better keep it cool about this Alicia chick." Fatherly advise from a young man barely able to tie his own shoes.

Dirk and Don went on to tell what the outcome of the trial was and that they were simply put on probation and would be expelled if the probation was broken. They laughed hysterically when Dirk told me that beer was not allowed in their probationary state. It became obvious that I had saved these two from nothing; they were always in harm's way.

But my mind wandered away to Alicia. It was her in the dream. But I had never seen her, how could this brown eyed, brown haired girl in my dream be real? Immediately, more important, what had my mentioning her name in my weakened state done to my relationship, or lack thereof, with Linda. It was foolish, but I got up and headed for Oakwood Hall, the dorm where Linda stayed. I was determined to get this in the open as quickly as possible. I guess there was pain in the shoulder, but the ache in my heart was overpowering. How could I be placing an unknown before a known? I questioned myself all the way over.

Outside Oakwood, I realized I had been followed the last few steps. It was the nurse from the medical center. She approached me with a smile, "It really wasn't a good idea to leave the center before you were released. Come with me."

I burst forward to the front door of Oakwood just as the door opened out. The door caught my shoulder square at the insertion point of the collar bone. The sidewalk instantly was nearer my face. Then I blacked out.

Tuesday I awakened in the medical center again. When I awoke there was no one around. For the rest of the morning, only the occasional nurse came by. About two forty-five in the afternoon, Linda came in with mail. She wasn't smiling. She laid the mail on my tray and walked away. On the top of the pile of mail was a pink envelope and the fragrance was unmistakable, Alicia. Linda was jealous, and I couldn't do anything about it. I called after her in vain; she was gone.

Chapter 17
<u>Tell It Like It Is</u>

I hurried off a letter to Linda as soon as I could hold a pen. Unfortunately, that wasn't until Thursday. In the meantime I called home and asked if Linda had contacted my parents. My mother said that she had, but had stopped calling on Monday after I was reinjured outside her dorm. Mom offered to come get me for the weekend, but by now I was concerned more about my love life than being comfortable and being waited on. From what my mother had said, I was not in Linda's plans any longer and that simply had to be rectified.

When the letter was finished, I called in the nurse and asked her to put it in the school mail for me. She had become a friend in this week's time and was happy to do the small errand for me. As she left the room, I thought out what it would be like if Linda were to understand and walk through the door at that very moment. It was a dream that was filled with soft music, hazy shadings around the picture's edges, and most of all a gorgeous blond coming towards me. Each time it ended with Linda giving me another letter and then walking away angry. My self-confidence in this matter was weak.

The rest of the day I spent reading books for classes that I was missing. It really was more difficult than it sounds though. There was no stereo playing, no screams in the hallway, no roommate asking for something. It was quiet. I accomplished virtually nothing. Beyond that, I kept writing a letter in my head to Alicia. She would understand the predicament that I was in and give me some good advice. Eventually, I gave in and started the letter:

Dear Alicia,

You are not going to believe this; a girl here at Manchester is jealous of you. She thinks that the letter I just got from you is from my girlfriend, and she didn't give me time to explain. I don't know what to do. We have never had a date since I spent the weekend in the hospital when we were to have gone out. Oh, yeah, I'm in the hospital with a dislocated collar bone. I was dancing with a semi-truck out on the highway, and it took advantage of me. You don't believe that do you? It was football and to make a long story very short - I scored and paid

for it. Help me please! I don't know my feelings
for Linda, by the way that's her name, but I never had a chance to find out due to the injury, and
then she picked up my mail for me and saw your
letter. She jumped to conclusions evidently and
walked out. I haven't heard from her since, and
she won't answer the phone when I call. What
should I do?

I went on with other information about
the past week and responded to her letter which,
by the way, was a friendly note telling me about
her pledge night at the sorority on the LaCrosse
College campus. She had many experiences that
were like the ones that I had gone through at
Calvin Ulrey, but the difference was that she
seemed devastated by them.   She was actually
talking about quitting college and just getting a
job. I wanted to kid her about her draft status if
she did and quickly erased that comment knowing that it would touch nerves that I have been
working to sooth.

I closed telling her that I really would
like to spend time talking to her and if that were
possible that she should let me know. We had
by this time a verbal agreement that neither of us

could afford a lengthy conversation on the phone, so writing was our outlet. But this was different, I wanted instant gratification. Only Alicia offered that. I finished the letter sadder than when I started. My interpretation of the situation at the time was that I was in love. I was confused who I was in love with.

The door to my clinic room opened slightly and a girl's hand was wrapped inwardly around the corner. Momentarily, Linda followed her hand around and came toward me. She half smiled, and I'm not sure what the other half was. As she approached the side of the bed, she slid herself to a sitting position next to my right side. No words, she just looked at me. Then, without any indication, she leaned over and kissed me on the cheek. Her lips lingered with the singular kiss, and she slowly pulled herself away. Tears were all over her face. The kiss had been a cover-up for crying. What was going on?

Standing and going to the window, Linda sighed as she wiped her tears away. I followed her as much as I could without positioning myself for pain. It took about a minute, but she eventually was able to say what she had come to say. "Alicia is more important to you than you know. While you were out, you didn't just mention her name, I could have handled that. There was an intensity, some kind of fire that was burning inside of you. I didn't sense that I was a part of that. I didn't have any way of knowing that you had never even met this person." She was crying again.

This was really more than I could handle. I couldn't effectively get up to console Linda, and I was absolutely sure my words were merely that, words. Words were all I had though, so I gave it a shot. "If we apply all you just said to the two of us, I think that you are going to see that I have much the same relationship with you, don't I?" Linda nodded in agreement. "When I was under the anesthetic, I was in another world, one that I can't live in. You are in the world that I can, don't let the other world get in our way." It was awkward saying "our way" since there had been no time to develop any relationship at all.

"Do you want to see me?" Linda was honestly looking for a commitment.

"Only if you want to see me?"

"Would I have stayed the weekend with you if I didn't?" It was a question that I had pondered myself.

"I guess you might just like to play nurse to poor invalids and then run away when they are in their direst need." Levity seemed appropriate by now.

An honest to goodness smile. Linda came to me, put her arms around my neck, and pulled back just enough for our faces to focus on the other. "Let's start again, okay. The nurse says that you can go back to your dorm tomorrow. Can I be here to help?"

"You don't have to if you don't want to?" I thought about what I said and quickly came back, "But you want to don't you? I mean, I want you to."

Linda stayed with me until it was almost midnight. She kissed me sweetly before she left. I felt good when the nurse brought my pain killer. It really was unneeded. But as I drifted off, the letter I had written caught my eye, and I dreamed of the brown haired girl.

Chapter 18
<u>For What It's Worth</u>

As November's days grabbed the trees and shook the leaves free, the campus at Manchester took on a different look. Navy pee coats took the place of jean jackets, and the flowering flowing clothes that epitomized the 60's were covered from sight. Less distinguishable also were the long locks of the young men who had seen their hair length as an outward sign of rebellion. I hadn't been home in a month. My hair had been growing since the beginning of my college days back in August. The Broadway musical "Hair" later explained this concept better than anyone ever would.

Linda, the radical "peacenik" that she was, saw in my long rebellious curls a statement from me about the Vietnam War. She had been on peace marches and stood up for her convictions numerous times in public forums. I was with her now. Following her to these meetings. I was a good listener, trying to decipher what this whole hubbub was all about. I really never committed myself to this at the time, but I put on the show for Linda. She wanted a hippie; I became one, at least outwardly.

The local SDS was meeting in the student union's lounge, and Linda felt that we should attend. I, however, was of the belief that I needed to get some studying done since I had lost some time with the shoulder injury which, by the way, mended nicely thanks to tender, and I do mean tender, loving care from Linda. My grades had fallen, and I tried to justify to her that it would do me no good to attend these meetings if the ultimate result would be that I would flunk out of school, get drafted, and go to Vietnam. Her response was what I found to be the usual: "I can help you with your school work anytime, but this is of national concern. We can make a difference if we just put in the effort." So I went to the meeting. It really is hilarious what a guy will do to be near a pretty girl.

I had written a report about the SDS for my political science class and was intrigued about the goals of the organization. I wasn't sure if the establishment press of the time period or the group itself gave off the apparent paradoxes of beliefs, but I could certainly see in them. They advocated peaceful resistance; and yet, almost every confrontation that they were in was violent. There were lofty words of freedom from oppression for everyone, yet they seemed to believe that their concept of America was the only true concept. I could go to this meeting in good conscience for only two reasons: Linda wanted me to go, and I knew in my own mind that the Vietnam War was wrong, at least our involvement in it. On that, the SDS and I agreed.

I hadn't received a letter from Alicia since I sent the letter asking her for help in the Linda matter. I had sent a couple of other letters, and still no reply. It bothered me, but I didn't think I should call her and I didn't know what else to do. So when I got the letter before Linda and I headed to the meeting, I was flabbergasted. I tore it open and read it as if I were hungry for the words.

I sensed hesitance. She was talking about my situation, how I had to go for this girl at all costs. She made my situation with Linda seem to be my last chance at a really good relationship. She suggested that maybe I shouldn't write her anymore and that she had come a long way and could get along just fine. There was more, but something in me was questioning the

146

motive. Greater was the intensity in my gut, so I tried to evaluate what was wrong. No matter how I looked at this, it was my relationship with Linda that had changed everything. The brown haired girl may have been smiling at me at the football game, but now she was crying.

I was back to square one. Alicia was in my thoughts; Linda was real and less than a block away. I couldn't lie to Alicia and say that I wasn't seeing Linda, and Linda already knew that my relationship with Alicia was only through the post office. At age nineteen I was trying to decide my future, or so it seemed. "Why couldn't they exist in my life together?" was the obvious question. Mulling it over and over, I came to the conclusion that they could, and I could handle it.

I had been doing all this while walking back to CU. I checked the bulletin board, a note from Linda reminding me to pick her up in an hour. Just enough time to write a letter I thought. Hurrying up the back steps, I was in my room and writing within seconds. The words were easy.

No letter I had written in my short life was as well thought out as the one on that early November day. What I was going to say was more than I had ever committed to any other person. I felt that Alicia needed to know that I needed her, and it had to be more than I had said before. Yet I had to stay away from seeming to want a relationship. Balancing this with my feelings for Linda was the crucial part. It was also the most difficult to word.

I went through fourteen sheets of paper before I hit upon the notion that a poem would serve me better than a group of words that were from the heart and yet muffled by confusion. The poem was easy:

> Choices abound
> Of life and death.
> Why is it hard?
> To find an easy path
> The way that the river does
> Winding its way
> Through the realms of non-resistance.
>
> Here is my now
> Ever here
> And yet it can leave
> At its whim.

There is uncertainty
Ever there
And yet filled
With possibility.

On the one hand there is hope
On the other hand there is hope
In my hands for the first time
There is love.
My choice is love
Everywhere.

I was impressed with the outcome. It
was a poem of love and yet wouldn't have to be
interpreted that way. It said I was intrigued with
Alicia. What it didn't say was that I didn't want
to lose her. I added that at the end. To do this I
used humor:
We've come so far and now you want to
dump me with no explanation. I think a dying
man is deserving of an explanation. But maybe
you already have found a new letter writer,
maybe one who writes clearer, better penman-
ship. Give me a chance, I can learn. You can't
throw me over for some calligraphist. I do have
other qualities you know. Off hand, I have
trouble thinking of any, but I'm sure if you spent

a day to a week you could find one.   Don't stop now, the brown haired girl with brown eyes is in my dreams.

My thoughts were interrupted by a knock at the door, and Nick called in to me. "Linda is down in the lobby, she says that your supposed to be down there. Better get your ass in gear."

The letter was in the envelope before I could even think. I vaguely remember writing the words, "I love you" at the bottom. Too late, the letter had to go out, and I wanted to say something like that anyway. I stuffed the letter into my coat pocket and put the coat over my arm while I searched for my keys. My psychology book was under them and was calling me to delve into some Freud. I grabbed it and was off.

Downstairs, Linda was not acting impatient at all, even though I was over ten minutes late. She rushed to me and threw her arms around me. The excitement of the evening gushed from her eyes. Sharing it with me was what made it special for her. This was her way of drawing me closer into her life. The thought of that was taking a hold in my heart. We were more than just friends now we were boyfriend and girlfriend. A fact that I made sure everyone knew as we walked across campus by putting my arm around Linda's waist. Immediately, she did the same.

The meeting had already started when we arrived, and there were no seats left. Looking around the room, it was evident that chairs were not the accepted form of seating. Crossed legged "hippies" were everywhere. They ranged from the long haired, stubbly beard types to the "John Lennon" glasses and tie die group, or abominations of the two. There were even a few faculty members among the crowd. I wasn't too out of place with the sandals, bell-bottom jeans, and t-shirt. There were no beads around my neck, no peace symbol and for that I was a little paranoid. I was sure that some of the radicals in the groups were pointing at me.

Loud words of hate and rebellion all tend to sound the same; it was no different that night. A guy named Sunshine Light was expounding the virtues of hunger strikes, marching on the state house, and taking over the administration building at Manchester. Each of the suggestions was given an appropriate amount of applause and discussion. But the lingering idea of the three on the college crowd was the administration building takeover. I personally liked the idea of going to the state capitol and marching around it for a while. Good publicity, and plenty of things to do in Indianapolis.

The decision was made, but no vote was taken – the administration building was to be bombarded by students at eleven that very night, and we would sit in any office in the building until we got other schools around the country to join us. Then we could really send our statement to the people of the United States and the world. Linda liked the idea and whispered to me. "Get a blanket and meet me at the Dean's office at eleven. Let's spend the night together."

Originally, this idea of sitting in the offices and not moving seemed like a poor idea to me. It seemed to me that it would be at the most ineffectual. Now, it had possibilities. The possibilities had nothing to do with protest of course. Yes, I really was remiss in my social consciousness, and Linda could use the support. "Sounds good. Should we bring our books?"

Linda laughed, "All you ever want to do is study. We'll be doing more important things." Who was I to disagree.

I returned Linda to Oakwood Hall at about 10:15. Not much time to get a shower, get on some cologne, and get back, so I ran. Back at the dorm Wayne and Dirk were in the hall waiting for me. This was not going to be the same confrontation as we had early in the year. Wayne spoke first, "Were you at the SDS meeting?"

I saw no problem with that so I said without hesitation, "Sure, what's the problem."

Now Dirk was ready, "Watch out Mark. Whatever they decided, don't do it. I just got word that one of the real radicals in that group is planning something none of you will be able to control. What it is, who he is, and when it is going to happen - none of that is clear right now."

My mouth was open. "They voted to take over the administration building at eleven. We are to go into the offices sit and not let anyone into them. What could go wrong with that?"

"Nothing if that is all that will be involved." The next part was hard for Dirk. "I will be there. Word leaked out early this afternoon. President Burgher called the governor; who called the national guard; who called me. I'm a guardsman. I don't like this war, but I be-lieve we need to defend our country. I'm not sure that I have to defend it from the SDS, but if my government says I have to, I will."

Dirk said these things for my benefit. He had come to like me, and I him. Wayne was standing there waiting. "Mark don't go. It can only hurt you and the friends you have here. It isn't that important."

They didn't say any more. They left me alone. Alone with my thoughts. I sat at my desk. It was almost 10:30. It was so crystal clear before. My decision would carry a lot of weight. I went over to my bed and hoped to sleep through the whole thing. Sleep didn't come. The Vietnam War knocked on the door. I had no choice; I had to answer.

Chapter 19
<u>Silence is Golden</u>

Every part of the plan that Sunshine Light had laid out went off just as he told us. For our part, Linda and I stationed ourselves in the Registrar's Office. The Registrar's Office is on the first floor at the end of the long hallway. We gained access when a stringy, long-haired senior whom I had seen around campus came along and pried the door open with a crowbar. The ease with which he carried this out amazed me on two levels. First, this office was supposed to be extremely secure because it stored all of the student records. Second, because this guy showed no remorse for breaking into the office. He actually seemed quite adept at his trade. I wondered where you would gain this kind of experience and quickly realized that I was in my apprenticeship.

There were ten of us in this office. File cabinets lined the east wall; the back wall had a large window overlooking the front lawn of the Administration Building. The door was on the opposite side from the window. Their was a railing on the inside of the door that had a writing surface on it for students, parents, or other visitors who entered the door. This kept a barrier between the registrar and the visitor. We and the other students could easily block access to this room with the barrier already in place. We all settled in front of the barrier, and Linda and I snuggled close.

Linda actually kinda encircled me and let out a soft cooing sound. This was her ecstasy; fighting for a cause with someone for whom she cared all at the same time. I was so glad that I didn't back out. At least for that moment, it was almost a religious experience.

We had been there for over an hour and had actually slept in each others arms for a while. That was until we were awakened by a loud commotion down the hall. There was a lot of yelling and students running in all directions. We really couldn't see anything, but we could hear the voices and the footsteps on the floor in the hall outside the door. With the door shut, we were unable to see what was going on. Then there was a loud cracking sound. More of the sounds repeated, followed by screaming and crying. By this time in my life, I had never heard the sound of a gun except on television.

But that is what I heard that early November morning.

I looked around the room; every single person's face was filled with fear. Linda was crying uncontrollably in my arms. What I thought was to be a lark; a campout with this beautiful girl, had quickly become a nightmare. Stupid! You stupid jerk! I was warned! I began to equivocate between my self-loathing in my mind and trying to comfort Linda. What had I gotten myself into? I didn't even have strong beliefs on this war, but now I was caught up in it. Linda looked into my eyes; I had to wonder is she worth it? She held me tighter. I had my answer; I was here for her.

A blast from a bullhorn turned our attention to the window. A girl across the room who had previously been in the same position with her boyfriend as Linda and I yelled to him at the window, "What are they saying?"

He was laying on the floor below the window, but he looked back at her and shrugged. He was visibly shaken like the rest of us; I wondered if he was here on the same pretext as me. He rose slightly to look out the window. As he caught sight of what was going on, he fell back to the floor. He began to gasp uncontrollably. Gradually, he gathered the presence to call back to us, "It looks like the whole United States armed services are out there! You can't even see across the street!"

They didn't know, but I did. I sat for a second weighing how to let them know. They deserved to know the truth. I stood up slightly, so that they could all hear me. "One of the guys from CU told me that he was a National Guardsman and that he was told to be ready to help out the college tonight if we actually did take the Ad Building. President Burgher called the governor for the Guard because her heard that there would be trouble tonight. I suggest that we get out of here as quickly as we can."

I got no response from any of them. Then I looked at Linda. She was not proud of me. In fact, she wouldn't say a word to me. Her body language said it all, "you are a traitor to me and the cause. Don't come near me." I tried to think quickly. I was on probation from the football game and the homecoming float, so I couldn't be caught here. But I didn't want Linda to think that I was backing out on her. I just had to get out of this situation and keep Linda's respect.

I reasoned with her. "How do you know what has gone on out there? What were those gunshots about? What do we really know about this Sunshine Light character?" This seemed like a perfectly good questions at the time. There was no way for me to know that the question I asked was being asked all over the campus.

There was disgust in her eyes. That disgust was for no one but me, and it burned right through me. It took her a while but eventually she managed to confront me, "Any cause takes dedication through good and bad times. How dare you question the man who really knows what it takes to get rid of this immoral war!" She paused for a moment of thought and came back at me, "Tonight, your presence here, it was for all the wrong reasons, wasn't it. You just wanted to be with me!"

When she said the words, it sounded so wrong. And had it not been for the tear gas that was hurled into the room through the window, I probably could have contemplated suicide or exile to a remote island and face no one ever again. The crashing window sent particles of glass everywhere. I reacted quickly and, no matter how she felt about me at the moment, I covered her to protect her from the shower of glass that was coming at her. In an instant, I was a blanket completely covering Linda. The stench of the burning fumes was immediate. I whispered to her, "Keep low, maybe the gases will rise. Let's try to get to the door and get some clean air."

She pulled away from me, coughing and hacking. "You're a traitor." She chose the torture of the tear gas to my protection.

I tried to reason with her, "You don't betray anything by just trying to breath clean air. Let me help."

Reason in the late 60's and early 70's was somewhat of a nebulous thing. She would have nothing to do with moving from where she was, and the fact that I suggested it further showed to her my lack of commitment. So I stayed. I don't know what I thought would change anything at this point, but I stayed.

My back was to the door when the creature came in the door. He was huge, masked, and armed. The gas mask covered all of his facial features; he was a perfect clone of the other guardsman running up and down the halls of the Ad Building. Huddled on the floor inside the

160

door, we had to look somewhat like third world refugees. His dominating stance, legs spread wide and arms crossed at the chest with a rifle cradled inside. His presence caused a tremor to run through my body. The tear gas had clouded everything, but I realized that he was not standing there alone. His words were simple, "The governor of the state of Indiana requests that you leave the premises immediately; if you do not, you will be arrested."

No one moved. I wanted to. I knew it was the right thing to do. I didn't. At this point, it wasn't Linda, but it wasn't the protest of the war either. I wasn't absolutely sure why I stayed, but I was sure that I needed to face this issue that I had put myself in. The towering hulk came toward Linda and I. My commitment was complete; there was no turning back.

One by one we were carried out. I had seen on television how to peacefully resist. I didn't fight it when the guardsman pulled me out of the building; I didn't help either. As I was taken out, I noticed bodies everywhere. None were dead. All were alive and protesting. I turned to see if Linda was behind me. She was nowhere to be seen. Did she know that I carried through on my commitment? Will she be taken to the same place that I will be going? Where are we going? Then I caught a glimpse of her as I was taken from the building. A guardsman had lifted her and was carrying her out. She fixed her eyes on me, but the look hadn't changed. My attempt to rectify things, left only a gaze that was yelling at me, "How could I have been so wrong about you?"

Two guardsman took me to a bus that we were all being placed in. We were instructed to be quite and sit where we were placed. We quickly found out that we would be transported to Fort Wayne because North Manchester or any of the other communities in the area couldn't handle this many arrests. That was when it happened. My mind finally calculated what was to happen next: my parents would be called! We were read our rights as a group. There were probably forty to fifty of us on this bus, all male. We were further told that we were being arrested for attempting to incite a riot, trespassing, and accomplices to a felony. Felony! What felony? The gunshots! My mind started to race.

Questioning my fellow prisoners was at best futile. They knew no more than I did. In fact, they were all pretty adamant that if there had been a felony, it had been in the name of the cause. Not me, I was suspicious.

We found out later the all of the girls at the sit-in were transported on separate buses to a jail in Huntington, a community south and west of Fort Wayne. I took some time to look at the faces on my bus. All of them looked vaguely familiar as Manchester students. Not one of them was Sunshine Light. Surely, he was arrested too! Then I thought that I wasn't sure how many protesters there were, so it was possible that he was on another bus. He had to be.

Even though it takes about 45 minutes to get from Manchester to Fort Wayne, it seemed much shorter. It seemed short because I spent the whole time trying to figure out how to get out of this without my parents finding out. We had just pulled up outside the jail when a face that I hadn't thought of in weeks came to mind – Ray. We hadn't been very close lately. He was spending more and more time with Julie, and I still was uncomfortable with that situation. And I was caught up with my relationship with Linda. He was my only hope in this situation.

The guardsman shook me from my plans when we came to a stop. "Each of you must be processed. It is a simple process; give your name, fill out the forms, fingerprints, and make your call." I didn't have to ask the question. A short young man at the front of the bus shouted, "You mean that we won't be held?"

The guardsman showed his frustration, "All of you on this bus are just pathetic followers. The real agitators will prosecuted to the fullest. If I had my way, all of you would be locked away until you rot."

I soon found out that I and the others were to wait in the holding cell to be processed, that the phone call would not be monitored, and that unless someone came to get you, you remained in the holding cell. My phone call was obvious now. I reasoned that if Ray couldn't come and get me, he could at least break the news to my parents, so I could alleviate some of the aggravation that would be imminent. I would have to face the music, but I could delay it slightly.

Fort Wayne had been my home since I was born. Not one of those 19 years had been spent anywhere near the city jail, at least from the inside. As we were paraded to the holding cell, a policeman came forward and unlocked a large, celled "room." He told us, "You all go in here. Wait until we call for you. And keep your hippy comments to yourself!" He further commented, "You can be released after we take care of the preliminaries and post bail."

That stopped me in my tracks. This time I was the one to ask the question, "How much is bail?"

The jailer looked at the sheet. "It looks like it will be $1000 for each of you."

Thankfully, I didn't ask the next question. It was a weakly looking, pimple laden faced boy who blurted out, "What if we don't have $1000."

He roared out a laugh. Then as he looked around the motley crew that came from Manchester he realized that none of us had been arrested before. "Guys, bail is ten percent of what is set. For those of you that can't figure it out in this case, you will need $100." He stopped and made a call. "Forget what I just told you. I checked. Everyone here will be allowed to leave without bond."

Boy was I relieved. I didn't even have the $100. Now all that I had to do was get through processing and make my call to Ray. I settled onto a slab and looked around. These ragtag members of the revolution had very little in common with me. Most had gathered to figure out how to top this protest. I wasn't one of them; it was more obvious now. What was I thinking! Oh yeah, Linda.

After about a half hour, the jailer came for me. I took care of the paperwork, gave them my fingerprints, and listened as I was told when my hearing date would be. I took it all in, but I was more than ready to get the chance to make my call. But it wasn't to be so easy. An officer in street clothes pulled me aside into a small room. He offered me a seat and began to ask me questions: Where was I when the guns went off? So they were guns! Did I see who was firing? It wasn't the police! But the final question was the one that brought all of the rest together, "Son, if you can give us any information on who stole the money from the school safe, we would drop any charges that we might have against you."

It came to me like a lightning bolt: Sunshine Light set it all up. He had no intention to be involved in a protest. He wanted to rob the school. He wasn't in the holding cell or anywhere else. He duped all of us, but more importantly, he took advantage of all the students who had true convictions. Students like

166

Linda. For a short while I pondered whether telling the officer what I knew would further infuriate Linda. In the end I had done a dumb thing in going to the Ad Building that night, I needed to rectify that. So I told the officer what I knew, what Sunshine Light had told us, what I had noticed, and most important, I gave him a detailed description of Mr. Light.

When I was finished writing my statement, I was taken down the hall to a phone and told that I could call for a ride. I called Ray's number. Thankfully, he was home and got to the phone before either of his parents. They were great people and liked me, but probably not at two o'clock in the morning. He was not really with it to start with, but when I told him where I was he came around immediately, "You're where?!"

"You heard me – I'm in jail. Now get your but dressed, get in your car, and get me out of here."

Through his sleepy coma, he started to laugh. "What did you do rob a bank?"

I was impatient at this point, "Listen, I will give you all the details when you take me back to Manchester. Just get down here and get me out!"

"Wait a minute! Do you really think that I am going to take a half hour to come get you, another hour to get you to Manchester, and then an hour to come home, tonight!"

Simply, I said, "Yes."

Just as simply he said, "Okay." With that he hung up. My assumption was that he was on his way. And he was. In the time that I spent waiting for him I reviewed how stupid I had been. I had let my hormones rule my brain, and I admit that I even went so far as to note that I had nothing to show for it. I looked around the cell. No one spoke. I didn't either. We had nothing in common.

When the officer came to release me, I was bored out of my mind. He walked me to the desk where I needed to fill out one more form. Standing there with a smile that told me I would never live this down was Ray. This was all a joke to him. " That's what you get for joining up with the hippies." My problem at this point was that I wasn't like them, but I had a similar belief about the war. That much of a commitment I could make. As we left I saw some footage of the "riot" at Manchester on the desk sergeant's TV. That was followed by a picture of Sunshine

168

Light. I wondered if I had been the one that gave enough information to find a picture. It didn't matter; my ride was there, and I was going home.

Chapter 20
Brown Eyed Girl

     The trip back to Manchester was any-thing but quiet. I had to detail for Ray what had happened including elaborate information about Linda. His questions were pointed, and I felt as if I were on trial. The only thing I cared about was that my parents would not be told about what had happened tonight. Ray quickly agreed to my plan, and I knew that I was safe at least from his angle on the situation. Manchester College administration might be another story.

     As we neared the campus, Ray pulled over to a parking lot for a small grocery store that was off campus. He stopped the car and turned off the ignition. For a second he said nothing, he was obviously collecting his though-ts. Slowly he began, "I really had hoped you would have been home one of the last two weekends so that we could talk this over. I think I understand what is going on with you better now." He paused and looked past me as if there were some sort of script behind me to read. "Damn, it! This was supposed to be simple: you write to her; make her feel good. You did that I know. Now she's miserable, and it's because of you."

I didn't let him finish, "We're talking about Alicia now aren't we?" He didn't need to respond. "What exactly is it that I have done?"

Ray was obviously astonished, "What do you mean what did you do? You got her to fall in love with you, didn't you? Then you go off with this Linda person and have the balls to write and tell Alicia all about it!"

"Now wait a minute, Ray! I never once led Alicia to believe our relationship was more than friends, in fact that is the way she wanted it to be. That is the way that both you and Diane wanted me to handle it." I was both angry and confused. Did she love me? What does that mean? What business is this of Ray's anyway?

"Whatever it is that you have said to Alicia has her thinking that you care more about her than she ever thought that she could have allowed. A month ago when I talked to Diane, she told me that Alicia was going to ask you to come with me next August when I go up to see Diane for the week. She wanted to know if I thought you would come, and if you would stay at her parents' house."

This was all news to me. News that I couldn't be happy about, but it was good news. "Well, if I was asked I would go, but how was I to know?"

"Maybe if you hadn't been concentrating so much on your hippie girlfriend, you might have come home for a weekend so that I could tell you!"

"You could have written me! For that matter you could have given me a call." I was defensive now. It wasn't entirely my fault.

"Listen, you haven't made contact with me since the last letter I wrote you back in October. I wasn't the only one not keeping in contact."

He was right, and I couldn't carry this any further. "Yeh, I'm sorry. Well, what can I do?" Then I remembered the letter that I had written just before all of this had happened. "Hey, I think that I may have solved this whole mess already. I sent Alicia a letter yesterday telling her that I still wanted to write and... I'm not sure..." and I wasn't, "I think I said 'I love you'."

"How could you not know if you said 'I love you'?"

"That is a longer story than you want to even hear right now, just know that I probably did. Now the question is how do I know that I love a girl that I have never met?"

This puzzled Ray much more than it did me. He could more easily understand the Linda situation than the relationship I had with Alicia. "Maybe analyzing this thing is more than we can do at this time. We have almost nine months before the two of you meet, why not just let things flow like they have been and see what happens?" I heard Diane talking in those words. She had obviously encouraged Ray to say something to me. Her motives were that she wanted Alicia happy and Ray's were to keep Diane happy. I wondered where my happiness fit in.

"No problem, that was my plan from the beginning; it is the August thing that still seems shaky to me. It is a different ball game to write a person a letter that you don't know. Going to Wisconsin would be a commitment to each other that would seem impossible right now." I had thought through these words, but when they were expressed out loud, they made a lot of sense.

Ray was almost pleading now, "If just for my sake, will you at least think about going?"

That was no problem, "Sure, but there is one thing that I ask, get me a picture of her. It's driving me crazy imagining what she looks like."

"I read your mind Mark. I asked Diane to send a picture of Alicia about a month ago, and I got it about three days later. I've held it until I saw you next, so..." He reached into his wallet and produced the picture. "Diane had someone take the picture and Alicia didn't know what it was for, probably thought it was for the family album." He offered the picture to me, while describing what was there, "You know Diane, so the only other girl in the picture has to be Alicia." The brown hair. The brown eyes. The girl at the football game. How could it be? How could I have known that she would look like that? It was eerie, but not for long. She was like no one I had ever seen before. The brown hair was shoulder length and tied back in a po-nytail. The brown eyes were surrounded by long dark lashes that were sculpted by nature not some cosmetic company. Alicia's face was one

174

that could be read easily. Her story was there and could be read by anyone who had a heart. Just by the picture I could see an empathetic person. I "was" in love. I didn't have to guess anymore.

"I take it that she meets with your approval since I can't get your attention." Ray was laughing at me now.

"This is my football dream that I was telling you about." It sounded stupid when I said it, but it was true.

"Well, it looks like your dreams will be coming true."

Ray started up the car and took me the rest of the way to Calvin Ulrey. We said our goodbyes, and I thanked him for getting me out of jail. I asked if he'd like a tour of the place. He declined saying, "Can't get to near a place that breeds pcople like you. See you next week?"

"Count on it." It was time for me to get back home for a while. This week would be my last before I would face the home fires again. My parents were going to find out, I figured, so I had decided that I would tell them everything. I guess that's called facing the music.

A lot was resolved that evening. There was ground that Ray and I could still stand on together. Alicia and I seemed to have feelings for each other that go beyond what we had thought our relationship would be. I was going to resolve my transgressions with the truth. Ah, if life were always this easy.

Chapter 21
<u>Think</u>

Sleep was tough on me that night. The brown haired girl had come to the jail in Ray's place. She held my hand and forgave me for going out with that hippie girl. We drove in my car for a long time until we saw mountains ahead of us. There were evergreen trees all around us. I pulled over to the side of the road, at her request, and she walked to the mountain. I waited for a long time, and she didn't return. When she returned, she was crying, and then she ran away.

That was it! I awoke and was sweating. My alarm had not gone off, and I was only three minutes away from missing my biology class. Instead of washing, getting breakfast, and brushing my teeth; I circumvented the process by just getting dressed and heading off for class. I had to have been a sight as I ran across the campus. My hair was uncombed, my shoes unlaced, and my shirt tail untucked. I reached the front door of the classroom with a minute to spare.

This biology class usually had around fifty students in it. As I sat down, it was clear we were not going to approach half that number.

I figured that some of the missing were still in jail cells or the equivalent somewhere still. My lab partner proved me to be somewhat in err. "Did your here about last night?" My lab partner was Charles Collier, the stereotypical science major. At various times in out nation's history he has been called "bookworm," "geek," and "nerd." His intelligence was one of the reasons I passed biology though. He had the answers; I just had to listen. "The SDS took over the Administration Building last night, and the National Guard was called in."

I acknowledged that I knew all about that, but I didn't offer that I had a part in it.

"Well, that wasn't all. Sunshine Light or whatever he calls himself stole money from the Treasurer's Office and no one can find him anywhere. A couple of his followers say that he took the money to fund the anti-establishment army somewhere in a secluded place. No one knew who did it until one of the protesters last night gave the police in Fort Wayne a lead."

I should have felt like a hero, and to some of the people, I probably was. To the rest I was lower than whale shit at the bottom of the ocean.

Just then Professor Milligan came in. He looked around the room and sighed. It was as if he were saying, "If only education could be that important." He went to the podium and stared at a note that was laying there. He looked up and spoke directly to me, "Mr. Logan it seems that Dean Grace feels that your presence is more important in his office than in my classroom, and I disagree. You can make your choice." With that I was in limbo. This man gave me a grade for this class; Dean Grace could say whether I stayed at Manchester. I wanted to discuss this with Professor Milligan, but he wasn't all that good at understanding anything that wasn't in a textbook.

I opted to stay. Professor Milligan could be an ally, I figured, and I was sure that I needed all the allies that I could get. So, I sat and didn't hear anything Milligan said. My thoughts were in that leather lined office that Dean Grace decorated with his own cold tastes. There were scary thoughts running around my head. I could be expelled!

Even though I had psychology immediately after biology, I made my way to the Administration Building. Just outside I noticed a number of National Guardsmen were still stationed around the building. I was let into the building only after I produced a school ID and was cleared by Dean Grace through a walkie-talkie. The halls were a mess leading to his office. Food, clothing, broken glass- everywhere were signs of the night before.

I was outside Dean Grace's office when I heard the voices of Wayne and Dirk. They were talking about me. Dirk said, "He didn't know what was going to happen. We talked to him beforehand, and it seemed like he was just going there to be with that girl, Linda Warner." Wayne added, "She persuaded him that this would be a peaceful sit in and nothing else, I am sure of that." With those words I knocked, figuring that I needed to speak for myself.

Dean Grace asked for me to enter. Inside, I saw that Wayne and Dirk were in their Guard uniforms. They had been there last night. I gave them a smile and went directly to Dean Grace. "I'm sorry I didn't get here sooner sir, but Professor Milligan said that his class was more important than whatever you wanted, and I felt like I would be unable to doubt him."

Poorly worded! I was surely going to get the full wrath now. Instead, Dean Grace patiently listened and pensively weighed his words. He began subdued, "Being late is of no consequence, breaking the law is." He turned his attention to Wayne and Dirk who were now behind him. "Your fellow CU men here say that you had no intention of aiding this Light character in theft. They think that your motives for last evening were, at the most, purely romantic."

The way he put the word romantic made it seem so immature and unlike what I wanted it to be. But it was the closest thing to the truth, so I told him that romance was the sole reason for my attendance.

Grace leaned back in his dark leather chair and apparently was surveying the ceiling. He got to the point, "I'm inclined to believe you; and in light of the fact that you were the one who led the police to Sunshine Light, I will let this incident go." Safe! It was too easy, but I wouldn't question the decision. He wasn't finished though, "I really could care less what your friends here felt about you. They are here for a different reason, and so are you. It is just fortunate for me and everyone concerned that each of you is in the position that you are. Mr. Logan, you have established yourself in our revolutionary community and the two of you are in the Guard. Among the three of you, we can more easily find this Light character."

Dirk spoke first, although we all were trying to ask questions, "What do you mean? Why would we be of any use to you?" That was my exact question.

Grace was cool in his reply. "Calvin Ulrey won the competition for float this year for the first time. Isn't that right?"

He knew it was. Don had been so proud when our idea "Prime the Pump of Knowledge" was chosen for the best of the dorm class. So what?

Grace went on, "The props that you used on that float were amazing and especially that pump. Can I ask you at this time where you could find such a pump?"

I offered the answer, "We borrowed it from a local establishment." Euphemistic, and yet to the point.

With that Dean Grace smiled and walked to his file cabinet against the wall opposite our chairs. He pulled out a folder with large letters on the outside spelling out "Calvin Ulrey - 1967 Homecoming." He opened it up and produced a picture of our float. "Is this the float that won the prize?"

He knew damned well that was our float. Dirk came forward, "So what, we won, we didn't cheat!"

"Ah, but you did steal, didn't you." His stare was equally divided among us. "In fact, this did come from a local establishment, Manchester Valley Cemetery. The grounds manager identified the pump in the picture as the one that was stolen from his cemetery and never returned. I looked at Dirk. He was in charge of the return of the pump. He shrugged his shoulders.

"It wasn't too hard for us to find once we started, and we didn't until after the football game with Taylor. I think you all remember that game. The barn that CU used to prepare the float was abandoned, but guess what was in that barn. I see that at least Mr. Thomas is aware of what was in that barn."

Dirk was holding his head in his hands. His face was covered fully. We were had. The only question left was what was to happen to us. Each of us was a three time loser and deeply situated in the Wilkins' doghouse.

Wilkins sat back down in his chair. He opened a different folder. "Sit down, men, this will take a while. You have no choice in this matter unless you want to be kicked out of college. If that is your choice, let me know right now, and I will go no further." He waited for what he thought was an appropriate amount of time for our responses. "I knew that you valued your positions here more than that, so I have an alternative for you. You will remain at Manchester on probation. Your parents will be informed as such. They will be informed that it will be for the pump incident. For you Mr. Logan that will be good news. I'm not sure what it means to the two of you."

I was impatient at this point for some answers, "So what do you want from us? This seems too easy."

"Ah, you want to cut to the chase huh? You, Mr. Logan, have ties to the radical community here at Manchester, whether you want to or not. Mr. Thomas and Mr. Renfroe are related to our country's armed services. You are friends. No one will ever suspect that you are checking with each other on the whereabouts of this Sunshine Light character. Mr. Logan will

184

never come to my office again. Your probation will be enough incentive to keep you straight is that clear," indicating that I would do as he said. "But you two will be constantly in this office answering to various questions, but will not be suspended. Your role here will be to convey any information on what is happening with this Light character. The information will be coming from Logan who will continue to date Ms. Warner."

Dirk was disturbed with this, "What gives you the authority to tell us to spy on fellow students. We're just students ourselves." He had a good point, and I chimed in with another, "If we find there is something very wrong, what can you do about it anyway."

Grace pushed the button on the intercom, "Miss Davis, send in the gentleman that has been waiting."

We turned to see a hulk of a man in a three piece gray suit enter. He was unsmiling and carrying a briefcase. He shook hands with Dean Grace. With a quick turn to view us, he captured at least my attention. and I noticed the others were staring at him as well. He got to the point, "My name is Lykins, special agent, FBI. What you have just been told is top secret. The

young man we want you to find out about is not
a student here, although he has established himself somehow in the community. He is,
however, dangerous. We have linked him to
robberies, bombings, and even a death. The
counter-culture sees him as a Robin Hood. We
look at him as a criminal."

Wayne spoke with a trembling voice,
"This guy is dangerous then?"

Lykins minced no words, "Yes. That is
why you are not to have direct contact with me,
and Mr. Logan will never make contact with
Dean Grace until this is all over." He was making this as sinister as he could. "By the way,
you cannot tell anyone beyond this room what
we have said, including your parents."

It hit me; this plan included my relationship with Linda. "I don't think that I can help
you that much though. I think I blew my
chances with Linda last night, and I'm afraid that
I portrayed myself as a traitor to the cause by
suggesting that we all leave when the real problems started."

Lykins found this humorous. "Don't you
think that we know that? We know. We made
some preliminary inquiries. That has been tak-

en care of. When you gave the Fort Wayne police the information last night, we investigated your situation and put rumors in place that you were actually a hero to the cause. Luckily, you were placed in the holding cell and the rebellious students sharing the cell with you were not in the Registrar's Office with you. They were sure that you were taken off and beaten, and that is why you were never returned to the cell. They are being arraigned this morning for no reason other than to get all of this in place." He stopped and looked me over good. "Your appearance is a help to our cause as well. You are dressed as you were last night; you haven't slept. Good scenario!"

It hit me. How did he know about the Registrar's Office. "How could you know about the Registrar's Office?"

"Your friend, Ray Osborne, didn't leave Manchester quite as soon as you thought last night. We spoke to him in this office for about an hour after he left you at your dorm. He filled in a lot of gaps for us. That is why we know that we can trust you."

I felt betrayed, and yet I knew that Ray had no choice. For that matter, neither did I now. One question was unanswered though, "You can't get Linda to like me again though."

"Again, we were lucky. The girls were taken to another location and before we let them go, we were able to tell about a young man who had enabled Sunshine Light to go free when he was seen going out of the lower level of the building. That is why your present attire is appropriate. You are probably the only person within a hundred miles that fits the description."

Now I was resigned to my fate. "I'll see Linda as soon as I can. She won't know much, but I'll try." I had little to say and was depressed that I must deceive Linda.

Dean Grace was of no mind to talk either. He showed us the door. If I wasn't a traitor before, I sure was going to be now.

Chapter 22
<u>Can't Take My Eyes Off You</u>

Linda was in the lobby back at CU when I returned. She looked tired, and there was a hint of dirt scattered on her white blouse. I stood looking at her, incredulous at what I was about to do. She was trusting, intelligent, and beautiful, attributes that are admirable in someone whom you would want to spend time with. Spending time with her did not even seem a remote possibility from this point on. When her eyes caught mine, my traitorous feelings crept forward, and I almost ran from the room. There was obviously too much at stake, so I approached her.

She jumped to her feet and wrapped herself around me. Holding me as tight as she was capable, she began to cry. "I'm sorry I said those things to you last night. I know you were just thinking about me. You probably think more about others than anyone I have ever known." She looked me over and hugged me close again. "What did they do to you? You're a mess."

"A lot of questions." I had to change the subject; lies were forming, and I didn't want to have to say them. "You're kind of out of sorts yourself. Are you all right?"

Her smile said a lot. Whatever she had gone through the night before was made better when she saw me. "I'm fine. We just had to spend the night. They released us without even charging us. But I heard that they were tougher on the guys and... well... we heard that they took you aside, and you weren't brought back all night."

Since she wouldn't let it go, I had to play out the script that was given to me. "The cops in Fort Wayne pulled me aside because they thought that I was the one that allowed Light to get away. They asked the same question over and over, just changing the way that they asked it. When they were finished, they let me go."

"You did help him, didn't you?" Obviously, this excited her because her voice went up an octave.

This was where the lie had to begin, "Yeh, I guess I stumbled into helping him get away. That's still what they think, but they don't have any proof. I'm not actually sure what I've done." That was the truth!

With a shudder, Linda pulled me close. "Let's not think about this right now. How about we go over and get a bite to eat?"

Needing a little time to think the whole situation out, I stalled, "I still have a little time left for my Lit class, and being so far behind, I better make a showing. How about I get a shower in and change clothes after class and then meet you at the Student Union for lunch?"

Linda looked herself over, "You know that sounds good. I haven't felt this grimy since losing the tug-of-war across the river at homecoming." A quick tug of my belt brought me face to face with her. "Don't take too long."

The kiss that followed was the most passionate we had ever shared. I didn't have to lie in the kiss. I let it all go, and my body reacted. She knew and smiled as she backed up. "We'll continue that emotion later, okay?"

Out of control, I shook myself to sanity, "If it is necessary, I can wait."

With a peck of a kiss, she was gone. Damn! I felt so good, and it felt like I was supposed to be doing it. But it was wrong. She trusted me. She wouldn't know there would be an ulterior motive all along. I was low. I was stuck. Then I wondered if it was alright if I fell in love with Linda? Would it mess up anyone's plan? Could I have a relationship with her? How far did I have to go to sell this charade?

I went to class, but by the time I got there, I only took a few notes, and we were out. I was in a daze on the way back to the dorm. In the process of thinking this all out, I made it to my room. Wayne was there, and we talked through our roles. He was vacillating as much as I was. He knew Linda. He knew how she was vulnerable and naive. We had the same deep-seated feeling of regret for what we were doing, but it did seem like the right thing to do, and we were caught up in our own actions.

I took the shower slowly. The myriad of circumstances danced around each other shoving for a place of permanence in my thoughts. Funny, Alicia Williams was the one person I didn't bring into all of this. She was out of the scene for now. The shower was long, but I didn't feel clean.

Wayne came in as I was drying off. "Message from Linda. Said she is going to be a little late. She got a call from her parents, and they are coming down to talk to her. Somehow they got word that she was involved." In a way I was relieved. Now I had the time I really needed to sort out everything.

"Did she say when she wanted me to pick her up?"

"Yeah, she said she'd call and something about picking up the pieces too."

I was back in the room and dressing when I was buzzed that there was a phone call. It didn't seem that Linda's parents would have been able to make that three-hour trip from Columbus, maybe she had made a change in the plans again.

The phone was down the hall. Since it was early afternoon, most of the hall was deserted, and it was unusually quiet. I picked up the phone and said hello. The hello in return was female, but it wasn't Linda. She said hello again. "Is there anyone there? Mark are you there?"

It was Alicia. "Yeah, I'm here Alicia. It is so good to hear from you!" I was serious about that remark. I so wanted to tell someone about this situation, and Alicia was safe being so far away.

My last two days were in another act of my life now. The stage now was a foreshadowing of the future, and I had little control of it. I realized that I couldn't tell her anything, so I told her what I wanted to and what I thought that she wanted to hear.

"I can't talk long, but I do want to straighten some things out." She hesitated and plunged forward, "First, I don't want you to stop writing," again a pause, "unless you want to." There was a feeling of relief coming through the phone line. There was a longer pause then, but I didn't feel that I could interrupt her. Finally, "Second, ...I ... would..., well I would like for you..."

I wanted to help her. It was such a struggle for her. I anticipated the end of her sentence for her, "Would it be alright if I come to visit you in Lacrosse this summer when Ray comes to visit Diane? I have never seen Wisconsin or you, but I have heard great things about both."

She didn't say anything for what seemed like an eternity. A terrible chill ran through me. Maybe I had anticipated her thoughts incorrectly. She then began to speak, almost in a whisper, "August is so far away. Mark, you don't have to come if you don't want to."

I quickly came back, "Nine months from now for one week, we will be laughing and talking face to face. Don't doubt that I want to be there." I hoped that the conviction in my voice would sell her on the fact that I was serious.

She paused for a second, " You know me so well. Thank you for that." It was evident that she was gathering herself for one last word, "I've got to go." Alicia was grasping for words now. "I love you." She hung up before I had chance for a reply.

It was evident now that the letter had arrived, and that I had indeed ended the letter with those words. Rollercoaster, thy name is Mark Logan! I was on a ride that was seemingly going to give me every thrill I would want. Is that what I want? That was my question to myself: Alicia? Linda? Nothing was resolved. In fact, I didn't want to tell Alicia about Linda, the FBI, or anything at all now.

After looking at my watch, I hurried back to my room to get dressed. As I pulled on my shirt, I caught a glimpse of Linda in the distance. She was coming to meet me half way. I tucked my shirt into my pants and slammed the door behind me. As I left the room, Wayne caught my eye as I passed him. I decided this was the time to

get started. I could not let this go on too long.
My emotions were distracted into too many
areas. Get the information and get out clean,
that was my goal.

Chapter 23
<u>Baby, Now That I Found You</u>

Linda greeted me much as she had left me. Stirrings inside me made me uncomfortable in what should have been a most comfortable situation. The elements of a true relationship were all there except the deception with which I was involved. My first true girlfriend, and it was a lie!

"My parents want to meet you, Mark. So I told them that they could join us for lunch. Is that okay?" She was talking fast, and the thrill of showing me to her parents was apparent in her whole demeanor.

I couldn't tell her no, even though I was unsure of how to approach any set of parents, let alone the parents of a girl that I was trying to deceive. I acted as if it were fine, "Sure, it's okay with me, as long as you don't mind them meeting a jailbird."

She grabbed my arm and led me toward the Student Union Building. "Remember, my darling, I'm a jailbird too. They know that, and they know that you were there with me."

"Won't that bother them? I mean, they might think that I am corrupting their daughter."

Linda stopped me with a tug on the arm. She looked deep into my eyes, "My father was a conscientious objector during World War II and spent many days doing just what we did. My mother was always by his side. They believe in what we are doing. They will never doubt us."

I swallowed hard. People with convictions had always been a problem for me, they made me seem so shallow. This would be harder than ever; they will see through me, and I would be embarrassed and exposed. I had no choice but to go forward, but sweat developed in places where I shouldn't sweat.

Inside the Student Union, near the student lounge, was an older couple. They waved to us, and Linda returned the wave. They were young looking. Linda's father was thin, a man who had the two most obvious signs of age teaming up on him: he was slightly balding and his beard was distinguished with gray streaks everywhere. Her mother had long hair that was blondish, and yet was creeping toward white. They were both dressed casually in slacks and flannel shirts. As we approached them, I saw the resemblance, they each were capable of displaying a smile that genuinely invited a stranger in. I was at ease for a while. They were not the enemy.

Linda introduced us and I shook hands with both. They had strong hearty handshakes that were sincere. Linda's father led us to the cafeteria line. "I want to pay for all of us if that is okay with you Mark?"

"You know how we students are with money. A free meal at anytime is welcome, sir." It sounded so formal, but my parents had ingrained in me respect for elders that I couldn't shake.

"If its okay, call me Bob," he asked.

Linda's mother added, "And call me Cheryl."

I was ill-at-ease calling adults by their first names, but I agreed.

We got our meals and found an empty table near the windows overlooking the football field. Bob said grace, and we began eating. These three were close. They kidded each other, and Linda had no trouble relating to them what had happened the night before. I knew my father, a veteran of World War II, didn't understand the protests to the Vietnam War and judged all adults to be of the same mind set. We had arguments about it often, even though I had never committed myself one way or the other. Yet, we were close in other ways. Linda's parents made me feel at home.

Cheryl asked me, "Linda tells us that you are from Fort Wayne. Why did you come to Manchester?"

"My parents both went here, and I guess I figured that what worked for them was good enough for me."

Bob was surprised, "Your father wouldn't be Pete Logan would he?"

He wasn't half as surprised as I was, "Yes, he graduated from Manchester in 1947 after he came back from his hitch at Okinawa. Mom graduated the year before."

Cheryl leaned back and laughed, "I'll bet your mother's name is Ann. They went to school with us."

I wasn't sure how to react to this. It was obvious my father's political bent was opposite to that of Bob, and my mother was far more conservative than Cheryl. Why, my parents even looked older than Linda's. "Are you sure? My parents lived in the married housing over where the new Garver Hall is being built. In fact, I was born in the Wabash hospital."

Bob was exuberant at this point, "We used to baby-sit for you. You and Linda shared the same crib when either we or your parents would have to go somewhere. You two have known each other longer than you know."

Oh great! Now I was betraying someone that I have a history with. We actually slept together, literally. This felt like family to me, but I was constantly remembering why I was there. I would have to wait to get to the mission. Maybe Linda would never know what was going on. Maybe someday these would be my in-laws. I responded genuinely, "My parents will want to know that I have met you. They have already met Linda."

Linda bubbled, "That's right, when Mark was hurt in the game I was telling you about, his parents, and I sat around and waited for him to regain consciousness. We never even talked about family background. What a small world it is!"

Bob looked at his watch. "Sorry we can't stay longer, this was just a stopping point for us. We've got crops to attend to and some supplies to pick up." He stood, and so did Cheryl. I stood, again out of respect, and reached out my hand. "Mark, Linda couldn't be in better company here."

"Take care of her will you? Someday I'd like to meet up with your parents again, wouldn't you Cheryl?"

She shook her head yes and bent to give Linda a kiss. Bob followed with a kiss on the forehead for her. Then they made their way out of the cafeteria.

Linda pulled my hand to her. "They love you, and so do I. Let's study together tonight, I'm behind in my studies and need some help. Think you can help me in lit and biology?"

My opportunity to get on the case was at hand. It wasn't my first thought though. I first considered: you bet I want to be alone with you tonight. Lecherous, pornographic reasons. "What time?" was my only reply.

She leaned over, kissed me and whispered, "Seven, my room, and remember your books." A devious laugh followed the word "books."

Leaving the building the way we came in, I noticed that the campus was fuller now. Was it my imagination or were all the rioters of the night before out there, finally released? A couple of the ones with whom I had ridden the bus went out of their way to shake my hand. Lykins had done his job. Linda was looking adoringly at me. I felt like shit.

Chapter 24
<u>On a Carousel</u>

The next few weeks were filled with letters and phone calls. Mostly letters. Both Alicia and I had developed our own language using everyday words but in our context. It wasn't really a language, but more of an understanding. She started to tease me with words that flirted with sexual innuendo. There were times that in her words I could swear that I could see her blush.

My grades were not as glowing as my correspondence, however. Not only had I managed to maintain a relationship through the mail, but Linda and I were getting closer and closer. At the same time the ominous task that I carried from Dean Grace was weighing on me as well. The result was that I was either missing classes or sitting in the classes and drifting off to Linda or Alicia.

In addition, Dirk and Don were constantly finding reasons for me to be doing anything but classwork. They even smiled knowing what they were doing to me. But they were built in excuses for my lack of motivation

204

and distraction. What was really happening was that I found myself writing more and more. Mostly poetry. And the poems were mostly about one or the other of the two young ladies in my life. That is not to say that some didn't reflect the times in which we were living, but my relationships took up a lot of the time.

The only grade that I definitely knew was the biology grade. Professor Milligan had pulled me aside last week and told me that if I didn't make up some of the labs that I had missed that I would fail. While he was telling me how tragic this would be, I was thinking of how to put this situation into a poem.

The other profs were either toying with me or so totally liberal that they just chalked it up to a freshman still looking to find himself. All I know is that I didn't feel a compulsion to worry.

The week before Thanksgiving I received a message that I needed to go to Dean Grace's office. For only having three months of college under my belt, it seemed that I had been in this office too often. This time though I noticed more. As I entered, I realized that Grace wasn't really that old. My earlier impressions of him were that of an old man who liked to get

under the skin of undergraduates. I had learned
that he, himself, had been a student at Manchester and had lived in Calvin Ulrey as well. He
had moved up the ladder from instructor, assistant professor, professor, and department chair
very quickly. When I saw him on this day, he
was wearing one of the double breasted suits
that he seemed to favor with a flowery shirt,
business-like with a flair for some fun. I had
seen him off the campus, and this demeanor was
not the same off campus. He wore jeans, t-shirt,
and sandals.

He was the enemy in this job though,
and as I waited for him to be free, I noticed that
his secretary was watching me in an extremely
disapproving manner. It was pretty obvious that
she felt that college students were all spoiled
rotten, and that I was a perfect example of her
stereotype. It seemed to me that she should be
placed with another office since she only saw
students who were in trouble, but that thought
probably didn't enter her mind because she had
all kinds of stories to take to the community
from this job.

My wait actually took almost fifteen minutes. In the time that I waited, I took out a piece of paper and started to write a poem.

> The door to the future is yours
> Fail to open it
> And the ingrates of the past greet you
> Are they such awful company?

As I sat there staring at my work, I was finally summoned by the secretary into Dr. Grace's office. I was so into the words that I had written that I was walking and reading the words as I entered the office,   "Enthralled are we by the written word?" Dr. Grace's words startled me into consciousness. He was standing just inside the door and indicated that I should sit down. He went to his chair and added, "A love poem no doubt?" I believe he was asking a rhetorical question.

" Uh, no, it's just a poem that I was starting while I was waiting." Letting that statement out, embarrassed me. Except Alisha, no one even knew that I wrote poetry.

He reached across the desk, "May I see your work?" It wasn't the question said in the manner of that student passing notes in class.

Grace seemed genuinely wanting to read my poem.

I gave him the poem, and he started to read it. He leaned back in his chair after reading the four lines. Pensively, he studied me for a minute. Then he leaned forward and questioned me, "What does this poem mean to you?"

I really couldn't remember what I had written, so I reached for the poem. Dean Grace handed it to me, and I read my own words. It seemed pretty straightforward to me. "I guess it means to me that the future doesn't have to be so important in our lives today. Maybe now is pretty important too." I felt a glow of accomplishment with my interpretation and the statement that I made.

Grace took the paper back from me and read the words. "Perhaps this somehow explains the trouble in which you now find yourself. The future has little meaning to you, so you don't see that your lack of effort in your classes will directly affect you and your future." He went back to his desk and picked up a folder, looked at some papers inside, and closed it. He then offered the folder to me. "Let's see if what is in here will put the 'now' into perspective for you."

It couldn't have gotten any colder in the room if a storm had gone through at that moment. My name was typed on the tab of the folder. Included across the top was vital information about me like my home address, my parents' names, and so on. It was the contents of the folder that I dreaded. The first page was a write up of my work in Professor Milligan's class. This information wasn't anything that I didn't already know. The second sheet was an assessment of my work in my psychology class. The sentiments there were much like what I knew would come from Milligan. There were other sheets from my other professors, none as bad as the first two, but they definitely did not paint a good picture of me either.

It was the official looking sheet in the folder that grabbed my attention. Blazoned across the top of the paper were the words: "Discipline Problems." As I looked across the issues that were listed there, I realized that I had become something that I never thought that I could be – Don! It was all there. A report that I wrote and recited a pornographic poem. My part in stealing a pump from a cemetery. My actions at the administration building were there in great detail. With that was a note that I had been helpful in looking for the perpetrator.

There were a couple of character references. One was from Mrs. Harrington the dorm mother. She called me a "sweet boy" who is influenced by that hooligan bunch led by Don Bates. The other was from Dirk, since he was an All-American, his word was still good at the school. A couple of years later after he had graduated, his name was mostly dirt. No matter what they said, I could figure out that this folder spelled out in big letters "**You're in trouble boy!**" I searched in mind for a way to get past this situation. Nothing. I sat there in a stupor.

While I had read the folder's contents, Dr. Grace had strolled to the window of his office. He was standing and staring at the front lawn of the Administration Building. When he began to talk, it was towards the window, but there was no doubt that he was addressing me. "Your SAT scores and grades from high school indicate that you can handle college work." He turned and looked at me, "The grades that I see in that folder are not indicative of the young man whom we admitted to Manchester." His pause at this point was for me to digest what he had said, and I did. It was true that I had changed considerably. But my intelligence was the same, it was my attitudes and emotions that had evolved.

He continued. "Change in students is to be expected between high school and college. It is one of the hardest transitions in our lives. A slight drop in grades is somewhat expected." He then looked at the poem in my hand and pointed to it. "This poem indicates the intelligence that we recognize in you. But it also tells me that you are not moving forward. You are stuck, and I want to help."

Help was not what I had conceptualized as my reason for being in Dean Grace's office, so I was stunned for a few minutes. At the time, I saw this man as the enemy. The guy who got mad at everyone. Obviously, I was wrong. "I don't see how you can help." That was all I could say.

Grace pulled a chair up right in front of me and stared into my eyes. "The real question is 'do you want help?'"

I was astonished at my response, "Why wouldn't I? I have dug a hole that I don't know how to get out of!"

He smiled, "Indeed." As he went further, he leaned back in the chair, "You should want to fix this mess. It is my job to help you and any other student get back on track" With those words he went back to his desk and picked up a second folder. As he opened the folder he explained, "Professor Milligan alerted me to your problems, so I checked with your other instructors. When I saw that you were in over your head, I worked with all of them to devise a plan."

He handed me the folder and indicated that I should open it. I did and found outlines for all of my classes. He continued, "Each of your instructors took the time to put together a plan for you to pass each of their classes. As you can see, in your literature, sociology, and physical education courses, you are getting off pretty easy, but that is because you had done more of your work in those classes. It will be your biology and psychology classes that you will have to really work hard."

The details of the outlines were very specific and the time lines for each were specific with little or no wiggle room. He was right; this was not going to be easy. Professor Milligan had me virtually doing the whole semester of biology over again, and I has less than a month to complete it.

My shock must have showed, because there was a look of concern on Dean Grace'sface. I swallowed hard, got out of my chair, and walked to him. "I've been wrong, and I deserve this. Thank you for the opportunity. You won't be sorry." I turned and went for the door.

Grace called to me, "That isn't quite all. You have to get all of this work done or you are out." The manner he presented this was not as a threat, but as advice.

I didn't respond. There was really nothing that I could say. It was in black and white. I shut the door behind me and walked back to CU. I wasn't thinking of Linda or Alicia as I went down the steps of the Ad Building. My mind was awash with ideas to get the work done. As I analyzed it, I could get all of the work done, but the biology would take more time than I had. That was when I decided that I would have to miss most of my Thanksgiving break, and that every weekend after that would have to be spent writing papers and getting labs caught up.

I had a plan and was finalizing it in my mind when a voice cleared my mind of all the work, "Mark, please slow down. I have to talk with you."

It was Linda, and she was smiling. She caught up to me and grabbed me by the arm. "I think that I owe you an apology." With that she stopped me from walking and put herself in front of me, face to face. "I found out this morning that you were right." Then she kissed me.

I had no idea what she was talking about. She could tell, so she added, "That night in the Ad Building, the sit in. You knew that there was something about Sunshine Light that wasn't right. I doubted your motives." She stopped and a tear formed. "I so much wanted to be a part of the changes that are coming in the world. I thought he was, well, I was wrong." She showed me the front page of the paper, "College Protester Found with Money." The article told about Sunshine Light aka David Simmons, wanted in four states for armed robbery and bad checks. It further said that the SDS had never heard of him. Simmons' accomplices had ratted him out because he hadn't split the money with them which was the plan. They further told the police that the idea was to distract everyone with the protest.

After I finished the article, it hit me. Grace would have known that Simmons was caught. I wasn't on the hook anymore, at least for that. He must have truly wanted to help me. Just as quickly, it hit me that I didn't have to lie to Linda.

But the folder in my hand brought me back to the current reality. I stroked Linda's face with my left hand, "I am so glad that this is all over, and I don't care about being right or wrong." I then indicated the folder, "I have to get to the library. I have a lot of work to do." Then I told her what had happened in Dean Grace's office.

The walk to the library wasn't long, but by the time we got there, Linda knew all about my problems. Before we went into the library, Linda grabbed my arm and looked deep into my eyes, "This is partly my fault, so let me help you. I was going to go home for Thanksgiving, but now I am going to stay and help you get through this." She didn't leave an opening for me to debate her on this, and I really didn't want to. I really wanted her to stay with me.

As we entered the library, I put this all into perspective. School was going poorly, but there was hope. Linda was with me, and we were happy. And then came the realization – how do I fit Alicia into all of this? I started to sweat. Linda smiled at me thinking that the anxiety of all the work had gotten to me. She hugged me and said, "It's all going to be all right now." I believed her.

Chapter 25
<u>Goin' Out of My Head</u>

It was the weekend before Thanksgiving Break. I was grateful for the hour in the car. I needed the time to sort things out. I was under the speed limit and was in no hurry to get anywhere. I hadn't heard from Alicia since we talked the other day and started to think that she hadn't really said what I thought that she said. It was a dream, and I was just confused because of all the things that had gone on at Manchester. I knew that wasn't true, but it made me less crazy than I was at the moment.

Linda had decided that, since she was going to be with me over the Thanksgiving weekend, she called her parents to see if it would be okay to celebrate their Thanksgiving the weekend before. They were fine with that, and it gave me the chance to clear up other parts of my life.

I wasn't expected home, so I went to Ray's first, I really needed someone else's perspective. When I pulled up to his house, I noticed that he had just returned home and there was a girl in the car. My first thought was that

Ray was cheating on Diane again, but in closer observation I saw that the girl <u>was</u> Diane.

Quickly, I got out of my car and ran up to Ray's. "Diane, what are you doing here? When did you get in?"

She looked me over. I had forgotten that she hadn't seen me in over a year. My long hair and bell bottoms were new to her. "My have you grown up, Mark. I flew in just a few minutes ago. Ray and I wanted to celebrate Thanksgiving together even if we can't be together on Christmas."

"That's great! You mean you'll be here all week?" I wasn't sure why I would care, but it was good conversation.

Ray stepped out of the car, "Diane will be here until next Saturday. Will you be available to go out with us tonight?" As he was pulling out Diane's luggage, I noticed a sideward's glance to me. It was only for me and I assume that it had to do with the riot at Manchester. He probably didn't want me to mention it to Diane, so I played along.

"Well, I haven't been home yet. Let me check and I'll call you. Okay?"

Diane spoke before Ray could answer, "At least come over after supper. We need to talk."

"Sure." It all seemed so ominous, but I was intrigued. "I'm sure that the folks will get over asking me questions by the end of supper, and then I'll be over."

Ray took the luggage in the house and Diane followed. I got in the car and headed home. An imbecile could see that this had to do with Alicia. Even if my parents had plans, I decided that I would have to beg off.

I pulled into the driveway and parked my car behind my father's. He had a '65 Chevy station wagon. It reeked of family, and I reflected on how much I hated driving that car. Yet it was the vehicle that our family depended upon on our many family vacations. In retrospect, we never used it for that purpose again.

I was greeted, if you could call it that, at the door by my father. This was extremely unusual when you consider that he seldom left his recliner once he was home. His face was covered with lines, and they weren't worry lines. The puffs he was taking on his pipe signaled that I was in trouble. Like a puppy who just chewed on a shoe, I ducked and headed for the sofa. As

I was sitting, mom turned the corner from the kitchen wiping the dishwater from her hands.

Dad started very slowly, "We have been told that your grades are dropping," he paused for effect, "and that you paid a visit to Fort Wayne and didn't stop to see your parents." While he was speaking, my mother brought a letter to me that had the return insignia of Manchester College. Written above the school's address on the envelope was Dean Grace's name. My father continued with a stronger sense to his message, "Explanations are necessary, and they better be extremely good."

With no preparation I went into my dissertation, "There really is no good explanation. I was in the wrong place at the wrong time and because of my involvement with Linda, my time in the clinic, and the cause, I got behind in my work. I can tell you now that I have met with Dean Grace and will raise the grades. Linda is helping me."

My mother almost had tears in her eyes. "How could you get involved in a riot. What were you thinking?" I think she wanted to know what jail was like, but she didn't ask.

"Mom, I was with Linda. She said the sit-in was a good idea. I guess I just followed her. Truthfully, I didn't even know what I was doing. If it will make you feel any better, I wasn't in the jail very long, and I will have no criminal record." I added that information thinking that it would get me off the hook.

Dad was furious. "Do you mean to tell me that you got yourself arrested to impress a girl?" Dad had a way of getting rid of all the garbage and getting to the meat of an issue. I was surprised by his next response though. He started to laugh uncontrollably. I was stunned, but not more so than my mother.

"I don't see what you can be laughing about! Our son was in jail and is in danger of flunking out of college." She was so serious that I went to console her.

My father controlled himself and spoke to her, "Don't you see? Mark was in love. He did the same thing that I did years ago in trying to get to know you. You do remember the day the recruiting officers came to Manchester? Do you remember what I did? Do you remember why I did it?" As he paused for her response, I perceived her smile was growing. "I see that you do remember." With that he turned to me,

"That doesn't mean that you are off the hook, however. Is it safe to say that you are aware of the severity of the issue?"

There would be no reason for me to shirk this issue. I hit it head on. "I cannot fail or I will be expelled. I won't let that happen."

After sitting down on the sofa next to me, dad put his hand on my shoulder. With deep sincerity he began, "I will work my hands off for my children so that they can get a better education than I had. I never finished college and neither did your mother. We want you to have a better life than we have had. That is what I'm talking about. We are committed to your education, we expect for you to be just as committed to it as we are."

It was easy to agree, and then I played the trump card. "I forgot to tell you. Both of you know Linda's parents – Bob and Cheryl Warner. They said that you were friends at Manchester."

From the look on my mother's face, I could tell that these people were dear to her. She came to me and put her arm around me, "The Warner's were our closest friends in college. They were much like us. Married. A

222

child." It hit her then. "How absolutely romantic that the two babies who were together in a
crib are dating eighteen years later." Then came
a big hug.

We discussed the Warners and what
they have done since Manchester. The talk continued through supper and would have gone
longer if I hadn't remembered that I promised
Ray and Diane. I made my apologies and
jumped in the car. I knew I wasn't totally off
the hook on the demonstration thing, but it had
been tempered pretty well.

Ray and Diane were sitting on the en-
closed front porch of Ray's parent's house when
I pulled up our front. They were talking as I
walked up the sidewalk. As I approached the
door, they stopped and Ray motioned me in.
They didn't waste any time as I entered the door.
Ray was first. "Mark have you lost your
senses?" Diane was next, only calmer, "I know
you meant well Mark, but everything's a mess
now." She hesitated and came back with well-
chosen words, "She loves you. She doesn't
know it. But in her eyes, it's there. The only
time she comes back to reality is when she looks
at the MIA bracelet that she wears for Nick.
Then she feels as if she is betraying him." She

stopped for second. Tears were welling up. She wiped them away and came to me. "I know you were helping because we asked. And I know that you did your best. But we have to find a way to end this."

I was dumbfounded. I knew what she said was probably true. I also know that in my crazy mixed up world of the moment, I actually wanted her to love me. It also hit me that Alicia had grown to need my letters for support. Even if I put a stop to the letter writing, I didn't want to hurt her. She had become important to me as well. The thought of her hurting in anyway tore at my soul.

I had been in my thoughts for a long time when I finally mustered a few words to Diane. "It has gotten out of hand, hasn't it? What can I do now? I can't hurt her. I care too much for her." Diane just shrugged and looked to Ray. Ray was disgusted with the whole thing, after all this was taking away from his time with Diane. He eventually grunted, " You need to think what could possibly come from this in the end. Maybe it is best to just end it now and everyone move on."

I was about to tell him how crude that sounded when Diane spoke, "It's true. Really Mark. The two of you actually coming together. Maybe once next summer, but never again. Even though I would like for you to come with Ray next summer. It makes sense to end it now, and you can move on too," she struggled for the name that Ray had obviously given her. I helped her, "Linda." She continued, "And I will help Alicia. She still has to face what she will eventually find out about Nick. Maybe that's enough for now."

I listened and could understand that they made sense. They made sense to a person who could logically ponder a situation. Not me. I was incensed. I went to the door and looked over my shoulder as I opened it to leave. "Have you noticed that Alicia and I are the problem? Not you two playing God with our lives. It was your idea to begin with. Now the way that we have created our bond makes us wrong! Fine, I won't write her! You explain it to her any way you can!"

As I struggled my way to my car, I thought of one last point, turned and was face to face with Diane. She spoke in soft words. "I wish that Ray loved me as much as you love

Alicia, and you've never met. Give her time. Give me time to help her. Live your life here." Then she kissed me on the cheek and smiled a knowing smile.

I spent Saturday at home, mostly alone with my thoughts and of course with my family. Being around family kept me busy and allowed me to think. I was now committed more than ever to Linda, if she would have a liar. I was going to tell her the truth about Alicia.

Chapter 26
This Guy's in Love with You

Linda had talked me into spending Thanksgiving Day with my parents. Her parents had even called and suggested that Linda spend the weekend with my parents, so Linda and I drove to Fort Wayne after classes on Wednesday. She convinced me that the rest of the weekend we could get my work caught up. I actually felt bad that she had to spend the time away from her parents. I mean, I know that she made the trip to Columbus the previous weekend, but it just seems that you should be with family on Thanksgiving.

My parents were very happy to have her with us, especially since they felt like Linda had been a part of our family all along. She got the full treatment that weekend. My grandparents, aunts, uncles, and cousins were all assembled as was the custom until my grandmother died three years later. My grandfather joined her a little more than a year later. So this was a special Thanksgiving, and we didn't even know it.

Being the oldest of all of the grandchildren, this meant that I was the first to bring a date to the festivities. Linda fit right in, even though she knew only me and my parents. She helped me to make the transition that we all must go through: from the children's table to the table with adults. The whole meal my cousins and siblings made fun of the fact that I had to listen to boring "adult talk." It didn't seem so bad actually, because Linda and I were the focus of the conversation.

I found myself trying to shield Linda from the comments of relatives. More than once I became defensive and irritated. The Logans are a loving family and enjoy each other's company, but that sometimes bordered on invasion of other's privacy. Before that day I had never noticed that, but I had never presented a young lady to the congregation before either.

Linda handled all of the confusion very well. In fact, she fit in better that day than I did. She laughed loud and hard when Uncle Bill told his usual Rodney Dangerfield self-deprecating jokes. When Aunt Mary was having trouble with two year old Jason, Linda was down on the floor with him rolling around and playing with him. They all loved her.

I was in the dining room standing in the doorway watching Linda playing euchre with my sister and cousins when my father came up beside me and put his arm around me. "She's something Mark! How do you feel about her?" Since my father had always teased me, in his own way, about dating, I didn't quite know what to say. So I surveyed his face to find that playful look that he would always get. It wasn't there. He wasn't kidding this time.

How could I tell him the turmoil that was inside me? How could I explain how I felt about Linda when I still couldn't explain my feelings for a girl hundreds of miles away whom I had never even met. I made a quick and decisive decision that Linda was here and so was I. That is what is most important. The other part of my dilemma wasn't important now. "Dad, I really like her a lot! She's different from any girl I have every known." It sounded slightly evasive, but it was true.

"Taking the conservative route, huh? Well at least in your relationship anyway!" The reference to my jail term was evident, but the way that Dad could get his little jab in and still refer to our relationship. He patted me on the back and started puffing on his pipe. Politically, we were starting to split, but we couldn't have been closer at the time. Later in life, I would realize that I was closer to him than I was letting myself believe.

Everyone admonished us for leaving that evening. I had made a deal with Linda that we would get back to Manchester by eight so that I could get some more time in getting work done for classes. Before we left, my parents invited Linda back for Christmas. Linda was gracious and told them that she would have to check with her parents and find out the schedule. As we went to the car, she stopped me and then she looked at me. "Do you want me to be with you and your family at Christmas this year?"

"You know that I do!" The words and my reaction to them were instantaneous. I took her in my arms and kissed her like I had meant to since I met her. I don't know how long the kiss lasted, but we did draw a crowd. By the time I was lucid again, my brother, sister, and cousins were all around us making obnoxious noises and making fun of me. They didn't say or do a thing to Linda. Just me. Thankfully, my mother came out and dispersed the crowd. She then hugged us both and sent us on our way.

The trip back to Manchester was short because Linda and I recounted all that had happened that day and reminisced about Thanksgivings past. In that short amount of time, I found myself learning more about this wonderful person than I had ever known about any of my friends from high school, even Ray. Half way back, Linda moved to the middle of the bench seat in my car. She snuggled up close to me. The heater in that old car never worked, but that day it was plenty warm.

As I pulled the car into the empty parking lot behind Calvin Ulrey, Linda reached over and grabbed my right hand. She drew it to her lips and then held my hand to her cheek. Then she looked up into my eyes. Her eyes were glistening in the darkness of the night. I brought my other hand to her chin and delicately held it. I spoke softly to her, "What's wrong? Linda did I say or do something wrong?"

I had learned her smiles by now. The one she gave me this time was the "no stupid" smile. I guess I knew that the tears weren't from sadness, but it was really important to know. She gathered herself enough to say, "Even though I couldn't be home today, I've never felt more as if I were home. Your family made me feel like I was a part of your yearly gathering and you, well, you have been you." Then the waterworks really started.

Instinct just took over. I turned off the car and pulled her closer to me. I began to kiss her hair first. That seemed to help. Then I kissed the back of her neck. Again, she cuddled closer, as if that were really possible. As for me, I felt responses in regions of my body that I had, up to this point, been able to suppress. Sometimes the suppression came from my own abilities to control the issue; at others it was the lack of participation of my date.

With automatic pilot working, all controls were being overridden. I found myself moving forward as my hand was under her shirt feeling for her bra. I found it! I unlatched it, and with no resistance! It was when my hand, under its own devices I can assure you, crept to Linda's breasts. Then Linda stopped me. She turned quickly to look at me face to face. I started to come up with excuses about autopilot, controls, and so on. I didn't get a word out, she beat me. "Why do we need to have our first time in the car? We have this whole campus to ourselves!" She stopped to see if I could put two and two together.

232

Four! Four! I got it, but my instincts were crippled for a split second. I just sat there and stared. What I now know was going to happen was monumental and my brain was trying to sort it out! Linda wasn't waiting, she slid to her door and got out. Finally, I reached for my door handle and was out in no time. Right there in front of me was Linda, her arms outstretched to me. She encircled my waist and pulled me so close we were in each other's pockets.

After a period of minutes , that might have bordered on a half hour, I moved back a little from Linda and murmured in her ear, "Thank you."

Quizzically, Linda whispered back. "For what, we haven't done anything yet?"

"Whether we do or not, right now I feel better than I have ever felt before. You're the reason, so, thank you." And I kissed her.

Linda started crying again. This time I was truly at a loss until she explained, "You can't be more thankful than I am. Remember, I'm the one that almost threw what we have away when I refused to let you protect me." The sobbing became worse. When she finished, she broke away from me and headed for CU. At the door she stopped and looked back at me. She indicated with a jerk of her head that I should have been right behind her. Soon I was.

Incredibly, we did get some studying done that night, but it wasn't all work that I had to do. Linda and I explored the world of our bodies and learned each other very well. I knew that making love could be wonderful and had fantasized what it could be like if it were right when I was in high school. One year later, I found out.

The rest of the weekend went much the same. Linda decided Friday that since there was no one in CU besides us that we could get more done if we were together night and day. She went to her dorm and got some clothes. She stayed in my room the rest of the weekend.

It worked so well. In the mornings we would fix breakfast and then go to the biology labs. By noon we completed the lab work and headed back to make lunch and activities that soon became synonymous with lunch. Since my father empathized with my plight, at least partially, he had given me enough money so that we could eat out each evening, so we did. Most of the businesses closed down in North Manchester when the college wasn't in session, so it was

234

hard to find restaurants that were open. We made do with what we had, and we got back in time to work on psychology for a couple of hours.

After the studying each night, we explored each other in as many ways as possible. Since we were in a college dorm room, sleep was a little harder. I had a single twin bed. We tried to sleep in my bed the first night, but we both ended up with sore backs and headaches. So the next two nights, I slept on Wayne's bed while Linda slept on mine.

By Sunday at noon we started to notice more activity on the campus. Students were gradually arriving back from the holiday. By this time, with Linda's help, I only had one lab left to complete and all of my psychology was done! The other classes had been finished for a couple of days. I was going to make it! To celebrate, I helped Linda take her things back to her room where we initiated her bed.

As we sat there on her bed, basking in our togetherness, Linda leaned in close, "Can it get any better than this?"

"I can't see how."

"I can!" She sat up and turned to face me. Her nakedness was accentuated as the suns rays caught her in profile. "I want you to come home with me for Christmas!"

It came out the blue, but it sounded good to me. "I would really like to do that. I will check with my parents and see what day they are planning so that we can maybe go to both of our homes for Christmas." When I said it, it sounded like I wasn't sure that it was a good idea and, for the life of me, I couldn't figure out why. My parents schedule had been the same since I was born.

Linda didn't seem to notice because she leaned over and kissed me. Then she swept the sheet off of the bed and wrapped herself in it. As she did she walked to the window and looked out. "Do you think any of them had as good a Thanksgiving as what we have had?"

I yanked the blanket off the bed and draped it around my waist. Then I went to Linda wrapped myself around her, tugging slightly at her. She let out a slight purring sound. I was looking down into her beautiful blue eyes, "I don't know about them, but this Thanksgiving could have been the worst of my life so far.'" I kissed her and continued. "Now, thanks to you, for so many reasons, I will always remember this Thanksgiving as the beginning of my life as me."

The process of lovemaking as we had perfected it was about to begin when the door opened. Standing in the doorway, looking at us incredulously was Linda's roommate, Heather Douglas. She started to speak as we fiddled with the bedclothes around us, "Sorry to interrupt, but your paradise is lost; I have returned." Seeing that I was in no condition to move at the time, Heather continued, "I will give the young man the appropriate amount of time to put on clothes and vacate, two minutes." With that, she went out and shut the door.

I hurried to my clothes. The rude awakening of the real world came in the form of a matronly drab looking teenager, fully equipped with braces on her teeth and saddle shoes. I was thoroughly frightened that she would return, and I would not be fully dressed. It took less than thirty seconds; I was fully dressed. I kissed Linda as I was moving out the door. I wasn't so much afraid of Heather as I was the rules that Manchester had for the girls' dorms. No man was to be in any girl's room at any time! Combine that with the fact that I was on probation, and I knew what I had to do.

The trip across the campus was invigo-rating. I was a changed person. Linda loved me. I knew it, even though those exact words had not been expressed by either of us. Then I stopped in my tracks. I had not said "I love you" to Linda, but I had to Alicia. And Alicia had said them to me. I forgot all about her. Then I remembered that Alicia was over. Diane was taking care of it, and I was simply to let it go. No problem. Alicia is gone. Linda is here, and I ... I... love her?

Chapter 27
<u>But You Know I Love You</u>

"Fair is foul, and foul is fair." Shakespeare couldn't have been more right. As Christmas grew near, I became more confident of myself in the classroom and as a result my collegiate future was looking brighter. And I owed this all to Linda. And she was so beautiful! But always, there was something hanging over our relationship. I thought it was Alicia, but for the most part, I had driven her from my thoughts.

Sure, there were dreams at night that the brown haired girl would appear. There was no denying that subconsciously, I had some sort of need for Alicia. What made me the most crazy was the fact that I couldn't figure out what overpowering need was drawing me to someone whom I had only talked to a couple of times. The reality of Linda was there in my waking hours, but in dreams Alicia came to me. More than anything I wanted to shake the dreams away, but they were there. My biggest fear was that Linda knew and would leave me. For that reason, I worked harder and harder trying to block out the dreams.

While I was getting closer and closer to Linda, I also found that I was getting closer to my friends at CU. The moments that I had with them though were few and far between since Linda and I started dating seriously. But I truly reveled in their laughter and good natured pranks, probably because I was no longer the focus of any of the pranks. Dirk became one of my closest friends at this time. He had a steady girlfriend, and so did I. We had gone through a few hard times together in the few months we had known each other, and he kinda took me under his wing, like a younger brother.

Basketball season had begun, and Dirk was into his element. I was his lackey. He let me hang around him and included me in what-ever he was doing. Probation hadn't really slowed him down. Since he was an All-American from his junior year, he felt invinci-ble. There was no doubt that he knew that he was the reason that there were huge crowds at Manchester basketball games which translated into big money for Manchester. This some-times made him cocky; and truth be told, reckless occasionally. To some, he came off as a jerk. But, at the time, I had an element of hero worship for Dirk. I really didn't recognize it then, but in the eyes of maturity now, I know that he wasn't what I thought he was. And that is what got me into trouble.

I occasionally was still getting a letter from Alicia. On my part, I had decided that I wouldn't write back. With the way that Ray and Diane had left it, and my feelings for Linda, it didn't make sense to carry the relationship any further. I decided that it was best to not even mention to Linda that Alicia was still writing. My thought process was that I didn't want to mess up a good thing with something that didn't matter anymore. I had a vivid memory of how Linda had reacted when I was laid up after the football game. It didn't make sense to bring up those memories. After all, I was going home with her for Christmas, so I felt like it was best this way.

My first finals in college were in full swing. I was on top of the world. My grades weren't great, but I was going to pass unless I really blew a final. Dirk and I had both finished most of our finals by the Wednesday before Christmas break. His last final was on Thursday afternoon and mine was on Friday morning. Since it was my physical education class, I really didn't have anything to do for the rest of the week. I was feeling like vacation was already starting.

The final basketball game before the break was Thursday night. Linda and I were double dating that evening with Dirk and his girlfriend Cheri Adkins. That means I sat with two girls during the game. There were no real plans for the evening, but I had grown to know that we were probably going to a local bar where Dirk would be treated like the superstar that he was. As a result, so would we!

The two girls spent he whole game discussing the clothes that the people at the game were wearing and occasionally the tightness of the shorts on the players. I loved the game and enjoyed watching Dirk in his element. His superior abilities in rebounding, shooting, and ball handling were the reason that many people watched the games. Unfortunately, Dirk's supporting cast was a little below average, so we did lose our share of games. This game, though, we were ahead by sixteen points at half.

There was seldom a halftime show at Manchester's games. So the crowd would either mill around, go to the student union, or go back to their dorms. Often they didn't return, so second half crowds were always smaller. Linda and Cheryl used the time to talk. All of a sudden the topic that they were on drew me in. They were talking about contraception!

This is an important element of a young man's life at the time. I had not been very responsible. My thought was that Linda had probably taken care of the precautions for me. I didn't even ask her if she was on the pill. I didn't know how to start that conversation. So I listened a little more intently.

Cheri was the first to offer, "If I left birth control up to Dirk, I would have been pregnant my freshman year! My sisters both got pregnant their first time! We Adkins are a fertile lot!" She laughed which allowed Linda to chime in.

"If my sister hadn't told me about the pill and help me get it, I would have headed off for college unarmed." I really hoped that she didn't detect the heavy sight that I let out. "It sure has come in handy." With that she grabbed my arm and smiled at me. I smiled back trying desperately to look oblivious to what she was talking about. She went on to another topic, so I got away scott free? In more ways than one!

Their discussion started towards areas of female domain that no man wants to go, so my mind drifted. And there was Alicia. I hadn't had time to pour over her words, but she was definitely distraught. She didn't understand why I stopped writing. Was I okay. Was I angry or upset with her. Evidently, Diane didn't get the point across. I decided that one more letter was necessary. I had even discussed it with Dirk. I had shared with him all of the story. His only advise was that you can't have enough girlfriends.

The second half of the game was the exact opposite of the first. We could do nothing right, and that included Dirk. He missed seven jump shots in a row. And then the unexpected came, Coach Davis benched Dirk. When Dirk approached the bench, he took the towel from the coach and threw it right back in Davis's face. It was an uncharacteristic move for Dirk, even though he had a trigger temper. Davis glared directly at Dirk, but said nothing.

The game never did get better. Dirk went back in with five minutes left in the game, but it was gone already. After the game, Dirk didn't come over to us as he had done in past games. He slowly made his way to the locker room, not noticing anything or anyone.

The three of us sat there saying very little finally Cheri suggested, "We have our jobs ahead of us tonight." And we knew what she meant. Then she asked me, "Mark, would you go down and see where he wants to meet us?"

It was my thought as well, so I turned to Linda and kissed her, "If I don't return, I want you to know the sex was great!" I kissed her again, and play acted the warrior going off to battle.

As I approached the door to the locker room, I immediately saw the note that had hurriedly been posted on the door. "Team meeting! Do not enter!" So I didn't. I waited until the door was officially opened and let more daring souls enter before me.

I wasn't a stranger to the locker room. Dirk had made it easy for me to get access by introducing me to the players and coaches. I actually kind of knew all of them. My usual function after a game was to provide the communication connection between Cheri and Dirk. Usually he would respond with a snide remark like "So the little woman is impatient again?"

As I came nearer his locker, I saw Dirk like I had never seen him before. It looked to me like he was beaten, emotionally. He saw me and indicated that I should sit on the bench next to him. The events of the evening were wearing heavily on him. Abruptly, he stood up and reached for his towel. He struggled for the right words, "I have never lost it like I did tonight. I don't know what got into me." He sat down again, leaned his head almost to his waist. "Davis didn't have to say or do anything. I apologized to him and the team. I called for the meeting." He was crying now. "I have done some stupid stuff in my life, but I have never upstaged a coach. Coach Davis doesn't deserve that. He has made me what I am." With that he headed to the showers. Just as he was turning into the showers, he called over his shoulder to me, "Mark, you and the girls go over to the student union. I'll meet you there.

"Sure Dirk." Nothing more needed to be said. I had no recollection of Dirk every being humbled by anything or anyone before. Not even the prospect of his being kicked out of Manchester.

By ten we were all in the lounge in the student union There was a roaring fire in the fireplace, Linda was curled up next to me on the sofa. So I would have been perfectly happy to stay right there and soak up the warmth. I know that Linda and Cheri felt the same way. But we knew that Dirk was in charge of the agenda. When he entered the room, he was being hounded by the usual alumni who were always after him for one reason or another. On a normal night he would at least pay lip service to these leaches. Tonight he was ignoring them as if they didn't even exist.

When he finally reached us, he leaned to kiss Cheri. They were a great couple. She was the high school cheerleader who completed his mercurial emotions with her knowing patience. Beyond anything else, they were devoted to each other, no matter what Dirk said. They are to this day.

He didn't waste any time. He pulled Cheri from the sofa and indicated that we should follow. "Let's go get shitfaced!"

The emotion that he put into that phrase set the tone for that evening. It meant that Dirk didn't want to go far. He wanted to get drunk, and he wanted to do it now. My place in this would be to drive the car. Since I was only 19, I was too young to drink legally and Dirk did not want to contribute to my delinquency, so it made sense to give me the driving duties.

As usual, we ended up at the Main View tavern. It was that bar that every small town has on its main street, the one that everyone frequents, primarily because it is the only one. At the time it was famous for its cheeseburgers and tenderloin sandwiches. It was an experience that I still look fondly on today.

We slipped into the booth nearest the front window, giving us a full view of Main Street, North Manchester. The bustle of people outside the window included high school students who were trying to get in and a group of factory workers fresh off of their shift. They appeared to have started their drinking before they hit the bar.

Dirk ordered for us – cheeseburgers for all of us, a beer for him, and ginger ales for the rest of us. Cheri didn't drink and really was opposed to Dirk's drinking, but she really hadn't been able to make any headway in getting him to stop. The drinks were before us almost immediately, and Dirk had his beer down before I even had a sip of the ginger ale. He ordered another, which was followed by five more before the food arrived.

The owner of the Main View, George Stillman, made his way to us eventually. He took his usual position next to Dirk in the booth. Their conversation never really changed much. It centered mostly on the game, how it went, in this case what went wrong, and eventually evolved into stories of how it was when George played. It was at this moment that we really benefited from these stories. The longer the stories, the more free food we were given. Pie, fries, and all that we could drink – it was all ours free, well we did have to listen to the stories.

By one in the morning, we were finally full – of food and stories. Dirk had literally drunk himself under the table. I asked him if he was ready to call it a night. Very slowly, he pushed himself to a sitting position and belched loudly, "Yeah, Mark, the time has come for us to move on to other activities this evening. Alicia and Cheri, get your things, we're going."

Linda had been holding my arm before Dirk made the slip. Afterwards, it loosened and faded from my arm. I consciously did not look at her, thinking that any response on my part would bring more attention to Dirk's mistake.

Cheri, obviously upset with Dirk, corrected him as she helped him slip out of the booth, "You have definitely had too much to drink. You called Linda, Alicia. We don't even know anyone named Alicia!" It was innocent, but Cheri's help might actually have made things worse.

Linda didn't say a word. Neither did I. But Dirk wasn't finished. He caught his mistake, and in his corrupted state tried to fix it, "Mark, I used the other girl's name didn't I?" He almost fell as he was trying to get face to face with me. His next comment was worse because he thought he was whispering, although anyone in the bar could have understood him perfectly, "Linda doesn't know about Alicia does she?" He thought about it for a second as he turned away and added, "Sorry!"

I didn't' respond. I couldn't acknowledge him, so I suggested, "You're drunk! Let's get out of here." I reached for Linda's coat to help her with it. Before she could get her arm in the sleeve, she burst into tears and ran for the bathroom. Cheri ran after her, not knowing what the problem was.

Dirk sat back down and stared up at me, "I screwed you up big time didn't I?" When he finished, he threw up all over my shoes. It was obvious that this was not going to be the last elimination, so I helped Dirk to the men's room. Once I had him situated, I went to the women's room. I talked to the door, "Cheri, is Linda okay?" I knew that wasn't the right question when I received no reply. So I tried again, "Linda, I need to talk to you." A few moments later, Linda came out sobbing with Cheri behind her. I indicated to Cheri the men's room, "Dirk's in there throwing up."

I went to Linda. She was trembling. Putting my arm around her, I caught her eyes with mine, "We've been through this before. Give me some time. I think you will understand."

She tried to pull it all together. We reached the car where I loaded Dirk in the back seat. Cheri took over, holding his head up. Linda was across the front seat from me, not looking at me. The ride back to campus was very quiet except for the occasional retching from Dirk. I had very little time to get the right words to repair our relationship.

Chapter 28
<u>Oh What a Night</u>

It wasn't the easiest thing to do, but I spent the next hour explaining to Linda about the name she had heard months ago and the story of how I became a correspondent with Alicia. I didn't leave anything out. After all, it didn't make any sense to keep anything from Linda now. If I were still writing to Alicia, I might have had to dance around the topic, but the writing was only coming from Alicia. My biggest problem in relating this confusing story was trying to convince myself why Alicia was important to me at all. When I was finished, I spent a few moments looking into Linda's trusting eyes.

Linda was silent throughout my dissertation. When I was finished, the tears streamed down her face. When she had herself under a little better control she said, "You had really good reasons to write this girl." she struggled to say Alicia's name, but continued, "I understand why you would do that, It's in your character." She paused to take a big breath and blow her nose. "I even see why you kept writing to her when she knew about her boyfriend being missing. But... why do you...what is it that...she's a total stranger." She searched my face for answer.

And I knew what she meant. I didn't have an adequate answer, so I changed the focus of the conversation to what really mattered. I went to her and knelt in front of her so that I could hold her hand and let her see that these words were the truth. "You need to know one more thing. You matter more to me. More than anyone I have ever known. Since I have been with you, my life has direction, and I am happy. You have helped my self-esteem and confidence." I stopped to get ready for what I really had to say, because I knew what I wanted to say finally and didn't want to mess it up. I took her chin in my left hand as I held her left hand with my right. "You have showed me what love is. That love that I have learned from you is now my love for you." I kissed her lips and finished, "I love you."

I didn't wait for any response because I still had some damage control to do. "Dirk's mistake tonight was the best thing that could have happened to me, but it wasn't so good for you. Now I see that I wasn't being fair to you or

254

Alicia. Both of you were a part of my life, but neither of you knew how you fit in my life. Be assured that there is only room for you, You are the one I love." The tears started again, and I wasn't quite sure how to interpret them. "I was a little presumptuous a couple of minutes ago and kissed you. I want to kiss you again, but I am not real sure that it is a good idea, so I will ask first."

Her smile, that one that I saw when I first met her in the student union a couple of months earlier crept out from behind the tears. "I want you to...if you want to." This time our lips met tentatively at first, but it almost immediately turned into full passion. We had been on the porch on the swing outside Oakwood Hall for over an hour by now. The warmth of her kiss and body next to mine helped to thaw my nearly frozen body. But, more importantly, our closeness calmed my fears that I would lose Linda. I had almost lost the only girl who had loved me unconditionally to a non-existent mistress.

The time was well past the freshman girl curfew of one in the morning. Luckily, none of the campus cops really enforced the rule unless there was a lot of noise or a fight. That didn't mean that I could afford to be caught with Linda. My probation would not be lifted until the end of the semester. We both realized this, so we headed to the door. I knew that there was one thing left to do though, "I will write one last letter to Alicia explaining that I love you and that it would just be wrong to keep writing."

She opened the door, but was firm in her resolve, "It may be the right thing for you to do, but you are not going to stop writing Alicia."

I couldn't believe what I was hearing. "It has to be done. She needs to know how I feel about you, and that ..." She didn't let me finish.

Linda tossed her hair back and laughed, "You can't let her go. I know that. She needs you, and so do I. As long as I know where you stand with me." She stopped for effect, "I do know where I stand with you?" From my distressed look, she knew where she stood, "There is no reason for me to be jealous. Your friends have explained it to her, and she just seems to need you as a friend. I see no problem." This time she stopped to think, "But I reserve the right to review any letters that you get from now on." With that she kissed me on the cheek and went inside the dorm.

I was walking away from Oakwood when I heard a voice from above, "Just don't hide anything from me anymore." She was about to close the window when she remembered something, "By the way, I think that you need to know – I love you too."

Had she not closed the window so quickly, she probably would have heard me yell at the top of my lungs, "And I love you Linda Warner."

That night I dreamed again. It was explicit. There was a wedding. A house and kids. Linda.
I slept very well.

Chapter 29
The Word Before Goodbye

Christmas that year was going to be hectic. The whole three weeks were planned to be with Linda either at her parents' home or at my house. After our finals Linda and I loaded up my car with our stuff and headed for Fort Wayne. We stayed the night at my house before we got up in the morning to drive to Columbus. Because Columbus wasn't my usual hour trip from Manchester, and dad didn't trust the Fairlane to make it the three hour trip, he loaned me the family station wagon. I never shared with him that I feared the Ford's ability to make it; he just offered the Chevy.

The trip was pretty uneventful. No ice or snow. The whole trip we spent the time talking about anything that came to our minds. When we started to talk about her family, I started to get concerned.

Linda's father was a farmer. Her two brothers were farmers. Carrie, her only sister married a farmer. Carrie was older and had left the family to go to Indianapolis. She attended college at Franklin, but ended up pregnant and came home. Linda wanted to get away from the farm, but not her parents. She obviously loved them. She did not want a part of the farm life though. That was good for me because I knew nothing about farming. But it would cause a problem for this week. What could I possibly talk about!

We reached the winding narrow road that led back to the Warner family farm. The farm was east of Columbus and easily reachable from the interstate. The roads back were quite treacherous though. It looked like parts of it had been washed out, and there were hairpin turns that only one vehicle could navigate at a time. I was a nervous wreck when we finally reached the farm. I didn't realize it until we pulled up, Linda had a hold of my arm as if to console me. She already knew me pretty well.

As I turned off the ignition, she squeezed my arm and laughed, "Didn't realize that you were involved with a hillbilly did you?"

That put me more at ease, "Well from what I have heard, you hillbilly girls are easy."

The Warner farm was in a valley protected on all sides by rolling hills. The evening before they had had a dusting of snow. It was beautiful. Wherever there wasn't snow, there was the beautiful contrast of greens and browns from the foliage. We had passed a number of family homesteads along the way. Many were run-down shacks. I wondered as we went past if people really lived there. I also wondered if this would be the type of home that Linda was from.

Linda's parents were on the front porch waiting for us. My father's car was one of four in the driveway. Obviously, Linda's brothers were here and waiting for me. I had met the parents, but brothers, that made me nervous all over again. Linda hopped out of the car and ran to her parents.

I, on the other hand, eased myself out of the car to take it all in. There was a stream to my left that came off of the hill that we had just traversed. To the right of the house was a huge barn. But what I noticed immediately was the perfect quiet. Coming from a city, I seldom experienced this kind of peace.

Peace and quiet at least until I heard Linda's voice beckoning me to "Bring the bags, we are going in the house." Not even married, and I am getting bossed around. It was her family, and she hadn't seen them in a while. So I did as I was told. We were traveling light; I had one bag; Linda had four.

As I brought the bags to the front door, Linda greeted me with two young men. "Terry and Kyle want me to let you know that you are safe at least for a while. The family shotgun is in for repairs!" All three of them laughed heartily; I laughed with them, hoping not to betray the level of my nervousness as the result of the joke and my already growing apprehensions. Linda began the introductions, "Mark, you already know my parents." She indicated them. Not absolutely sure what to do, I went to his father and shook his hand. As I moved to her mother, she pushed my hand aside and gave me a big hug. Linda continued, "The guy over there with the mustache is my brother Terry, and the other one is Kyle, he's too young to even think of facial hair." As I shook both boy's hands, I noticed that the family all had the infectious smile that I had grown to love on Linda. They settled into their normal routine, and as a result, I felt at home.

Terry took me to his room. There was a cot set up for me, but Terry told me that he would sleep on the cot. I could have the bed. We debated it for a little while, but eventually gave in graciously because it appeared that he wanted to do this for me. After I settled in, Terry gave me a little more background on the family. Terry was to have graduated this year from high school, but he was a year behind. Last year his father had a serious injury falling off of the tractor, so Terry stayed home to work on the farm until his father was back on his feet. It was a tough time for the family. As he told me the story, you could tell that this family was extremely close. "I don't mind waiting to graduate. Around here, this type of thing happens all the time." He paused for a second, "It really got hard when we knew that Linda was accepted to Manchester. There was no money."

Linda, for whatever reason, hadn't shared any of this with me. "I had no idea. How did she make it then?"

Terry smiled, "She did most of it herself. She got a job at a factory in Columbus and was paid very well. The rest came from Manchester. She probably didn't tell you that she was valedictorian in high school either?" He smiled when he could tell that she hadn't shared that information. "She is actually embarrassed by being smart, but it sure helped her get into college and get scholarships." What he was telling me let me know that this family adores Linda. I translated that for myself, "Do not screw this up. This is one special young woman!"

Terry led me to the living room where Linda was on the sofa talking to her mother. She patted the open section of the sofa next to her, indicating that I should sit next to her. She kept on talking to her mother, "...and everyone is so helpful, especially the guys from cities." Obviously, she was referring to me, but since I didn't know that context of her conversation before I came in, I smiled and tried to act humble. It actually seemed to come off more like being a jerk in my estimation. Linda continued, "By the way, where did daddy go?"

Mrs. Warner sighed, "Since your father has been given the clean bill of health, he thinks that he needs to catch up on everything that he didn't get done before in a month. I think he's out in the barn cleaning up. He'll be in by supper." Then she turned to me. "It really is so good to see you again. And we are happy to share Christmas with you. Linda is so happy. You two are a great couple."

Linda was embarrassed, but not so much that she didn't hold me tight. She did change the subject, however, "Is Carrie coming over with Matt and Michael?"

Mrs. Warner had gone to the window. "Well, you don't even have to wait. They are just pulling in the drive right now." Linda's mother was in her element now. Her whole family was about to all be under one roof again. It was obvious that she couldn't be prouder. The strains of the last year weren't evident even though she was probably the one that held everything together. She had that quiet kind of strength. Her grandson came into the room in a fury and went right for grandma.

Somewhere to the back of the house, I heard a phone ring. No one heard it, and I didn't feel like I should impose. After four rings, Linda heard it and ran to get it. That left me alone with people I had just met and total strangers. As Carrie entered the house, Mrs. Warner introduced us. Matt was right behind her, and we were introduced shaking hands. By this time Michael was hidden behind grandma wondering who this stranger was and why grandma wasn't doing something about me. We played peek-a-boo, and he gradually eased from behind her and smiled at me.

Linda came back and came directly to me. She pulled me aside. "The call is your mother." A chill went through me. She hadn't meant for her words to weigh on me, but they did. "Your father fell at work. They have taken him to the hospital. It's his back." She grabbed my hand. "She's still on the phone and needs to talk to you." We went to the kitchen.

I didn't waste time when I picked up the receiver, "Mom, what happened?"

As usual she was composed, but I could tell from her inflection that she was shaken, "Your father was clearing the ice around the front door at work. Evidently, he slipped on the ice and as he was falling, he hit his back on the cement ledge next to the

266

door." She stopped short of finishing, probably to collect herself. "the ambulance just took him to Parkview, so we will know more later. What we do know is that he is paralyzed on the left side." Again she stopped. She may have been waiting for me to say something, but I was at a loss for words. She went on, "He can talk and said that the pain isn't so bad, but it could be because of the paralysis."

Instinctively I asked, "Did dad do his usual schedule for the holidays?"

"Yes."

It was then that I knew what I had to do. "There's no one to run the station for the next two weeks is there?" I didn't wait for an answer, "I'm on my way."

She was definitely crying now, "Mark, I really hate to interrupt your time with Linda and her family. You probably just got there. But I will have to be at the hospital and taking care of your brother and sister. I really need you here." She came back quickly to amend her plea, "Please do not come home tonight though. The roads around here are treacherous. They say that it will be better in the morning."

I promised her that I would wait until conditions improved. She told me to apologize to the Warners.

I hung up the phone and turned to Linda. Through my part of the discussion, she knew what was going on. Tears were streaming down her face, so I reached for her and held her to me. "I have to go home."

She shook her head to let me know that she knew. Then she looked up to me, "I'm coming with you."

I really did want her to be with me, but her family needed her too. I held her at arms length and gazed into her eyes, "Even though I want you to go with me, I really want you to stay here. Terry told me what you have gone through with your family since your father's injuries. You need some time with them. Besides, it looks like I will be working most of the time, and when I have free time, I will probably be at the hospital with dad." The harsh reality was just getting through to me: there is a possibility that he won't recover. The thought overwhelmed me.

Linda could tell. "We have a full lifetime together ahead of us, but every second that I am away from you seems like forever."

Those words gave me hope. Just knowing that Linda was there for me, turned my negative thoughts around. I smiled at her, "You're right. Everything will work out."

She hugged me, "I heard you say that you would leave in the morning. I'm glad that we will be together tonight."

Just then, Linda's father came in the back door and saw us. "Linda, what's wrong."

Linda took his coat and hung it up. She explained about what happened to my father and that I would have to get back to help out. I finished off the explanation, "Dad doesn't usually hire a full crew over the holidays. So he usually works more, thinking that it helps his workers. I will need to fill the gap."

While Linda and I were telling him the story, the rest of the family had migrated to the kitchen as well. Each had questions, and they all offered help. If the situation wasn't so bad, I probably would have appreciated what a close family Linda had.

I searched all of their faces and begged off, "As much as I would like to stay and celebrate Christmas with you, I will need to get going early in the morning."

Linda added, "I really want to go with you." She turned to her parents to see what they thought. "You understand don't you?"

"No, you need to be here with your family." I knew I wanted her with me, but I also knew that it didn't make sense for her to come with me.

Mrs. Warner calmly interjected, "No decision needs to be made tonight. Dinner is ready. Let's sit and eat. Then we will figure out what will happen." The she spoke directly to me, "Mark, no matter what happens, let us know what we can do. Your father, your mother, and you are very important to us."

When she pulled me to her with a motherly hug, the tears I had been holding back flowed unimpeded. I felt so foolish and vulnerable, and I knew that the display had to be embarrassing Linda and her family. Gradually, I composed myself and indicated with a wave of my hand that I was alright. With that we all went to the dining room table.

We had pot roast and potatoes. It was good, but it reminded me of my mother's cooking. Yet eating kept me from crying. Small talk started slowly, then family stories began. I loved to listen to them. They drew me in and allowed me to forget for a while what my father had to be going through..

After supper, we all gathered around the fireplace in the living room and continued family stories. I filled in the gap of time since they last saw my parents for the Warners. I also confided in them that dad was pretty strong, so I knew that he would come through this just fine. Eventually, Carrie and Matt announced that they needed to get home and get Michael to bed. This was evidently the signal for everyone else because within a quarter of an hour, the living room was left to Linda and me.

Linda spoke first, "You're right, and I know it. But I don't want to be practical, I want to be with you."

To be logical and in love at this moment was tearing me apart, "If I hadn't met your wonderful family. If you didn't know how much my family means to me. If I didn't love you so. This would be so much easier. I pulled a package from behind the sofa. I had hidden it there as we had entered the house. I handed it to her, "It looks like Christmas is today for us. It isn't much really, but it is from me."

She took the present. As she opened it, a tear ran down her cheek and fell on the present. She just stared at the unopened box. "You don't have the money for a present." The necklace that I had picked out slowly came out into her hand. I helped her put it around her neck. Again she cried, "It's so beautiful." In a second she was wrapped around me.

I tapped her on the shoulder. "That's not all. Look at the bottom of the box."

The poem was an afterthought, but in retrospect it was far more important. Linda read it softly out loud:

> Time ran quickly by me
> As loneliness sang for me alone
> I searched stranger's faces
> For an answer
> For anything.
> Searching was a mistake
> All I really needed
> To catch time
> To silence loneliness
> Was to listen to you.
> You gave me new life
> You gave me love
> Nothing I can give you

Can match that.

Merry Christmas and all my love.

Mark

Her tears let me know that my words had hit the mark. She scooted over to m, held me hard to her, and wouldn't let me go. Then she whispered in my ear, "Thank you Mark. I love you so much." Immediately, she turned very sad, "It just feels like when you leave it will be forever, and I don't want to lose you. Please let me come with you."

Even though reason was the last thing on my mind, somehow I fell victim to it, "To go with me would be exactly what I want. But that is selfish. You need to be with your family as much as I need to be with mine. Your father is better, and you really haven't had time to spend with him at all." Whether I wanted to leave her here or not, it was what made sense. "You know that I will call you every day, and if dad's condition improves, I will come back, I promise."

I got up and went to the window. When I looked back, Linda had curled up into a fetus-like ball on the sofa. It was obvious she was preparing for me to not be there. Slowly, she spoke her thoughts, "I can't help it. It seems so lonely here already." She arose from the sofa and came to me, "At least spend the night with me." Her eyes pleaded with me to answer yes.

As I surveyed the beautiful scenery that was the Warner's land, I became aware that the snow had begun again. Picture post cards couldn't have matched the splendor of the setting. Here I was in this locale with this girl, and I was about to say goodbye in a few hours. Again, logic came in to override these thoughts, "I am a guest here. I barely know your family. I cannot betray their trust in me."

Linda laughed almost to herself, "My mother offered for us my room when we came in the door. She almost immediately withdrew the idea realizing that you would probably be embarrassed if she offered. I am sure that having two brothers breathing down your throat doesn't help either." I nodded in approval of that sentiment.

A compromise came to mind and I submitted it to Linda for her thoughts, "Nothing says that we can't be here on the sofa and fall asleep together though."

She broadly smiled, grabbed my hand and took me to the Christmas tree. There she picked up a package and extended it to me. "I hoped to give this to you Christmas morning, but this will have to do." We went to the sofa, and I opened the box.

Initially, all I saw was the book. I pulled it from the package and opened it. All of the pages were blank. Linda beamed with her explanation, "The empty book is for you to write your poems in." She went to the poem I had given her. "And I would be very happy if this were the first poem in the book."

"There is nothing I have ever written that should come before that poem in this book." I pulled her head to mine and kissed her long and with the deepest passion yet.

Linda then went to the box and told me to open the rest of my present. Under tissue paper I noticed a necklace, something that I had never worn before. As I pulled it out, I noticed that it had a pendant like none I had seen before - a man holding an umbrella. Linda's eye's were boring into mine, and she explained, "I fell in love with you before I ever called you for that dance we never had. When you read that naughty poem and held that umbrella, I knew that you were the one for me."

Again, we embraced, kissed, and it lasted for over an hour. Somewhere in the process, it hit me that she knew that she loved me all along. When she called me for Breakaway weekend, in the hospital nursing me, and more importantly when she was hurt by thinking I had someone else. I ached for the pain that I had caused her and realized that no present that I gave her could equal what she has given me.

We did fall asleep together on that sofa that night. We were one soul with our lives together ready to be planned. The next morning came much too quickly, but it did and with much pain I told her goodbye, again promising to call, write, and come back. In the rear view mirror I saw her crying, her head on her mother's shoulder. Her father consoling her on her other side. That picture won't leave my mind or the song that I heard in my head as I drove away, "The Word Before Goodbye."

Chapter 30
<u>The End of Our Road</u>

No Christmas before or after that Christmas has had the profound effect on me. By the time I was back in Fort Wayne, I was a nervous wreck: worried about my father and missing Linda. When I pulled into the driveway at home, the place looked deserted. No cars, nobody. So, I unloaded my suitcase, changed into my work clothes, and headed to the gas station.

The station that dad managed sat on the corner of two busy streets: Anthony and McKinnie. In those days there was a gas station on all four corners, and they all did pretty good business. Dad drew people to his station like food draws flies. From the time the station opened in the morning at 6:00 until it closed at 11:00 at night, there was always someone there sitting in the front room telling stories. During the day, the best story teller was my dad.

The only problem with all these people hanging around all day was that they seldom bought anything. In fact, over the years, many of them asked dad for money, a job, or both. He was so trusting, he gave credit to everyone including one man over and over again and after each time he declared bankruptcy. It wasn't that dad was stupid; he was just generous. Unfortunately, most of these people took advantage of this bigheartedness.

So when I arrived at the station, I wasn't surprised to find that the place was loaded with many of the regulars for late morning. There were the two guys who were actually working: Carl, the assistant manager and all-around great mechanic and Gary, the high school drop-out whom dad befriended with a job to keep him off the streets. The rest included Pete, Tom, and Gerald: factory workers who were there wasting time before they started second shift. Wasting time might not be the best description of their activity; they were telling stories and making plans for the weekend and a future that most of them

280

wouldn't have because the factory would move to Ohio in a few years and dad would have to close the station at about the same time.

Gary greeted me, "Mark, your mother told us that you would be coming in. As you can see, right now there isn't much to do." The others all nodded in agreement. "Have you gone up to see your dad yet?"

"I really didn't think that I should do that until I was sure that you guys didn't need me to help out first." The truth is that I really didn't like to work at the station. It had been my only job since I was 12 years old. Dad had me start then pumping gas, washing windshields, checking the oil, and anything else that was full service and expected then. When I got older, I learned to change oil, mount tires, balance tires, fix exhaust systems and brakes, and do tune ups. The thing that probably bothered me the most was that dad didn't really pay me for doing any of this until I was 17. Sure, there was the candy bar on occasion, the lunch from Charky's, but no paycheck until the summer before my senior year.

Whether it was the lack of pay or the fact that the job seemed so demeaning, I just hated it. Part of me went to college so that I would be able to find a career that didn't include pumping gas. I never expressed that to mom or dad, but I am sure that they knew.

And I never really had much in common with anyone who worked there. Sure I had great fun listening to their stories, and I occasionally could bring one to them. But I pretty much liked school, they didn't. I was in athletics, they weren't. I played music, they didn't. Looking back now, I feel that maybe I was less than fair to them, but at the time I pretty much tolerated them because I worked with them. They were pretty decent people who I know looked out for me on more than one occasion.

Carl pulled me aside, "Go see your dad. Gary and I have this under control. After you have seen him, then drop by. Derek and Jason come on at three. If you could be here then, it would really help because neither of them knows how to close." I had closed the station since I was sixteen, before I had a license, so that made sense.

"That is what I will do. Thanks for your help Carl." I shook his hand and waved to the rest. When I got to my car and looked back, I saw a loyal network of friends who were taking on the challenge for my father. When he died thirty years later, every single one of those guys were there to say goodbye to my dad.

Parkview Hospital is on the other side of Fort Wayne, but it is a straight shot down Anthony. It took me less than ten minutes to get there. The only time I had ever been there before was when dad had suffered some sort of poisoning from an open cut. It is a good place, but from that experience I developed a dislike of being around hospitals.

At the information desk I found out that dad was on the second floor in room 241. Forgoing the elevator I bounded up the steps. After negotiating the maze of signs indicating rooms, I found room 241. Jane and Billy were there with mom. To my amazement, dad was wide awake. They all greeted me, mom hugging me and my siblings talking words that I was not even trying to listen to. After mom let me go, I went straight to dad, "How bad is it? Are you in much pain?"

Dad smiled, "Well hello to you too! Go right for the negative!" I reflected that the choice of words was not the best. He touched my hand, "It's going to be alright. I have feeling again. The doctor's are pretty sure that all I did was bruise my spine and that there is no permanent damage. In fact, they may even let me go home for Christmas." I turned to mom for verification in case my father was being overly optimistic. She nodded yes, but I could tell that this made her nervous.

She added, "He still will need to be on bed rest for at least two weeks and return to the doctor before he will release him to get back to work."

284

Of course, I was relieved and added, "You don't need to worry about the station. I stopped by before I came to the hospital. Carl is doing a great job, and I will go in this afternoon to help the afternoon crew."

Mom came to me almost crying, "I am so sorry that you had to leave Linda and her family. This morning, Carl called me and told me that he had talked to some of the guys and they have volunteered to cover the time over the holidays. He said that he will only use you when he can't find anyone else."

"Carl is a great guy, but I know that to have that extra person costs you and dad more money, so I am going to let him know to schedule me regularly." That was the reality that I knew - I came cheaper than any of the rest of these guys, and I needed to fill the time anyway.

She patted me on the shoulder, "Well, we don't have to decide anything now." She indicated my brother and sister and said, "Take them home. I think they've had enough hospital for one day." To that they both jumped to their feet and were at the door.

I countered, "You have been here for a while too. I just got here and want to spend some time with dad. So why don't you take them home, and I will stay for a while. Besides, I'm not working until three, so why not spend the time with dad."

Dad chimed in, "That makes perfect sense to me. Maybe I can get some sleep without all the chatter."

It was determined that I would stay until dad fell asleep and then head home to rest a little myself. Jane, Billy, and mom said their goodbyes, and I was left with dad alone. At first neither of us said anything then dad offered, "I really do want to get home as soon as possible, so maybe you can go back to Linda's. When do you have to be back to Manchester?"

"Jan term begins January 6. But I can drop the class, it only lasts a month, and I can make up it up later."

Dad was adamant: "You will be back at school for Jan term! There is no reason to stop your education because I screwed up." This truly upset him and in turn seemed to intensify the pain he was feeling.

"Whatever you say. But I don't want you to hurry back to work without being fully recovered, so there is no way that I will go back to Linda's before school starts and that is final" I realized that this was a compromise and that he would have to take it.

He did. And even though I wanted to return to Linda more than anything in the world, other than my family of course, I knew where I was meant to be for the time. We talked about the Warner's and how I pulled out fall semester for a while, but gradually the pain killers took over and dad graduated into a peaceful sleep.

As I was on my way back to work, I had no way of knowing at the time that the compromise that I had just brokered would not be fulfilled. Nor did I know that my world had just crashed and burned.

Chapter 31
<u>Traces</u>

As was the custom when I closed the station, there were just two of us. You never closed alone for fear of being robbed too easily. Two years later, we were robbed, and I was able to get a good description of the robber while Gary was unloading the drawer. Once the station was closed, I drove home.

It was well after eleven when I arrived. I was surprised to see that all of the lights in the house were still on. There were two other cars in the driveway. I recognized them both. One was Grandpa Logan's Olds 88 and the other was Grandpa Schmidt's Studebaker. Immediately, my thoughts were that something had to be wrong. Both of my grandfather's lived with a mile of our house and seldom, if ever came over at this time of night.

I entered the living room to find both of my grandfather's sitting there with my

288

mother. The serious expressions gazing at me let me know that there was a story that needed to be told and that I was the listener for whom they waited.

"What are you doing here? Did something happen to dad?" There were probably other questions I had, but I couldn't find a way to express them.

Mom slowly stood up and came to me. She took my shoulders and placed facing her. She hesitated and looked back to my grandfathers. They both indicated she should go ahead. "Mark, Cheryl Warner called about an hour ago. It was about Linda." A cold chill ran through me. Mom started crying and lost control, dropping her hands from my shoulders, she walked away. Grandpa Logan stood and took over. He indicated that I should sit in the chair across from him. After he resumed his seat he said, "The story as I understand it is that Linda was going to the store with her brother," he hesitated and turned to mom, "His name was Terry is that correct?" Mom indicated yes between her sobs. Grandpa continued, "The roads evidently were very slippery. A semi-truck crossed the center line and," I willed myself not to hear the next words to no avail. "Both Linda and Terry were killed instantly…" Grandpa went on and all three came to console me, but I heard nothing else. I felt weak; the strength of two ministers kept me from falling.

The rest of the night and early morning was a blur. Mom and my grandfathers each pledge support for me. Whatever I needed. But I could say nothing. When my grandfathers had gone and mom went to bed, I got in my car and started to drive. I didn't know which destination was my goal: Columbus, to discover for myself; to Manchester, to hide; or to Ray for advise. I chose none of the above.

Foster Park is on the southwest part of Fort Wayne. I often went there to sit, reflect, and ponder my future. There is an area near the river where a cement dike had been placed probably before World War II. It was a place where I could watch the river without the world getting involved. That dike wall created for me a world that I was safe, and at that point I needed to disassemble everything that I knew so that I could carry on.

I was there for over an hour when a car pulled up behind mine along the road. It was near dawn, but I still couldn't make out who was getting out of the car. As the driver came closer, I realized that it was Ray. When he got to the dike, he sat next to me and put his arm around me, "Your mother called me. She's worried about you and wanted me to find you. I told her that I knew where you would be." To be truthful, this was our spot. This is where we solved the world's problems. He continued, "Your mother told me what happened to Linda." He struggled for what to say, "Do you want to talk about it?"

"No" was all I could say. We didn't really talk for quite a while, at least I didn't. Ray kept trying, but he couldn't draw any response from me. Eventually, I assured Ray that I was alright and that I had something I just had to do. He wanted to come along; he wanted to help. But I was intent, "Ray, thanks for trying and more important thanks for being here with me. If you really want to help me now, just tell mom that I am okay. Tell them that I will be home in a couple of hours."

Ray and I had mulled over many situations before, but nothing this serious. He could tell that the line had been drawn. Unquestioningly, he said that he would relay the message. As he went to his car and I went to mine, he stopped and yelled to me, "Whenever you need me, whatever you need, I'm there." Ray didn't wait for my response, he got in his car and was gone.

I put the car in gear and drove to my first stop. The hospital. Dad was my rock. I needed to see him. Visiting hours wouldn't start for another two hours, but I never let anyone stop me. Dad was awake and watching the early morning news. Maybe this was a mistake. There he was in traction, very vulnerable, and I was coming to him for help. Then it happened, tears that I had been holding back since I had heard about his accident, since I had to leave Linda to go home, since I heard that Linda... I was totally out of control. A heartbreaking rage came over me. The hurt was unbearable. Dad could do nothing to help me.

When dad could see that I was able to hear him he suggested, "Come over here and sit down."

I accepted and apologized to him, "The last thing that you need is for me to come to you and act like this. I am so sorry." I paused to collect myself. "Dad, I don't know what to do."

I wasn't asking for him to help. In fact after my remark, I was ashamed realizing dad had his own problems. He offered help anyway, "Mark, there is nothing that you can do now. Life throws us curves all the time. You're just getting them all at once." Patiently, he continued, "All I can tell you is that you will get past this. It won't be easy and most of the time you won't feel very good. You will probably question your life and its worth." The pause this time was for the tears, "Believe me, I have been lying here with those thoughts in my head." I seldom had seen my father cry, so his tears created mine again. "I love you, Mark. You are a great son. I wish that I could take your pain away. If I put it with mine, how bad could it really be?"

It was his strong support that held me up. Then I realized, "Dad, helping you to get home and keep the station running may be the only way for me to get through this."

He smiled, "Sure, but you have to face your grief for Linda too." He was right, but for the moment I needed to focus on what I could control and that was helping my father to get home.

When I left him, dad was scheduled for physical therapy. I drove to Manchester. I wasn't planning to stay long. I had hoped to go to Linda's room, but the dorm's were locked down for the holidays since all students had gone home. What I managed to do was to go to the registrar's office and drop my Jan term class. When I pulled in the driveway at home, I had everything taken care of, but I no longer had Linda.

Chapter 32
<u>The Tracks of My Tears</u>

I worked at the station every day. I didn't really need to, but there I didn't see the faces I saw at home. There sentiments didn't gush whenever I looked sad. Customers just wanted service. My coworkers may have known that I was depressed, but for the most part they let me take care of it in my own way.

Dad came home on Christmas Eve day. Whenever I wasn't working, I spent the time helping him. Retrieving things for him and helping him with his exercises became a daily routine.

One day was spent in Columbus. I went for the funeral. My sister went with me. When we entered the Warner's home, I felt like I had never been there before. I was introduced to family that I had heard about by Cheryl Warner, but I wouldn't be able to remember any of them ten seconds later. The house was empty without Linda. Jane, though two years younger than me, was my rock. Whenever I was unresponsive, she filled the void.

When we were to go by the caskets, she provided the crutch that kept me from stumbling.

That wasn't Linda. Since I had never been to a funeral before, I had no idea what I would see, hear, or sense in any way. That wasn't Linda. Someone had played a joke on me and everyone else. The beautiful, effervescent young woman that I loved had to be somewhere else. I wanted to scream, "What have you done to Linda?" Jane grabbed my elbow and pulled me away. She looked at me like she had never done before, "It's too much for you isn't it."

I simply said, "Yes."

Jane protected me the rest of the day. When it was over and we were ready to head home, she asked if she should drive. "No, it's time for me to be your big brother again." I took the keys, hugged the Warners, said our goodbyes, and were on the road. A quarter of a mile down the road, I saw two crosses. It had to be the place, so I pulled over. We never said a word, but we both got out and went to the crosses. I said a silent prayer for Linda and Terry; I am sure that Jane did too. It was there that I felt Linda's soul trying to reach me. I cried, and I smiled.

From that moment the relationship between Jane and I had changed. Her help and guidance that day, the fact that she shared the experience on the side of the road with me - she was now more than my little sister, she was my friend. That has never changed over the years.

On New Year's Day, I decided that I had to talk to the Warners. It was Cheryl who answered. "Mark, it is really good to hear from you. How are you doing?"

"I'm making it. It helps that I work at the station each day." I was hesitant, not sure what to say. "I just called to...to...you know, I guess I don't really know why I called. I just felt the need to talk to you."

This woman who had just lost two of her children interrupted, "Mark, don't worry about it. Actually, I have some things I need to tell you." There was a heavy sigh on the other end. "Linda was never more happy in her life than from the time that she met you. On her last day, she felt that the world was right. My husband and I hope that you realize that you are a part of our family now."

Tears were rolling down my cheeks. She had one more thing that I needed to know. "Linda was buried with the necklace and poem that you gave her. She would have wanted it that way."

Because I could no longer control my hurt, Linda's mother allowed for me to compose. When I felt that I could talk, I kept it simple, "Thank you. Now I feel like I am still with her." We did spend a little time talking about family, and I promised Cheryl that I would come to Columbus over spring break.

By hanging up the phone I felt like I was moving to the next stage of the process. That's even what I sensed. Life was putting me through some course of action. I had no control. And when I interacted with family or friends, I was amazed that they didn't see it.

By the end of January, I was prepared to return to Manchester. Dad had been given a clean bill of health and was to gradually build back to his regular schedule. That took two days - definition of gradual for my father. I wasn't needed at the station, in fact mom and day were encouraging me to head back a week before to get myself back to being a student. Until it was imminent, I really hadn't given returning much thought. So I packed without contemplation of what this would mean.

Just as I was finishing, I saw Ray pulling up. Neither he nor I had made contact throughout the whole ordeal. I didn't because I really didn't think that Ray would have anything to offer at the time. I am sure that is the way he felt as well. I met him at the door. "Good to see you, Ray."

"You too. How are you doin'?" Genuine concern from Ray.

"I guess I am making it day to day. I have never felt like this before." I stopped to see if I was going to take this too far emotionally. "I miss her so much." It was too much so I just brought it to an end.

Ray took over, "Looks like you are getting ready to head out?" He was the master of deduction, so I smiled and nodded my head. He continued, "I guess there is no good time to bring this up, especially now, but Diane called and wants me to tell you how sorry she is for you and all that has gone on. I have been keeping her up on what you have been going through."

"Thank her for me will you," is all I could think to say.

Ray was a little uncomfortable in continuing, "Diane wants to know how to handle Alicia. She has been asking Diane why you stopped writing. Evidently, she has sent you multiple letters in the last few weeks. Diane will tell her why you haven't written back, but she wanted to make sure that you didn't want to do it yourself. Is that what you want?"

I really had totally put Alicia out of my mind until now. With everything else, I still couldn't find myself writing to her. She didn't have my home address, so she couldn't have written me here. I sensed an obligation that I needed to complete. "I will write her back when I get back to Manchester. Just tell Diane that I need a little more time if she could stall Alicia."

Of course, Ray said it could be done. Then he helped me load up my car. Even though I hadn't planned to leave until later that day. I said my goodbyes. As I put the car in gear, I realized the chapter of my life called "Linda" was over. But it really never went away because the blond haired girl with the big blue eyes still smiles for me in my memories. Few miles between Fort Wayne and Manchester were tearless.

Chapter 33
<u>What Becomes of the Broken Hearted</u>

Word of Linda's death spread around the campus without my intervention. In fact, I stayed to a strict schedule the first few days: class, library, cafeteria, room. For all of their faults; Don, Dirk, and Wayne were my salvation. They insulated me from the outside world. By the end of the first week, I was a hermit among a throng of people.

I didn't write Alicia or call her. I couldn't do it. I would go to the phone, dial, think of Linda, and hang up. A call seemed like a betrayal of Linda, and a letter was just too painful to write. That first week back was nothing but lonely. Friday, I was packing to go home. The weatherman was calling for a blizzard, so I was hurrying. To spend the weekend alone was just too unbearable. I was almost ready to go when Wayne came in with a message from the desk. "You've got a phone call, Mark. Terry at the desk says its a girl. Do you want me to see who it is?" Wayne had gotten used to his role of Mark Logan protector.

I couldn't let it go on. "I'm going to face things starting now. Thanks for everything, Wayne, you've been great."

The walk to the phone created a shifting sensation in my stomach. Each step caused a little more sickness to grow inside me. Touching the receiver and pulling it to my ear, I almost tossed my cookies. The voice on the other end was Alicia. What could I say?

"Mark, is that you? Please talk to me." There were tears in her words.

Timidly, I responded, "I'm here Alicia. How...how are you?" It sounded too trivial to be talking small talk.

There was an obvious pause. Alicia got right to the point, "Mark, what is going on? I haven't heard from you since before Christmas. I thought something awful happened to you. Didn't you get my letters?"

I knew that I had to face the situation because this had obviously hurt her. Slowly

I unfolded the whole story of Linda and I and that the I had told her about in my letters was Linda. "I knew that," she matter-of-factly told me.

I went on. I told her about going to Columbus, my father's predicament, and through a lump in my throat, I recounted the story of Linda's death.

Neither Alicia or I spoke for the longest time. I was drained and Alicia was obviously stunned. Eventually, she expressed her sorrow, "Mark, I would have had to be a fool not to notice how you felt about Linda. Your letters gradually betrayed the casualness that you started with. I knew all along." Somehow she knew that I needed to be aware of this knowledge that she had. "I didn't say anything about it to you because," she struggled at this point, "because, it really was selfish, I wanted you to be there for me. I was afraid of losing you." There were no more words, just sobbing.

As much as I wanted to respond, I didn't know what to say. Silence was filling the void again. It was Alicia who spoke first, "Diane knew all about this didn't she? She kept telling me to be patient."

"Well, I told Ray; I'm sure he told Diane." I reached deep within to finish my story, "I told Ray that I would write you when I got back to Manchester. I didn't. I just couldn't make the call. I couldn't bear telling you or facing Linda's memory again."

Alicia had obviously composed herself. "Mark, when we began this whole thing, you wrote me to help me get through my depression over Nick. No one helped me to get to this point more than you." I was crying openly now. "I still need you. But more importantly, I have to help you now. I want to joke with you and make you smile like you did for me. But now is not the time. Let me be here for you. I'll take back 'I love you' if it will help. No strings, just friends."

We were full circle now. I knew that she was right. Our words had been crutches for us before. But now I needed stronger support. "You don't mind starting our relationship from the beginning again?"

Softly, Alicia reassured me, "The beginning was easy the first time. This is as much for me as it is for you."

We talked for over an hour. Alicia reprised her letters, although I opened all of them after we hung up. I told her about dad and my family.

It was just good-bye when we ended the phone call. Although we had taken a step back in our relationship, there was a break in my depression. I didn't go home. I faced the world I that I now had - without Linda. Don went to the package liquor store and bought me a bottle of Ripple. I got drunk for the first time. It didn't feel good, but I lost the weekend.

Chapter 34
<u>Something Stupid</u>

Alicia's letters came steadily, at least two a week, and I tried to reciprocate as often as possible. The tone of the letters were markedly different now. She had become my support; my emotional sounding board. Seldom did I think of her as anything more than my faraway friend. In fact, before I signed my name I put in "Your friend." Without Linda, that is where Alicia fit.

My campus life was pretty simple. I had delved into my studies, a fact not lost on Professor Milligan whom I had the good fortune to be associated with again; this time the course was zoology. More than once he took me aside to compliment me on the change of attitude. Most of the time he patted himself on the back for the way that he handled me during the fall semester. Nothing was further from the truth; I had learned to play the college game. So I acknowledged Milligan's presence and ideas when he required it. Each day in my prayers I thanked Linda over and over again for being the savior of my life, deeply in my soul I wanted to tell her in person.

Socially, I didn't exist; nor did I have any reason to improve it. After a couple of weeks, the guys in at CU had pampered me enough. They were fed up with my sulking and left me to my own devises. Except Dirk, Don, and Wayne. They became my drinking buddies. Either Dirk or Don were more than willing to buy me wine. They thought this was there way of including me, but more often than not I sat with the wine staring out the window listening to music. Rod McKuen's poetry was interspersed with my own As I started to fill up the book that Linda gave me, I started to realize that if I filled it up, I would no longer have the strong connection because it would be done, so I drank more to slow down the process.

I stopped going home for weekends altogether. I reasoned that they wouldn't understand where I was at this point, and I don't think that any of them would get me anything to drink. But that is what led me to the student union the first Saturday of March.

I hadn't attended a dance or any other activity the whole second semester. Everyone, especially Wayne, would try to get me to go and at least enjoy the music. I would usually beg off with "I have a lot of work to do" or "I need to get my laundry done." The truth was that I couldn't face a girl, any girl for any reason. I found myself even diverting my eyes if I thought a girl might want to talk to me. But that night was different. Don had a brilliant idea and in the short time that I had known him, I knew that I would follow him and that I would be in trouble.

The idea was formed while I was driving with Don to the local liquor store. Immediately after he asked me what I wanted, that mischievous face of Don's went into overdrive and I quickly dreaded what might be coming. "Mark, we are finished with all this melancholy shit. It's time for you to move on. You're going to the dance tonight and enjoy it."

I politely dismissed his proposal, "You and I both know that the last two people on Manchester's campus that should go to a dance are Mark Logan and Don Bates. Now just get me something to drink." Don's aversion to dancing was legendary on campus so I knew that I had him there.

Don's glow and smile increased, "Ah that is very true when I am sober." His low cackle laugh intensified as he went into details, "You are a novice drinker. I on the other hand am a professional. We are going to get plastered and enjoy a dance."

I was not impressed with his plan and, since I no longer was fully enamored with the pressure he used to place on me, I made my stand, "You do what you want Don, I am going back to the dorm, kick back on my bed, and listen to music."

He reached across and grabbed me with both hands on my collar and pulled me close for effect. "You bet your ass your going to listen to music - at the dance!" His nostrils flaired, "Either you have fun tonight or every single night for the rest of the school year you will spend in your closet with shaving cream, cologne, and Ben Gay eating away at your genitals." So much for Don Bates compassion.

He exited the car and entered the store. He came back with my choice at the time, Bali Hai, and his Bacardi and Coke. From the floor in front of him, he brought his ever present thermos and mixed his favorite. Just as quickly it was empty again. By the time we had reached campus most of the Bicardi was gone.

I, of course, waited until we were in the parking lot to begin my bottle. In no way was I nearing the same league as Don, but on that day I tried. It didn't make sense for me to act this way, but one thing that Don had said was in my mind. I hadn't really realized that my friends were tired of my attitude. I didn't even realize that I had an attitude.

312

We departed my car artificially happier than we had left the campus. Don was sure that we could head straight for the Student Union and be on time for the dance. I, on the other hand, noticed that my bladder had grown to capacity. Try as I might, I couldn't get
Don to turn back to the dorm for relief. Actually, he responded, "You know I think I have to piss too. Look around!" We were now just outside the science building. He continued as he worked with his zipper, "Mark, you see anybody around?"

Without really looking very hard, but laughing at Don almost falling over trying to open his fly, "Nope. Go ahead."

Once he had the gate to the dam open, Don relieved himself on the wall of the science building. The shear suggestion of release of the tension building in my bladder overwhelmed any reason within. I hurried to be next to Don and joined him in watering the plants. Unfortunately, I missed the wall and the cover it presented me. In my drunken state I had faced myself to the

Student Union. In front of me were four couples walking my way. I might have noticed their laughing if I hadn't felt the tap on my shoulder. I wheeled around before I had finished to see who might want me. Staring me directly in the face was Dr. Grace. After his shoes were well soaked, I came to the realization of the severity of my actions. I tried to express to him how sorry I was, but all I could manage was to throw up on his wife's dress. I was just about to keel over into Dean Grace's chest when I was caught by two arms. I searched my savior's face expecting to see Don's. What I saw was a girl's face, a face that I had seen before.

Whoever she was, she sat me down and toke Dean Grace aside. She talked with him for a long time, at least it seemed like it to me. As they talked, I looked around for Don. What I saw was his body lying among the bushes, passed out. No one had even noticed him, and he was so out of it, he knew nothing.

The conversation continued. I tried desperately to remember where I had seen the girl's face before. My head was just starting to really hurt when I saw Grace head in my direction. He knelt down next to me. The expression on his face that I had anticipated was anger, what I got was a mixture of anger and compassion. "I understand that you have been under considerable stress of late, Mr. Logan. I, like the rest of the campus was very sorry to hear of the death of Linda Warner. I guess that I hadn't realized that you and Linda had grown so close." He paused and looked back at the girl who had helped me. "Heather assures me that you are not really yourself lately. What I know about you is that you are doing better in school and now you mess it up again." Whether he was pausing for effect, he didn't need to, "You are back on probation. The only reason you will not be expelled is because Heather thinks this is only temporary.

With that Dean Grace and his wife went to his car. I was left there with Heather. I remember the name too! But where?

Heather…Heather Douglas! Linda's roommate who was so rude that day back in
November. I thought that she hated me.

I moved to the bench. I was cold and
probably pretty pathetic looking. Heather
came over and sat next to me. This time she
offered a smile and patted my leg. "Why is
that every time I see you, you are doing
something that you aren't supposed to do?"

Of course, she was right. Over the
last couple of months, Heather had treated
me as a necessary evil. But today, she offered me tenderness instead of the scowl that
I was used to. Maybe that was why I didn't
recognize her. "Thank you. Heather, I
don't know what to say, but thank you."

She began to cry, "I should have
talked to you weeks ago. We should have
helped each other. She was my friend." I
put my arm around her, and she snuggled
against me. When she gathered herself to
speak again, she directly at me, "You have
been hurting for so long now and so have I."
The tears started again, "She loved you so

316

much, and I know how much you loved
her." A heavy sigh introduced what she really had to say, "It is time for both of us to
move on. I need a friend right now, and
from what I have just seen, you do too. We
need to help each other get past this. Do
you think that you could handle me as a
friend?"

The big bear hug that I gave her was
the only answer she got. It felt like Linda
sent her to me. I could feel her crying. The
deep down tears and hurt that I had held
back for over a month began.

I don't know how long we sat there
commiserating with each other. The snow
had started, and we were covered. Heather
pulled away and I suggested, "I do believe
that I am sober now. Would it be okay with
you if we go to the snack bar and get a cof-
fee? I'm buying."

From the person I had always
thought personified a frown, I saw a faint
smile, "How about Dutch.?"

I understood, "Yeh, Dutch."

We spent the night at the snack bar, at least till it closed at midnight. We continued talking at Oakwood until I was kicked out at curfew. In just a few hours, Heather and I had been able to unload burdens that we had carried since Linda's death. For the first time in the months since Linda's death, I slept the rest of the night all the way through. Talking with Heather gave me the chance to get Linda back and get a new friend all at once.

Chapter 35
Only the Strong Survive

Heather was symbolically my sister. She was my salvation. I told her everything, and she reacted to it all rationally and yet not detached. Early on in our relationship we came to the understanding that we were two people who shared a common tragedy that cried for constant release.

I was free of the persistent well wishers wanting me to "go out" or "do something." With Heather I was safe because they all thought we were lovers. We never were. She was engaged and devoted to Dan Zigler, a senior who had used his last year in college to join the Peace Corps. He was stationed in Cambodia, teaching the Cambodian children English in a missionary school. His letters were often the entire focus of our discussions. Heather read them with a tone in her voice that betrayed her desirous wish for him to be next to her. There were times the letters embarrassed me; I felt like an intruder on their private feelings.

I didn't bring up Alicia until almost the end of March. As was our custom, Heather and I were studying at the library. We would study and reflect. Alicia just never came to my mind. Somehow my ambiguous relationship with Alicia didn't stack up to that of Heather and Dan. When I did tell Heather about Alicia, she smiled that knowing smile my mother used when she was had read me long before I put anything into words. "What took you so long?"

"What do you mean?" I was dumbfounded and just a little confused.

"Linda told me about Alicia." With those words she swallowed a heaviness that had accumulated in her throat. "Linda told you she was okay with your letters to Alicia. Yet, she really hated the fact that you were writing Alicia."

An uncomfortable sensation welled up inside me. "If she had told me not to write, I wouldn't have. She had to know that."

"She did. She also knew that Alicia needed you and saw that a girl hundreds of miles away was really not a threat." Her pause was for effect, but it was obvious that Heather was almost in tears. "I didn't tell you that I was out looking for you that night you soaked Dr. Grace's shoes. I had been keeping close tabs on you. Linda would have hated what her death had done to you. I just had to do something...for Linda."

She was right. I hadn't given much thought to the future before Heather saved me that night. Since that night I gave up drinking altogether (I never liked that stuff all that much anyway). I still kept pretty much to myself. But I still had my friends and I had added Heather. "I don't think I have ever adequately thanked you for that night. Thank you."

"No need. In fact you just thanked me a few minutes ago. You trusted me with your story about Alicia."

All I could do was stare at her.
"How in the world can that be thanks.
Every time I think about Alicia or bring it
up, it just feels like I'm betraying Linda."
Those words came especially hard, so I
stopped.

"Linda wanted you to be happy. She
loved you. Do you really think she would
want you to be crying for her and keep up
this vigil of yours. Linda saw so much more
in you." I was so shaken by her words that I
didn't realize she had taken my hand. "Mark,
when you could see what was going on in
the administration building and tried to protect her, Linda knew that you were special.
There are a lot of causes out there. Alicia
may be yours for now." With that she
beamed that big broad smile of hers. "We
could use you in the march against this war
also."

The war in Vietnam, Civil Rights,
student demonstrations - they had all been
foreign to me the last three months. If it
weren't for the letters from Dan, I would

have been a total illiterate on the state of the world and the country. Heather's joke stirred in me a desire that had been repressed since I was a child. Conviction! "I want to become more involved in the anti-war movement. Linda barely got me started." I stood over her and vowed, "For Linda's memory and my own values, get me involved."

That was the start of Mark Logan, outspoken political activist. Heather kept me informed about situations from that point on. We would disagree, and I wouldn't follow a cause just because she had chosen it. All-in-all, I was a blossoming caretaker of this world. At the least a person who cared what was going on around him.

The best example of my new found awareness came when Heather explained the significance of Martin Luther King, Jr. who had come to the Manchester campus to deliver a speech on racial equality and student involvement in February. She led me through the words that I had heard. Through her ears and eyes I was able to take in the fluency of his speech and the spirit of his words. Blacks students had been around me since I had started school. I had never noticed that they were any different from me. All the hullabaloo about racial equality in the papers seemed a bore to me. It wasn't in Fort Wayne, so why should I care. I was changed when I reflected with Heather about that February morning in the auditorium.

As would be the case with any neophyte revolutionary, the next day I searched out Nathaniel Briggs for verification of the black dilemma. We had gone to junior high school together and played on the football teams. We went our separate ways in high school, Nathaniel had graduated from Central High School a rival of my alma mater, South Side. We had been rivals on the football field, but friends at Manchester, but in the last couple of months were no more than passing acquaintances on the campus. He was at Manchester on a football scholarship. When I stopped him in the commons area, he flashed an amicable grin, "Mark, how's it hangin'?"

In junior high we had the kind of relationship that would have allowed us to start somewhere other than with small talk, but I was on a mission so I delved into my business, "Nathaniel, it really is good to see you and talk to you, but...well...I have started to work through the words and ideas of Martin Luther King."

"Yeah, I was there. He's quite a talker isn't he?"

I was feeling more uncomfortable, but I had come this far, "We haven't been real close in the last few years, and after last night, I don't think I ever really knew what life was like for blacks in Fort Wayne, or anywhere for that matter."

Nathaniel laughed a robust laugh. His six foot four frame was carrying more weight than it did in high school. No doubt a weight training program. "Mark, you were pretty insulated. But, don't feel bad, so was I. Black athletes are treated differently than other blacks. Look around this campus.

How many blacks that are here aren't athletes?"

I thought it over. "The only ones I can think of are the foreign exchange students from Nigeria and Botswana."

"Bingo. It sure is amazing how all of us ignore facts that stare us in the face. I get an education because I can carry a football. My sister is back in Fort Wayne working at the grocery store for minimum wage. She's the smart one in the family, but no athletic ability."

We talked all the way to the Student Union Building where I headed for my mailbox and Nathaniel went for the bulletin board. The anticipated letter from Alicia was there with a letter from mom. As I was opening Alicia's letter, I looked to see what Nathaniel was searching for on the bulletin board. He was searching the "Rides" section. I worked my way toward him. "Do you need a ride home?"

I think he was as surprised as I was that we had not thought of it before. "Are you going home for the break?"

Quickly, I offered, "You've got a ride home if you want it."

Nathaniel reached out to slap my hand as was the convention to show agreement at the time. "Man, you're a lifesaver. I thought I'd have to hitch or stay here on campus the whole vacation. When will you want to leave?"

"How about three tomorrow?"

"My last class is at noon, so that will work out fine." With that we went our own ways.

After Nathaniel had gone, I opened the letter from Alicia. Alicia's letter was not unlike the others of recent vintage. Very supportive and understanding. It was only the recurring dream of her (it never stopped) that kept me being interested in the situation at all anymore. With Heather's help I realized that a trip to Wisconsin to see Alicia was what I really needed. So I had written a letter that was totally out of character for me in my new state:

> Dear Alicia,
> I am going to be brief. I know that I haven't been my jolly self for quite a while, but that is going to change. I have it from a very reliable source, you and I are star crossed. I think that means we should meet. Now you could come here and save me a lot of time and money, or I could come out there in August with Ray. I chose the part about me going to
> Wisconsin. Spring break starts to-morrow. Write me at home this time. I don't want to miss one letter.

> Mark
> P.S. If you don't agree with what I said, pretend that I was being held captive with a gun at my temple. Pretend they made me say these things.

This letter that was in my hand was a response to that letter. It was a warm letter. The kind that you would read in front of a fire on a cold rainy night and fall back dreaming of the face on the other end.

Mark, the time will never come that I won't want to see you. My only regret is that it will take until August to finally meet. Until then your words will have to be enough. Your in my dreams and thoughts. Hurry!

As I packed to go home for the break, my mind flashed back and forth between Alicia and visions of her at the end of a road, open arms, waiting for me; and my memories of Linda and the Thanksgiving weekend we had together. The joy and hurt together brought me to a conclusion that I am forced to believe by what I think is my inner voice. Things are in my path for a reason; it would be foolish to avoid them. And that I realize that it applied to the trip home that spring as well.

The next day Nathaniel and I got off right on time and traffic was almost nonexistent due to the fact that most students were on the interstate on their way to Florida. The trip from Manchester to Fort Wayne had become a nightmare since Linda..., so Nathaniel's company was welcome. He had a great sense of humor, at least until we had a flat tire.

Fortunately, we were within walking distance to a small town called Smithsville. If the spare tire had air in it, we would have just been able to change the tire and go on our way. It didn't. The walk was probably good for us. I had offered to go alone, but Nathaniel said that he didn't want to be left in the car without a white person in it as well.

The only garage in town was able to send a tow truck out and took care of everything relatively quickly. In the time we waited, I suggested that we go and have a bite to eat at the cafeteria across the street from the garage. Nathaniel was not exactly thrilled with the idea. He even inferred that it might be dangerous.

I couldn't see how going to get a bite to eat could be dangerous. But it could have been. As we entered the place, the woman behind the counter ducked behind a door to the back of the restaurant. In very little time a rotund man dressed in the white accouterments of a cook made his way to us. The wetness of his face and the filth all over him encouraged my stomach to crawl with the very thought that he was working with food.

His words were not eloquent, but they were concise. "No niggers in here. No nigger lovers either."

I was intimidated at first, then outrage took over. I looked for Nathaniel; he had left. I looked back to the slovenly gourmand. "There were no niggers in this room, just fat ass ugly bigots." I felt good for voicing my displeasure. But when I saw his fist headed for my face, my feet gave me a much better feeling.

Why I thought I could find asylum in my car showed my inexperience in civil rights demonstrations. "Mr. Blimp" and a couple of his belly-protruding buddies were coming toward the garage. Nathaniel was in the car as I approached. "Is the tire fixed?" My eagerness to know superseded my common sense. A quick look in the direction in which Nathaniel was pointing revealed the proprietor of the garage putting the a lug nut on .

"How much?" I yelled as I started the car.

The mechanic reached behind him for the bill. "Well, let's see, for the tow it will be..."

"Bottom line, how much? We're in a hurry."

"Twenty-eight dollars, including tax."

I threw three tens at him and pealed out. He was waving and yelling, "But there are only three lugnuts on that wheel."

On the road again, I was speechless. Nathaniel sensed my shock. "First feel for prejudice?"

"I guess so." I had never thought about it. No one had ever treated me or my friends like that for any reason before. "Nathaniel, do you have to deal with that kind of thing very often? Doesn't it hurt your feelings?"

"It hurts a lot more than feelings, and it happens a whole lot more than I can stand sometimes." He turned away from me and looked out the window. "I've had white folks say those words to me after they have broken into my own house."

Silence filled the rest of the trip. When we pulled up to his house, I was taken by how simple and strong the old two story was. "This house is filled with pride isn't it Nathaniel? Could I sometime meet your family?"

As his large frame unfolded from the old Ford, Nathaniel flashed me a smile. "Careful now Mark, that guy back there in Smithsville will end up being right after all -

Nigger Lover." He shut the door behind him and walked up the sidewalk. Then he stopped and walked back a couple of steps. "Mark, you've just learned something that I've known all my life. Just being here with my family won't help anything. Your welcome anytime, but come as a friend, not a researcher or social worker."

The words hurt a part of me I didn't know I had - the white man part. I could never really be able to experience his life because I embodied all that had hurt him. We traveled back and forth to Manchester for the next three years. I grew as a white man to understand a lot, but in the end I was Nathaniel's friend and nothing more. Of course, that was good enough for me and Nathaniel.

Chapter 36
<u>Hair</u>

It was an early spring for Indiana, and I was spending most of my vacation working for my father, and with whatever time I had left, I spent it with Ray debating the world. I told him about my letter to Alicia , but he was only concerned about his own trip and saw me merely as another driver on the long trip.

I wrote Alicia every day. I was intimidated by the "I love you" that had come months before, but was able to say "love" before I signed off. Our letters took a one hundred and eighty degree turn. Gradually, we started to become intimate. My deepest secrets were for her and hers were for me. Nothing that happened to either of us was too insignificant. The funny thing was it was never boring, to write or read.

The vacation was nine days and by the end I had seven letters to show for it. Ray caught me reading one of the letters when he came over once, "Doesn't she ever take a day off?"

"I'm sure Diane sends you regular letters too, so don't make such a big deal about how much Alicia and I write each other." For some inexplicable reason he had irritated me, and I knew that it showed.

"Listen, big shot lover, I'm engaged, and it makes a whole lot more sense that Diane write each other more often." As irritated as I was, it didn't even come close to the anger in those words coming from my best friend.

"What's the real problem Ray?" I searched his eyes for the answers. He diverted them away from me. "What have I done to get you so pissed at me this time?"

He spun around and let me have it. "You write too much." He stopped and looked away again. "You write too well." Plopping himself on my bed, Ray emptied his conscience, "Alicia is telling Diane about your letters. Not details. Just how you bare your soul to a complete stranger. Diane can't understand why I can't tell her how I am feeling like you do." It made some sort of perverse sense. Ray was jealous of me!

I went over next to him and put my arm around his shoulder. "Remember one thing about all of this Ray, you always get the girl. You have to be doing something right."

He smiled and agreed, "Most of the time that is true, but this time you are in control. Linda was in love with you and now so is Alicia. To Diane you are some sort of Casanova who not only gets the girl but wants to keep her an her alone." Ray shoved my arm away and continued, "I think I'll look bad next to you this summer."

I blurted out loud and quickly realized that this could be taken wrong. "Ray, Diane is so in love with you that no one is even in her field of vision - you know that. Now get off it! If necessary I'll knock Alicia around a little to look bad, okay?"

Though he didn't really acknowledge me, I sensed he could see how silly his feelings about me were. When I left for

Manchester on Sunday, he was his old self and gave me a map to look over so that I could help to plot our course of travel for August.

I picked up Nathaniel, and we were on our way. Smithsville loomed in front of us, and we made plans. Childish as it seemed, we wanted some revenge, at least I did. In the center of the small town, I slowed the car as I slipped off my pants. Nathaniel worked his way into the backseat and disrobed below the waist as well. It was orchestrated perfectly. I screeched to a halt, yanked down my pants at the exact same moment that Nathaniel did so in the back seat, and we each pressed our cheeks against the side windows as I blared on the horn. We held the position for no more than ten seconds, but the "interracial moon" was a success that day.

Nearing Manchester, we debated the need for a return engagement of the "moon." I was for it; Nathaniel didn't want to push it. His experience in protest won out.

338

I unloaded my luggage and "care packages" from my mother while I listened to "Hair" by the Cowsills on the radio. The words to that song hit home as I found myself looking in the mirror. My clean shaven face was now speckled with stubbles of a beard. The haircut that made everyone say that I looked so much like my father was replaced with much more that was totally unruly. "Give me a head with hair, long beautiful hair..." Linda would have liked the statement I was beginning to make visually. Anymore I knew that it wasn't for her that the statement was being made. After all it was my hair and my life.

My brief moment of narcissistic thoughts had to be interrupted. There were things to do. Get to my mailbox. Find out if Heather was back yet. Get some supper.

Heather wasn't in her room and the cafeteria wasn't open yet, so I headed for the Student Union building and my mailbox. The campus was coming back to life, but it was still pretty eerie how quite it was.

Only one letter was in my mailbox. It was pink stationary. Alicia. I was like Pavlov's dogs by now. Pulling the letter from the box, it became immediately apparent that this was not a letter from Alicia. There was no stamp. It was interschool mail. Still the handwriting was familiar. When I opened it, my stomach fell to my toes. Heather! Her words weren't meant to hurt, but they did.

Dear Mark,

I'm writing this letter before spring vacation. I wanted to tell you this in person, but I couldn't do it. We became so close; you were like my family. Dan worked some angles to get me to join him in the Peace Corps. I knew about it back when I was saving your ass that night. At first I didn't think you would care if I left or not, and then I felt you were becoming too dependent on me. That was when I decided that I would have to leave you this letter.

You were special to me. I found out that a guy and a girl can be friends without being lovers. You're a special person Mark Logan. I don't want to lose you as a friend, so I've given you my address with the Peace Corps. Please write and tell me how things are here at Manchester.

Your friend always,

Heather
P.S. I could never have done this if you hadn't told me about Alicia. She's going to help you more than I ever could.

Endings have always been a problem for me. But there had been too many in my short college career. Linda was gone. Heather was gone. Alicia was too far away. Setting goals for myself began at that point. Perspective was what I needed. Alicia was only a few months away. My college work was improving. I was now politically aware.

I was alone.

Chapter 37
First of May

Until school was out in May, I was on campus, the longest stretch of my collegiate career. For the first time there were no girls involved in my days or nights. In fact, other than studying, there was little distraction at all. That was until May Day festivities. I sort of went overboard there.

May Day was a celebration at Manchester covering a number of "rites of spring." Graduation would soon be taking friends and sending them all around the world. Marriage would ensnare others to apartments off campus. The school year was winding down and everyone was outside in varying forms of clothing. It was, in retrospect, a last fling for all of us to be sheltered by the fantasy world of academia.

Finals were two weeks after May Day, and I was prepared, so I was like the rest of the campus: throwing Frisbees, laying in the sun, playing practical jokes. It was the last that got me into the most trouble.

Denny Shellhouse, the big lovable freshman who had been so helpful with the pump for homecoming, was becoming a regular jokester, pulling pranks on everyone. He wasn't even afraid anymore of Don or Dirk. When his latest prank, a closet door rigged with a bucket full of cow shit, ended up with me as its target, I began my plan. It was simple and precise - Denny loved to drink Mountain Dew, and he would leave a bottle sitting everywhere. I would just wait until he left one in a place that he could never blame me for refilling it for him.

I did refill it for him; it looked just the same. He had left it in the CU lounge, and there was a bathroom next door. I went to the desk in the lobby and talked to Dirk who was working and appraised him of the situation. His job was to tell me when Denny came back and picked up the bottle. I would then go around the corner and duck behind the desk to see the whole thing unfold.

The signal! I walked leisurely around the desk and slid behind it. Denny went right for the bottle and began drinking it immediately. He chugged it once and stopped. He looked at the bottle. Then he looked around. That would have been enough, after all, I was already having trouble containing myself. But, he took another drink and chugged the rest down. He wiped his lips and came towards the desk where Dirk was laughing so hard he was unaware of the fact that he was directly over me and fell over backwards. Between Dirk's laughter and Denny's acceptance of the fluid, I was unable to contain myself any longer. Dirk and I were rolling around the floor unable to contain our laughter.

In the meantime Denny put two and two together and dove after me. I was out of his reach with one roll to the left. He was out of control, so I bounded down the hall and up to my room. I locked the door. Safe and secure. Outside my door was heavy breathing - Denny! He was calm when he

344

finally spoke, "Your day will come, and it won't be today. You won't even remember, but I will get you." With that he left.

He was true to his word. I passed him in the hall and campus often. Yet, he did nothing. It was in the middle of May Day festivities that Denny took his revenge. The dorms were in competition with each other in a number of events. We had completed the greased pole climb, unsuccessfully. The bike race was a disaster as well. When we got to the tug of war competition down at the river, we knew that CU was out of the running, so we chose to swim across the river and tug from that side. Everyone assumed that it was sportsmanship, but Don figured we could tie onto a tree over there and no one would know. He was right. We won the tug of war.

It was during the tug of war that we all heard an explosion. It came from the direction of CU. At the time we all were concerned, but we explained it off as a number of things like a backfire or a chemistry experiment that had gone wrong. It wasn't until afterwards when I unlocked my dorm room that I could see the destruction that had ensued. Denny had set up a timer to start a match, that would light a M80 which was under a box, which had shaving cream and rubbing alcohol on it. ...The paint on the walls was being eaten away. The stain on the doors was alternately dark and light.

I had to repaint that room before I could leave for home that summer. I never once asked Denny to help or blamed him. For some reason I felt he owed it to me, and I got what I deserved. Denny went home before I did to his folks house in Cleveland. He got a job for the summer at a local dive motel as a night manager. Denny was shot to death by a doped up druggie who was in need of money for a fix. Denny's murder was the day after I finished remodeling my room. I never had the chance to tell him I was sorry.

Chapter 38
Hello, Goodbye

The Beatles were singing "Hello, Goodbye", and it was all over. My freshman year was over, and I had survived it, barely. I loaded the car with mixed feelings. Here I was just two and a half months away from being with Alicia. The excitement of caused me to have trouble sleeping. Then there was the drama being acted out around the campus.

Don's parents were down the hall helping him get all of his accumulated "treasures" loaded into a rented truck. They were yelling a lot, but there was a sense of pride in them as well. You know, Don was smiling quite a bit as well. He had actually graduated, and he even had a major in education! He became a teacher, then a principal, and finally a superintendent of schools. A heart attack took him before he was 50.

Dirk was gone already. He had a tryout for an NBA team. He never made it, but it was a thrill to think that I might have been a friend of a NBA star. Actually, he took over a Dairy Queen franchise in the Manchester area and started to coach PAL leagues. I saw him years later and barely recognized him, and he didn't seem to know me at all. He did have his NAIA All-American ring on and talked freely about his days as a star. He and Cheryl have been married for over 40 years.

Wayne and I weren't really saying goodbye that year. We still had three years to go. A particularly sorry time of my life came a few years after graduation when I found out through the school newsletter that Wayne had died a vagrant, homeless, in New York City. I guess he had lost some of his glamour and ability to talk his way out of things. His business failed; his wife left him and took his kids; and knowing Wayne, he couldn't put all together again.

Everyone else on campus was in varying degrees of ecstasy and pain. In retrospect, each year had its own pathos and bliss. But none of the four years were as traumatic as that one for me. As I packed, Manchester looked better, though nothing had changed in its appearance. Manchester was home now. In future years even though I had a chance to move to a brand new dorm, I couldn't let down the memory of all the Don's and Dirk's that had come before me and stayed at the old dilapidated Calvin Ulrey. Besides it held my memories of the freshman year. The dark and dingy halls manifested the spirit of Linda as much as the rest of the campus did.

There was one last letter in my mailbox. Of course, it was from Alicia. She was working at her summer job, a secretarial position at an insurance agency. In various ways she repeated how much my writing to her meant and how much she loved me. The letter told about how she and her parents were getting along, but how she really did want to move out on her own. In this she envied me for going away to college. More and more when I received her letters, I became anxious and in need of companionship. Not once did I feel the need though to compensate with someone locally. As if I had a pact with Linda, it felt like the only person that made sense had to be Alicia.

Once the car was packed, I looked around the campus first to see what I was leaving. "It was twenty years ago today..." was playing around in my head, as though I was at my college reunion. I couldn't drink in the meanings of the time enough. Finally, getting into the car was imperative, or I would never get on the road and home. As I pulled out of the parking lot, a girl with a guy jumped out in front of the car. It was Heather!

Heather came to my side of the car and bent down to the window. "Mark, were you going to leave without saying good-bye?" She smiled and not waiting for an answer she continued, " this is Dan, Dan this is Mark." We exchanged pleasantries and Heather went on to tell about their Peace Corp work. Then she got to the point,

"Thought we might be able to convince you to come with us. There is a commune in the northern peninsula of Michigan near the Canadian border. A large group of anti-war people are meeting there to set up a command post and live off the land. Doesn't it sound great?"

Heather had affected my social consciousness, so it was hard for me to decline. Yet, I couldn't envision myself as a communal member. I tried to explain. "Heather, this sounds perfect for you and Dan. To be truthful, I have a lot to sort out in my live, and I think that being home at this time is important to me. Is there any way that I can visit though?"

She smiled that motherly knowing smile that gave comfort to me in those days after Linda's death. "Alicia, I forgot. Sure, come and see us." She reached in her purse and pulled out a pad of paper and drew a map and wrote instructions. "Just remember, this isn't a college romp. If you come, be as committed as you were when I left." With that she leaned into the car and kissed me on the cheek. "I'll never see you again. But it was good to know you Mark Logan." Her eyes burned into mine. She was right, and I knew it. There was a part of me that wanted to become active and the other that was worrying more if I would ever find out who I was. As she left and got into Dan's Volkswagen bus, I was overcome with finality. To this day I don't have the faintest idea what ever happened to Heather. She didn't return to Manchester, and I never went to the commune.

The trip home was a blur of friends, lovers, and circumstances. In no time at all I was pulling into my parent's driveway. Mom and Dad were in the doorway, smiling. I couldn't help but wonder if they had gone through what I had when they were younger. I never asked them. Many small chips of our lives are not meant to be shared I guess.

Chapter 39
Can I Change My Mind?

I worked that summer for the state highway department and got as good an education there as I did in many of my school classes. Ray kept telling me that I was just learning what he had learned the previous year - the work world is where real life begins. I would leave at six-thirty every morning and get home at five every week day. It was a grind and was a prime motivator for my return to college. The cozy walls of academia were looking even better than when I left them.

My relationship with Ray deteriorated that summer and almost affected the trip to LaCrosse. It was hard for me to understand Ray anymore. He was self-indulgent and easy to anger. Yet, every Friday night that summer when we were off work, we would spend the time together at movies, drive-ins, going to the lake - almost as it had been when we were in high school together. He'd bring up work or I'd bring up school, and it was like another world. Neither of us could understand the other.

On the Fourth of July, Ray and I went with Julie to the fireworks together at the park. Julie fixed a picnic for us, and we sat and talked about old times. The crowd got bigger and bigger until we were surrounded by families, couples, and scattered individuals. There was an old-fashioned band box set up near the fireworks area with a Dixieland band playing patriotic tunes. The war in Vietnam had not changed any of the enthusiasm in Fort Wayne. In fact, there were quite a few people proudly showing their beliefs on both sides. American flags and peace medallions were everywhere.

It was a great day. The sun was beating down and the breeze was perfect out of the southwest. Ray and I went off to throw the Frisbee without falling over people; Julie wanted to just lay in the sun and get a tan. Near the golf course that is adjacent to McMillen Park, there was an open field where everyone went to have tug-of-war matches, sack races, and so on. There was plenty of room for us, but Ray wasn't interested in playing anymore. He motioned me to a bench. He couldn't find the words to tell me what was on his mind.

After what seemed too long for me, I asked him, "What the hell is going on Ray? What do you need to say?"

"Things are so easy for you, you know that?" Ray was serious. His eyes evaded mine. "Sure, you've had problems, but they always work out. Julie didn't work out; along comes Linda. Linda dies... Poor example." It was getting harder for him to find the words, and I was beginning to get irritated. "I don't know if there are the right words to say this, Mark. We aren't going to Lacrosse this summer."

All I could come up with was "You have got to be kidding!"

He got up from the bench and walked away from me. With his back to me, "At least I won't be going. If you want to go, that's your business."

"Ray, what could possibly keep you from going to see Diane? Both of you have been waiting for this as much as Alicia and I have? I thought you said you were going to set the date finally." At this my temper flared and I jumped off the bench, went to Ray, and spun him around to face me. "Ray what have you done? What is going on?"

He was crying. The tears were flowing down his face. He took both hands and rubbed them away fiercely. "I love Diane more than anyone in the world. I do. Yet, I keep doing things to hurt her." By now he had started to hit himself in the leg with his extended arm. "I was lonely. You know how I get lonely. I guess I'm just weak." His pause was to collect himself and to get my eyes to connect with his. "Julie is pregnant with my child." The tears came again this time in a torrent. He tried to go on, but the words were muffled with sobs and cries.

Stunned, I tried to make sense of this. "Ray, do you love Julie?"

Exasperated with my question, he grabbed my shirt and pulled me close, shaking me. "NO! I don't love Julie!" His words were slow and deliberate. Then he released me. "I'm sorry. I don't know how to feel. I feel responsibility. I feel shame. I feel guilt. But most of all, I'm scared."

"What are you scared of?"

"You. Julie. Diane. Mostly Diane. This time I have really screwed things up."

I was groping for the obvious question and a discrete way of putting it. It was too important to let go. "What have you and Julie decided to do?"

He answered quickly, as if the question was there for the asking all along. "Nothing. We have decided nothing. I've told Julie that I love Diane. She understands, but says that she wants to have the child. I asked her if she wants me to marry her. She says that it isn't necessary."

"That sounds like Julie. If that is the case, then what are you so worried about?"

Then I noticed a side of Ray that had never come to the fore previously. "I can't have a son or daughter of mine out in this world without me. Don't you see? This is my child! I can't ust walk away from it. Could you?"

My response didn't take any thought at all, "No, I couldn't." We both just stood there for a while until I broke the silence, "So what are you going to do? Have you told Diane?"

He drew up his hands to his face as if to hide from all of this. "That part of the whole puzzle is not even turned over yet. That is why you are here with me now. I need advise badly."

"But what advise could I possibly give you in this situation? I don't have any answers."

We started to walk and Ray begrudgingly asked of me what he needed of me. "I can't face Diane. But I don't want to lose her. Still, I may lose her anyway. You know Diane; you know how she will react. What should I do, tell her? Should I act like it never happened and keep it a secret?"

This was uncomfortable. I wasn't prepared for this and had little advise that was very valuable. "Seems to me that the truth is always best, especially since Julie is determined to have the baby. Better to face it now than sometime in the future." It hit me after that statement. "Wait a minute! You've already decided not to go to Diane's. Obviously, you know that you don't want to face her."

He hem-hawed around for a while, then confessed, "I had hoped that since you and Alicia are getting along so well that, well..., maybe you would go and plead my case with Diane. Maybe she would listen if you were doing the talking and not get hysterical or anything."

"Let me get this straight. You want me to travel all the way to Lacrosse, Wisconsin alone, to a place I have never been, and while I am there, you want me to tell your fiancée that you have fathered a child and don't know what to do. Is that just about it?"

He was desperate now, "I knew how your relationship with Alicia is going and that you would go now whether I did or not." He stopped to collect himself. "I can't face her or talk to her."

I put my hand on his shoulder. "Ray, how do you expect to explain the fact that I will be there without you?"

The first glimmer of hope came to his face. "I have that all worked out. I joined the Army reserves in May and arranged that my basic training will begin in August. I can't possibly go and that will give me time to think things over. It will also be perfect if you smooth the waters for me."

"Exactly how far along is Julie," I simmered.

"Three months."

"You asshole! You've known since May that you were not going with me!" With that I stormed off.

Loudly and pleadingly Ray called after me. "Mark. You have to help. I have no one to turn to. Where are you going?"

Over my shoulder and not looking back, "I should be going to Julie and expressing my condolences, but I couldn't bear to face her. See you again someday." With that I blocked out anything he said and got into my car. As I hit the gas, I saw Ray in my rearview mirror, standing in the middle of the road. He and I both knew that I would help him somehow, but I didn't have to stay there and get more and more angry at him.

At home I didn't hesitate to call Alicia. She was at work. I really wanted to get this off of my chest, and Alicia was the only person in the world left for me to talk to about this.

Discretion came over me however. There would be no reason for Alicia four hundred miles away to keep the knowledge that I would give her away from her best friend. And I was still Ray's best friend and couldn't do that to him. Besides he was good enough at it himself.

At my desk I found Alicia's latest letter. There was nothing profoundly different in the letter, but by now it was gratifying that she would tell me everything about her life. For some reason I began to think about Julie. How alone she must feel. I had to say something to her someday. Of anyone in this situation, I started to empathize with her. She was the one no

one wanted. Diane wanted Ray; Ray wanted Diane; and Ray wanted the baby. I began to wonder if I wanted and needed Julie. As I thought about it, it all seemed so abstract -To want someone just to make them feel better. Is that the relationship that Alicia and I have? Alicia did seem to need me, and she there for me when my life was at its toughest. I began to wonder if being needed was enough for the type of commitment in time and travel I was about to make.

It sounded selfish when I thought it, but I found myself trying to justify my relationship with Alicia to myself. With very little thought I took out a piece of paper and began to write:

Dear Alicia,

No matter what happens after you read this letter, I want you to know that you have been a Godsend for me. When my life was at its lowest point, you kept me going. There is nothing I can say or do to thank you enough. Accept my deepest thanks for that.

There is now a possibility that I will not be able to come out this summer. It arose today. Since I found out about it, I have had a little time to reflect on you and I. I have noticed that we both talk about how we need each other. How we depend on the letter that we get from each other to make it through the day. I am worried that we are building something between us that doesn't have any foundation. (Boy does that sound pretentious!)

I almost am sure that at times (actually quite a few) I have deep feelings for you that might be love , and yet we have never even met. Does that sound strange or what? Can it be? Is that dangerous?

Maybe what I am saying is - this is your chance to back out. And I guess its my last chance too. Let's think it over.

Love,
Mark

I decided that I couldn't wait to think this letter through. I got out an envelope and addressed it, put a stamp on it, jumped in my car, and headed for the post office. On the way my jumbled thoughts went from Alicia to Julie, from Ray to Diane, from Linda to Alicia. The brown-haired girl is starting to go out of focus more and more.

Chapter 40
<u>Let's Live for Today</u>

     The letter came air mail. The usual pastel colored envelope was missing as a clue. But the letter was from Alicia there was no doubt. I stood at the mailbox debating whether to open it there or to wait until I was sitting down. I was never very good at waiting. I tore open the letter.

Dear Mark,

     I know what is going on there, and I want to help. Diane came over just before I got your letter. Ray can't come because of basic training, right? If that is the problem, then I have to let you know that his presence is not necessary as far as I am concerned (except that it would make Diane happy). For your information Mr. Logan, whether we ever meet I know that I would be able to fall in love with you. Everyone is looking for someone who is kind and understanding, funny and able to laugh at himself, and finally, a person who cares, not just about how you are, but about what life is like and how people react to each other.

You better be here in August or I'll never see you again.

With all my love,

Alicia

My assessment of Ray went even further below what I had already considered it to be. Now he had left it to me! All of it. Should I tell Alicia first? Should I see Alicia at all? It felt like a betrayal of her to perpetuate this hoax that Ray had created. And what about Diane? No matter what, I was the one that would have to tell her.

I was dialing the phone immediately. Ray answered and I tore into him. "You creep! How dare you tell Diane that lie. You knew she would tell Alicia. Now you've put me in a situation where I can't get out, without looking like more of jerk than you." I couldn't place why exactly this made me so furious, other than the fact that Ray had taken advantage of me. I didn't wait for him to respond though. I hung up and went out and got into my car.

What was the problem? Obviously, Alicia cared about me. She expressed that very well. She wanted me to be there in August. I tried and tried to locate the cause for my fury, but itcouldn't be found. Beyond that, I had no idea where I was going.

Eventually, I found myself in front of Julie's house. It was the one place I could find some clues as to what I was feeling. Julie and I could always talk to each other, at least until this latest occurrence. Maybe there was something she could say to help me. The thought was ironic. In her condition and in this situation, it would seem she would need to talk to me.

I walked slowly up to the door. Knocking as unobtrusively as possible, I hoped against all hope at this point that no one would be home. No luck, Julie's mother answered the door. "Well, hello Mark. We haven't seen much of you since last fall. How did school go?"

I always liked Julie's mother and father. They both had infectious smiles and loved to be around young people. I had to get around that though; I had a mission. "School went very well. Mrs. Merideth is Julie here. I really have to speak with her."

My urgency must have been genuine enough, because without a word Mrs. Meredith called upstairs to Julie. Then she turned back to me, no smile now. "Mark, see if you can find out what is wrong with Julie while you are talking to her. Her father I have noticed that she has been crying a lot lately and has been very moody. I think it has something to do with Ray."

By the time that Mrs. Meredith had mentioned Ray's name, Julie was standing behind her. "Mother, could Mark and I be alone, please." I always liked that quality about Julie; no matter what the situation was, she could still be cordial to everyone.

Mrs. Meredith left the living room and went back to the kitchen. Julie indicated that we should sit on the sofa. What looked to be streams of tears were still on her face. She spoke first, "I know that Ray told you. We had a fight last night about the situation." She reached for a tissue; the tears were flowing again. "He won't marry me, but wants me to have the baby. I want to have the baby; but I want there to be a father also. He knows someone who can get me to an abortion clinic in Detroit, but I have heard horror stories about what has happened in places like that. I wanted to call you, but your life has gone so far away from mine that I didn't know whether you would care." The tears came even harder and faster.

Mrs. Meredith looked in from the kitchen. I saw her over Julie's shoulder. Julie didn't know that she was there. I motioned that I would take care of her, and reluctantly Mrs.

Meredith retired to the kitchen again. Then I turned to Julie, "Your parents don't know, that is all to obvious. When do you plan to tell them?"

With an ironic laugh, Julie struggled to answer, "I don't know. I have no plan. I want a child someday. I want to marry a man that I love someday. Neither of those situations fit right now." She apparently stopped to reflect on the other choices. "I can't have an abortion. It just doesn't seem right. The answer is probably an adoption, but that would mean facing my parents, and I don't know that I can handle looking into their faces."

I was at a loss. Placed in a position to give advice again. I needed Heather; she was the one good at this. I tried though, "Your parents are great people who care about you very much. There is nothing they wouldn't do for you. I'm sure that they will be disappointed, but they are the one's that will help you with this, certainly much better than me." After I said it, I knew that I had made sense. "In fact, if you want I'll sit with you and give you moral support, if that would help."

A broad smile came across her face. She reached for me and pulled me to her. "I needed a friend and you were there. Thank you." She kissed me on the cheek, and then we set down how best to handle the situation. There was a mixture of hope and fear in her words as we talked over what should be done. She really was beautiful, and more than ever I was drawn to her, even though it was probably too late for both of us.

That night we sat in the living room and alternately told her parents about what had happened. I tried to defuse any anger they had by showing the mistakes that I had made. Julie was straightforward and truthful. In the end they were exceptionally angry, but the anger was directed at Ray and not Julie. I think that Julie and I had mapped it out that way. There was even talk by Mr. Meredith of shooting Ray. The cool composure of Mrs. Meredith won out though. They all thanked me, but decided that from that point on they would make the final decision together.

The ride home was the most calming I had experienced for a while. No matter Julie's decision now, I knew that I could face Alicia and maybe even Diane if I had to. It was time for a letter!

Dear Alicia,

Nothing will keep me away now! Your words caused me to see that my place this August is by your side in the Lacrosse sunlight and moonlight. I'm sorry for the last letter, but with the news that Ray brought me, I was afraid that everything was going to fall apart for this summer. I had been looking forward so much to this time with you that I became despondent. Mark your calendar for August 14. That morning you will see Mark Logan at your front door. (What a horrifying thought!)

In the meantime, be thinking this over- what could you and I do to make these our "Moments to Remember." I know I have some ideas.

I skirted the Ray and Julie situation and still got my point across. All that was left now was time, and money. Had to scratch up enough to make the trip. No help from Ray. No help from Ray at all.

Chapter 41
Last Chance to Turn Around

By August 13 a lot had happened. Ray had tried to talk to me on a number of occasions, but I could find convenient reasons to be busy or leave as the situation called for it. I had received thirty-two letters from Alicia and three phone calls. But most important was what happened to Julie.

Julie kept me informed on what was going on in her world. Her parents eventually accepted her dilemma and talked her into two proposals regarding her baby. The first involved Ray. Their suggestion was that Ray was not fit to be the father of her child and shouldn't be regarded as having any choice as to what happens to the child. This seemed pretty vindictive for a couple of people whom I would have considered before this incident to be fairly liberal. What was surprising about this suggestion was that Julie went along with it from the very beginning. When she told me about this part of the decision, I asked her if she was willing to write Ray off so easily. She was quick to reply, "Ray Osborne is no more than a child himself. How could I trust him with this decision let alone my child." Ray was out of the picture; I wondered if he knew. Maybe if I answered his calls I would know.

The second part of the deal was that Julie would give the child up for adoption. Julie told me that this was a much harder decision and even called me to ask what I thought about the idea. Even though I was aware of how much she loved the idea of having a child of her own, I also knew that she was better off by putting it off for a while. So Julie and her parents met with their lawyer to set up the adoption and what Julie would have to do in the mean time.

I assumed that Ray knew all of this, and I didn't want to discuss it with him. Yet on the thirteenth, while I was packing to get myself ready to go, Ray showed up and my mother, oblivious to what was going on, escorted him into the room. Ray was subdued and under control for a change. "Mark, I owe you an apology. I've been trying to make this apology for the last three weeks. I know what you must be thinking about me, but I was in a situation that backed me into a corner. Now that situation no longer exists, you do know what Julie has decided, don't you?" I nodded that I did. "Well, I want to go with you to Lacrosse again if you will have me? I just have to see Diane."

"That's just great. Except aren't you forgetting something, like the Army Re-serves." I was packing more furiously, probably in a vain attempt to control my contempt for Ray.

He plopped himself down on my bed just like he used to; I didn't find it funny an-ymore. Leaning back lacing his fingers behind his head, "That went away too. If you had been answering your phone lately, you'd know that I'm "4-F." Seems my knees are both in bad shape. They don't want me." He sat pensively for a second and laughed.

"Been a lot of that going on around me lately."

That I found funny. "You brought it on yourself, you know."

"Just don't hold it against me. I'm still the Ray that was your friend before all of this happened. Let's go together; it'll be a blast. Two beautiful women and two best buddies." It
was that easy for him. Virtually no remorse.

I pressed him for the only condition that I had, "You have to tell Diane what happened here the last few weeks. She deserves that. Because if you don't, I'll guarantee that she does get it from Alicia or me. Bet on it!"

With all the indignation he could muster, he cried out, "What the hell business is it that I tell Diane? It will only hurt her and our relationship."

I looked him in the eye and waited until he was intent on what I had to say. "Listen, you arrogant asshole, you have hurt one friend of mine already with this. Imagine how bad this will be later after you have married Diane. Will she take it better then? I don't think so. I'm leaving tomorrow morning at six. If you agree to my only stipulation, be in the car loaded up by that time or I'm going alone."

"But, Mark..."

"No buts or any excuses this time. Agree or no. For now, just leave will you. I have to decide if there is any possibility that you are still a friend, and every time you open your mouth it gets to be more debatable."

Like a whipped puppy, he turned tail and left. It was so simple for him. I would understand and take him back, just as he expected the same from Diane. I was determined about this one though. Diane had to know what she was getting into. Maybe by the time we got to Lacrosse a miracle would have happened, and Ray would have grown up.

After a restless night, I was up at five and eating breakfast. As usual, Mom got up to make sure that the breakfast I had was nutritious. She was at the kitchen window, wheeled around and came to me, and whispered, "there are two legs hanging across the front seat of your car." I cautiously approached the car; it was Ray. It looked like he had slept there all night.

Breakfast was finished, and Mom had loaded the "care package" of goodies for the trip. It was time to leave when she touched my shoulder. "You have done some things lately that you didn't think that your father and I were aware of. Julie's parents told us." She was starting to cry. "You have done us proud, son. That is one of the many reasons that we trust you on this trip." She started crying again. "I just wish it wasn't so far."

There wasn't much that I could say. "It's only a week. Ray will be with me... Not much consolation, huh?" She smiled and shook her head. "I'll be home in no time. But I have to go, you understand don't you?"

She did. Then she pushed me out the door with a kiss on the forehead.   "Call when you get there, will you?"

"Sure, Mom." I wanted to tell her how much what she had said meant to me; I wanted to tell her I loved her. Instead the mature young man that I was got into the car and waved goodbye. In my rearview mirror I could still see her face as I pulled down the street. It really hurt to grow up.

Chapter 42
Expressway to Your Heart

We were on the road for what seemed like forever. At no time in the trip did Ray or I refer to Julie or the situation back in Fort Wayne. It was like an unwritten truce between us. We talked about old times. We talked about Vietnam. We talked about the countryside. But the subject of any girl was taboo.

Ray was no longer a confidant or comrade in arms. Our conversation represented a link only to a past from which both of us were moving. The trip existed merely as a trip down memory lane, a place we could endure as old friends. There was more than one time along the way I had twinges of melancholy as I looked into his face. I gradually became aware that this trip was my rite of passage when it really should have been Ray's.

Lacrosse loomed ahead of us. It is a small town on the Mississippi with one large cliff overlooking the river at the town's western side. Otherwise, the town was nestled in a valley that neatly encompassed the entirety of the little village. It looked like a postcard or the hamlet from a fairy tale. I became entirely engrossed in it, taking in all of its nuances.

Ray woke me from my reverie. "In a matter of minutes we'll be at Diane's. I can see from your face that you're as excited as I am." He was wrong. I was much more excited than he could ever comprehend.

Diane was waiting on the front porch. When she saw us, her face beamed, and she ran to the driveway, jumping at Ray's side of the door before he could even get the car to a stop. She pulled him to her and kissed him to the point of suffocation. When she let up, she couldn't stop talking. "I thought you'd never get here. I've been on the porch waiting for almost two hours. Oh hi, Mark! Alicia was here until she had to go to work. We'll pick her up at the office at eight. For some reason she had to work the afternoon shift." She grabbed Ray again and kissed him. Just as quickly, remembering, "Oh yeah, she arranged it that if she worked this afternoon, when she didn't have to she could have the week off to be with you."

Ray appeared to be a bit put off by all of this. "Come on Diane, let me out of the car. I have to get out and stretch and hold you right."

Realizing he was right, Diane backed away, but only so that he could open the door. As soon as he was out of the car, she did her best to enter his body by force. Ray was not resisting in the least. Feeling that I was a cog that was of no importance to this process, I extricated myself from the car and walked around the yard. The stretch felt good.

A voice from inside the house boomed out, "Get that stuff off my front lawn and get those boys in here now." A body followed the voice. It was a man, probably in his late fifties, just starting to bald and considerably shorter than Ray and I. He came to me and grabbed my hand with a firm handshake. "You must be Mark.

I'm Jon Fisher, Diane's father. Want to come in for a drink of lemonade? It could be a while before those two will be joining us." He obviously had forgotten that I met him years ago when his family lived in Fort Wayne. They had lived just a few blocks from me and just around the corner from Ray. That was when Ray and Diane had met. Incredulously, they kept in touch over the years and got back together three years ago. The rest just fell into place.

When Diane and Ray were finally able to tear themselves away from each other, it was almost seven. In the meantime I sat around talking to Mr. Fisher. The rest of the family came by from time to time. Most of them remembered me and recounted stories to Mr. Fisher to jog his memory. He didn't have the vaguest notion of me until Mrs. Fisher told him of the incident in their back yard in Fort Wayne when Ray, Diane, and I had dug the hole that was supposed to be our passage to India. What I remembered as anger years ago manifested itself in rolling laughter from Mr. Fisher as he heard the story.

From that point on I was like a child on Christmas Eve. "Is it time yet? Is it Christmas yet?" Only my questions were mostly inward - "Is it eight yet? Can we go now? Can I finally meet Alicia?" Ray and Diane were so self-absorbed that I was of no concern to them. Everyone else was there, but I wasn't. Mentally, I was picturing what it would be like when Alicia and I meet.

At ten till eight, Diane relieved my tension. "We better get going. Alicia gets off in just ten minutes." She pulled me out of the chair where I was sitting. "But you knew that already didn't you?" I tried to hide the fact that this had been all that was on my mind, but I betrayed this when I fell over the footstool that had been in front of me for the last hour. Diane helped me up while Ray laughed his head off. She whispered to me, "Between you and I, Mark, Alicia has been falling over things lately too." Her smile was so sincere and the thought was so welcome that I finally was able to compose myself.

The insurance office where Alicia worked was across from the town square. Ray pulled into a space that angled directly towards the front door of the office. I was conflicted as to whether to search the office from the back seat of Ray's car or act cool and wait until I got out and went to the door. I couldn't wait, of course. I craned and shifted, without any inhibitions. Back to the rear of the office was a girl with brown hair. She had her back to me, filing papers in a drawer. She was wearing a white blouse and a grey skirt. They fit her perfectly. If this wasn't Alicia, then those months of picturing her were a total waste.

As if she knew we were waiting, the girl whirled around and waved in our direction. Even though she was eighty feet away, her green eyes seized mine. I don't have the faintest idea how I got out of the car or when I walked to the door, but we were face to face, her eyes and mine still connected. She got to her voice before I could. "Mark Logan, I presume."

"You amaze me. Not in one letter did you ever tell me you had psychic powers." Stupid comment. Her very presence was freezing me. She was beautiful.

"And you didn't tell me that you were so handsome. In fact, we have to do something about your self-concept." With that she closed the door and grabbed my hand. "You're mine now aren't you?"

I was dumbfounded and the only way to express what I wanted to say was, "I hope you don't mind that I'm not as formally dressed as you." I held the door for her to get into the car; her dress slid up her leg slightly and showed their flawless angles.

She caught me staring at her legs. "I planned on going home first to change, but maybe you wouldn't mind if I wear the skirt."

Ray piped in at that. "That is a good idea. I'm hungry. Let's head to a pizza place."

Diane punched him in the arm and turned to Alicia. "If you want to go home, we can tak you and wait." I agreed with her.

"Oh, no we won't wait any longer." Then she scooted over on the backseat to be next to me. Alicia put her hand in mine and said only to me, "There's so little time for us." She paused, did I detect some remorse? "I want every minute possible to be with you."

I can't explain it, but I couldn't think of a thing to say. I just looked into her eyes. They were so close. I could see the eyes of the girl in the dream. They were the same. The same thin lips were set inside an impeccable face. Her cheekbones were high and accentuated by a light rose color. All of this conveyed the warmth that her words had given me all that time in her letters.

"Hey dope! You ever gonna say anything?" Ray was needling me, but it didn't matter, I was in heaven. Diane punched him again, and he put the car in gear.

It took a little while, but I eventually put my arm around her. The I held Alicia close. It was a desperate hug. It was like neither of us wanted to let the other go for fear that this would all end. For me, Linda came to mind, I was sure that she had to be thinking of Nick. Briefly, I worried that we were in a storybook and that this wasn't real at all. I squeezed this stranger as if I had known her all my life. She squeezed back. It was pretty obvious to me that she was aware of the same feeling. At the time I didn't really notice all that was going on, but it retrospect I now see that there were tears in her eyes too.

Diane navigated Ray to a pizza parlor on the edge of the Lacrosse College campus. It was pretty empty because even summer school was out. We had the place to ourselves after a while. Diane sat next to Ray, and Alicia was next to me. If an outsider had been told that one of the two couples at the booth was engaged to be married, that person would have been hard pressed to distinguish between us.

We spent the time catching up on what had happened recently. Most of what Alicia and I had to say, we had gone over in our letters. But it didn't matter, the stories were better coming from her voice. Diane was oblivious to much of what Ray had been doing, it was noticeable. He knew very little about what had happened to her in the last month as well. I looked at him to coax him into remembering what he had promised me. He nodded and indicated that this wasn't the best time.

From the pizza parlor, we took in a late movie. "The Graduate" was in town, and since none of us had seen it, the logical thing to do was get a ticket. We lucked out. Seats in the balcony! At least it seemed lucky, until the bat that inhabited the upper regions of the theater began to attack us.

Diane started screaming. To be truthful, Alicia and I weren't paying a lot of attention. I was staring at her most of the time, and she was gripping my arm or getting my attention in some other way. We hadn't kissed yet, but we had linked up with our eyes about when Dustin Hoffman was staring at Anne Bancroft's legs. We both jumped out of our skins. Ray was flaying around at the bat with a popcorn box, without much luck. I took my stab at it before the bat came right at my face. I alertly remembered that I was deathly afraid of bats. Composure wise, I was a mess. I had to make a good impression on Alicia, but I had to protect myself from this horrid monster.

I felt a hand on my back. I turned to Alicia who was smiling up at me. "Thank you for protecting from the bat Mark, but I'm not all that afraid of them." I gazed at her to see if this was just for my sake and realized she was telling the truth, so I sat down and let Ray be a hero.

Yet, I couldn't keep up the pretense. "I may be committing suicide in our relationship, but I have to tell you that if I don't get out of here, that bat will make me jump off the balcony."

The sweat on my forehead must have backed up my story because she led me out of the seat and said to Diane, "Mark is taking me out for a walk to get away from that awful bat."

Diane was amazed, "You're not afraid of ..."

"You're mistaken, Diane." She winked at her, and Diane winked back once she figured it out. Alicia continued, "We don't really need you two to chaperone us anymore anyway. See you tomorrow. I'll make sure Mark gets where he needs to go." It was a strange thing to say. Where do I need to go?

Outside the theater Alicia placed herself directly in front of me. There was no smile, but the sincerity was there. "You don't have to prove anything to me, Mark. You did that a long time ago when you agreed to write to a mixed up girl who spurned your caring initially. I don't think you'll ever know what you have done for me. Don't protect me; just hold me." Her arms enfolded me. It was a long embrace and through her body I felt tears.

392

And then I held her just far enough away to allow my lips to get near hers. Seldom does passion that strong manifest itself without sex being a close follow-up. Since we were downtown on a public sidewalk, we couldn't and didn't. But had we been anywhere else, it wouldn't have changed anything. This kiss was one of understanding, a kiss that was dreamt of by both of us, but it seemed that it would never be a reality. When it was real, neither of us would let it go.

At an undetermined interval of time, we did stop. We stopped simultaneously and smiled at each other. I spoke first, "My dreams weren't better. If there were no other days than this, I would feel great about my life."

Alicia coiled her left arm through my right, and we began to walk. "Thank you for coming to Lacrosse. With all my friends, including Diane, I was lonely. Sure, your letters kept me going, but a few weeks ago it started to get hard. Especially, when Ray told Diane that he wasn't going to be able to come. I thought... Well, I thought that you would have a reason not to come." Her tears started to flow.

We were near a park bench. I helped her to sit down. Then I cupped her chin in my hand, wiping away the tears with the other hand. "You can ask Ray, that was never a possibility. In fact," I debated on whether to go further. What the heck, Ray was a jerk who would definitely not tell Diane himself, "when Ray was looking for excuses not to come, I told him I would go without him. I almost did." I stopped just short of telling her about Julie.

A puzzled look was on her face. "What do you mean 'looking for excuses'?"

I realized that this was not the time or place. "It wasn't much. Let's call it fiancée jitters. You know how guys get when they think of commitment."

She accepted the explanation because it hit her what the rest of what I said meant. "You do want to be here then. I'm not just a charity case?" Strangely, her smile vanished, but she was searching my eyes for something.

"Ah, but what a beautiful charity case." I leaned over and kissed her again.

The kiss didn't last as long, but that isn't to say that it lacked in intensity. Alicia collected herself, "You have to be tired. Let's go home." She stood, and I froze.

"I guess I never asked anyone where I was going to stay. I know that Ray is staying at Fisher's. I just assumed that I would be too."

Dragging me along, she laughed, "You were going to stay there until just a few minutes ago. My parents said it would be alright, but I, well, I wasn't so sure." She stopped and came close and pulled me to her. "I'm sure now, okay?"

Like there would be any doubt!

The walk to her house took over an hour. We talked about all things that you talk about with someone you have known for a long time: family, friends, but mostly each other. I was desperately in love. I think she was too. Playfully on her front porch, she teased that her bed was just a twin bed. I was speechless. That caused her to laugh, and then hug me. "Mother and father will love you. By the way there is no way they would let you sleep in the same room with me. The same house, yes, but never the same room."

Inside, I met both Mr. and Mrs. Williams. They had been waiting up to see if they would be meeting the mysterious Mark Logan they had heard about in the last few months. They were a nice couple who more than once stared at my straggly hair. I felt that Alicia's father was sizing me up compared to Nick. When I found out that he had fought in Korea, I knew he indeed had probably done the comparison.

They made every attempt to make me feel at home. They did seem to be in a hurry to get me put away for the night though. I assumed it was because they either wanted to get the lowdown from Alicia or that they were just plain tired. The next morning it became all to clear why they acted the way that they did that night.

I didn't fight it though. Alicia led me to the basement where her father had built in a bedroom for guests. She helped me to make the bed and her mother brought me a pair of Mr. Williams' pajamas. "Couldn't help but notice you didn't have a suitcase, "she said.

That was the first that I realized that my clothes were all at Diane's. I was quick to let her know that I wasn't that uncouth. "My stuff is at Diane's..."

"No need to explain. Alicia already told us what happened." With that she bade me goodnight and left. Was it just my imagination that she looked over her shoulder at Alicia and gave her a stern look?

I sat down on the edge of the bed. Alicia came over and sat next to me. We both smiled at each other. She spoke as she ran her fingers through my hair, "They didn't like your hair much, but they do like you. I can tell." Pause. "So do I. Very much. In fact ..." She began to cry. "In fact, I love you." We held each other for over an hour. My instincts told me that her tears would stop if I held her tight. The whole hour the tears never stopped.

Slowly, she disengaged and held my face in both her hands. Lovingly she kissed my forehead. Eventually, as if she was trying to freeze the moment, she grudgingly got up and went to the door. She turned at the stairs to speak before she left, "Thank you, Mark Logan. I owe you so much. I'll never be able to..." The tears started again, and she was gone.

I went to bed that night and slept a restless sleep. The brown haired girl returned to my dreams. She was walking away. I could here her crying. I called to her, but she never answered me, never turned around. I never saw Alicia again.

Chapter 43
Both Sides Now

I caught a bus back to Mount Jefferson the next night. Ray and Diane came over to Alicia's and said that I could stay at Fisher's house with them. Diane even suggested she had other friends that would go out with me if I stayed. I never even contemplated either suggestion. The only option that made sense for me was to go home.

That morning I woke late; it was nearly ten. Why had no one awakened me? The house was quiet, so I made my way around silently. When I reached the kitchen, Alicia's mother was sitting at the breakfast table her head in her hands, crying. I didn't want to disturb her, but it was obvious she was upset about something, and I wanted to help in some way. I walked over to her and hesitated, but eventually put my hand on her shoulder. "Is there something wrong, Mrs. Williams?"

That's when I noticed the envelope in her hands. It had my name on it. She looked at me and handed me the envelope, as if it were the hardest task that she had ever been given. "She couldn't face you. But she did want me to give this to you." I think she wanted me to respond but I couldn't. She continued, "We are really sorry for all of this." Her eyes told me that the sorrow was deep and that I was about to learn something that would throw me for a loop.

Before I opened the envelope I had to know, "Alicia's gone? When? Why? Where?"

Her eyes were just like Alicia's. I hadn't noticed that the night before. They were sincere when she spoke, "She said the letter would explain everything, but I'm not so sure. Let me explain one thing that Alicia could never have expressed well enough in that letter." She indicated that I sit in the chair next to her. After a deep breath she began, "The letter will explain the why, when, and where. You need to know before you read it that Alicia loved… loves you. You have meant so much more to her than almost anyone else. I could feel that when the two of you came in the door last night. I also could tell that you loved her. Some-day... Well, sometimes things do work out." She couldn't bear it anymore. "Sometimes they don't." She left the room leaving me with the letter.

Dreading opening the letter, I put it off by thinking through the night before. What had I done? I thought we were getting along so great. Wait! Just before I went to bed, she was upset. What had I done then? I wracked my brain, I was comforting her. Isn't that what she needed.

I had to open the envelope. As if the paper were too thick to tear, I struggled with it. It fell open. It was her fragrance that I smelled. It was so familiar now. The col-ors. The flourish to her written strokes. It was what I had left of Alicia, and I didn't know why. Only reading her words would give me the answer.

Dear Mark,

There is no other way to tell you, and I am truly sorry that I couldn't face you to tell you. I couldn't bear to look in your eyes and see your reaction when I tell you. A wire from Nick came two days ago. He's back, alive, and in a hospital in San Diego. He also wired me a ticket to come out and see him. He says that he is okay, but he needs to see me. After all of our letters, you know that I need to go to him.

I wanted to call and tell you not to come. I even had the phone in my hand more than once and dialed. Part of me told me that it would be better if you never came to Lacrosse. The other part of me told me that we had to meet. I weighed what you would want to do. It was selfish of me. I wanted to see you and be with you, even if it was only one night.

You need to know; Ray and Diane had no idea. Diane thought that I took the week off work to be with you, so I didn't correct her.

By the time that you read this, I will be in San Diego. I know that you'll understand, that among many other things, is why I love you. I do you know. Always remember that is a fact. I also know that none of this will probably make sense to you. Right now it doesn't make sense to me either. I won't promise anything, like "I'll be in touch." I do know that I can promise you that I will never forget you. Please, never forget me.

      Love,

      Alicia

      P.S. Think of me when a bat is around. I'll protect you no matter where you are.

      The rest of the day was a blur. Alicia called Diane to let her know what happened so that I wouldn't have to explain what happened to her and Ray. That is why they showed up that afternoon. Diane talked. Ray talked. All the while, both of Alicia's parents were sitting and listening. When they were pretty well talked out, I replied, "I think that I will just go home. All I need is a ride to the bus station."

Before Ray or Diane could respond, Mr. Williams spoke up, "If you don't mind Mark, I will take you." Neither Ray nor Diane knew what to say. Actually, Ray seemed relieved. I read his mind, "Diane will pay attention to you and feel all sorry for you. What about me? I'm going to have to drive home alone."

That is how I ended up at the bus station with Mr. Williams. Ray and Diane could have been there, but they weren't. I was rude to Ray because I told him that all I wanted from him was the truth to be told to Diane. He hung up on me. Never did tell her the truth as far as I know.

With Mr. Williams help I got my suitcase checked and a ticket for Fort Wayne through Chicago. Before he left, he shook my hand, "My wife and I owe you more than you will ever know. When Alicia said that she still wanted you to come after she heard from Nick, we were sure that it was a mistake." His pause was obviously to put his words together, "Sometimes we have to open a door to shut it. Does that make sense to you?"

For the first time that day, I smiled because it made sense. Both Alicia and I had to shut a door that would only open once.

Chapter 44
<u>Summer Rain</u>

The trip home was lonely, but in some ways filled with friends. Linda visited me in my dreams along the way. She still loved me. She held me tight. Alicia was there too. She was looking everywhere for me, but I couldn't be found. Funny thing was, I was looking for her as well. We were in the same room but never found each other.

Toward evening, the bus pulled into Chicago. Since I had a to wait to make my connection for about an hour, I wandered around downtown. As I got near the Miracle Mile, I had a thought. I have a week off work. I'm in one of the best cities in the country. Why not stay? I retraced my steps and went to the ticket counter. I exchanged my ticket for that day, for another in four days.

After I grabbed my suitcase, I headed out to find a hotel. After a search near the Miracle Mile, I found a place that fit my budget. Amazingly, I was thinking very clearly, which caused me to search my bill-fold for Diane's phone number. I couldn't have anyone calling my parents to see if I got home safely. Then everyone would worry needlessly.

After one ring, Diane answered. I got to the point, "Hi, Diane. I need you to help."

She hesitated, "Are you home already?"

"Actually, I'm in Chicago. That's why I need your help. Mom and dad don't expect me home for four more days, and…" I needed to bring my thoughts together to fully explain my actions. "I really don't want to answer questions right now. For right now, I want them to believe everything went fine. In the meantime, I want to experience Chicago on my own."

It was obvious that Diane didn't know what to say. I think that she was also trying to decide if Ray needed to be privy to the plan, so she asked, "Well if that is what you want. Do you want to talk to Ray?"

I hadn't really thought about it, but the less Ray knew, the better this impromptu trip would work. "Just tell him that I made it home. I will get home before he will." I still had to tell Diane one more thing, "I think that I know you pretty well, so I am pretty sure that you are starting to blame yourself. Don't. I got to me Alicia. We had a great night. Now I can have an experience on my own. All in all, this could be a growth process for me."

Diane responded, "Is it okay if I still worry about you a little?"

I hoped that my smile could transport through the phone line, "Sure, but it won't be necessary. Tell Ray hello and goodbye."

Then we said goodbye.

Without the pressure of worrying everyone, I felt a weight off my shoulders. I was now free for four days to… what exactly was I free to do? I had no plan. Then it hit me, that was exactly what I needed. I grabbed my notebook and a pen and headed to Grant Park.

Chapter 45
Sure Gonna Miss Her

That night in Grant Park, I walked until instinct told me to stop. The first stop was just on the other side of Michigan Avenue. There was a isolated bench facing the towering skyscrapers of the city. I sat and jotted thoughts - all the people, all the concrete, my place in that mass of humanity and structure. I focused on one building that was dark and alone in all the rest. I pondered its story. It told me its rejection by the world. It drew me towards it.

The walk wasn't as short as I thought it would be. A couple of times I thought that I was there, but saw lights in the buildings that I found. After a half hour of walking in the direction of the building, I found it. Its desolate condition was no better when I was closer in proximity. Even though it sat among other buildings that were vital and alive with human inhabitants even at night on a Monday, this building sat

410

starkly alone. The lower two levels were boarded up and there was a sign on the main lower level door. I traversed the crosswalk and moved toward the door.

The sign was pretty simple: "Condemned. This building is deemed unsafe for any occupants. Demolition scheduled Sunday, August 25 at 5:00 AM." I don't know what made those few words so sad to me, but I backed up step by step, and with each step I took in the grandeur of the building before me. In all the windows I saw the ghosts of the people who had worked there. They stared down at me as if they wanted me to fix the unfixable. It was almost unbearable, so I lowered my head. As I did I saw the sign inside the large front window.

"Future site of the first high rise retirement community of Chicago." In those words there seemed to be hope. A place in downtown Chicago, near everything the people of Chicago have grown used to; how perfect. The juxtaposition of the old building and the new inspired me to write. There was a bench next to the building's boarded front door. In my notebook I wrote the poem "The Retirement of Hope." It was completed in about five minutes. But the muse in me kept going. From there, I wrote about the loss of Linda and its meaning to me. Then my mind lead me to Alicia and her future. The poem had no element of me in it.

By six in the morning, I had a collection of fifteen poems and two short stories. I hadn't even noticed that the city had awakened with many pedestrians glancing at me as they hurried to their jobs. I remained unaffected by them until I started to imagine their lives as they hurried by me. I created their stories on paper and by noon I had written three more short stories.

It was at that point that my stomach protested and my eyelids betrayed how exhausted I had become. The two body parts fought me as I made my way back to my hotel room. Along the way, I found a donut shop. A couple of donuts and orange juice later, I was in my room and flopped on the bed.

Later, in the light of day, I retraced my steps from the night before to the building that I had written about. As is the case with any light shed on darkness, the muse did not return. It didn't really matter. What I really wanted was for that to be the starting point for the rest of my investigation of the world.

That is when I realized that Chicago could actually provide the world to my exploration. That day it was the Art Institute. There I experienced the interpretations of artists for hundreds of years. Art had never spoken to me before. For some reason, I knew the language and allowed myself to converse with Monet, Picasso, and DaVinci. They all taught me more than I thought that I could ever learn in a lifetime.

The next day I spent at the Field Museum and The Museum of Science and Industry. Both of these museums had been a part of trips that I had made to Chicago with my family. I do remember elements of these wonderful sites, but nothing like I did when I experienced them alone. I took in all that I could, and when that wasn't enough, I sat and wrote my impressions of what was there. That evening, rather than hurrying back to my hotel room, I went to the beach off of Lake Shore Drive near the museums.

By that time there were few swimmers, sun worshippers, or even boats. I could walk the beach from the museums north to Grant Park. This when I first started to notice couples. In the two days of the Chicago experience, I somehow blotted out the couples around me. Once I had navigated the Soldier Field area, I settled at Buckingham Fountain in Grant Park.

My eyes jumped from one couple to the other. They were everywhere.

For the first time in this journey, I was at a loss as to what I was to learn. I had let my feet and destiny create my education and experiences. Well, my feet and destiny seemed to take me back to what I was trying to … to what? That was when I really saw

414

them, the couples. They were just as much my textbook as the paintings and displays. These people unknowingly were my professors. The problem, at the time, was that I was trying to learn the wrong lesson. So it never sunk in until much later.

The last two days I spent at a Cubs game, Shedd Aquarium, and downtown at the various stores of the Miracle Mile. On Friday, my bus was leaving at three in the afternoon, so I took the L and arrived at two. Sitting in the bus station, I took out the notebook to see what I had written. I decided to look at the most recent, so I turned to the last page I had used. To my surprise, I had filled all but two pages in the 50 page notebook. As I surveyed the work, I honestly didn't even remember writing most of it. But when I read the unfamiliar pieces, I heard my voice in them.

By the time the bus had left the terminal, I had filled the last two pages. One was a poem about a young mother who was traveling with her young child. The other was about the people who ride on buses and where they go.

On the over three hour bus trip home, I worked through how to explain what the week was like to my family and why I hadn't told them what I had done. I kept wanting to retain this experience just for me for some reason. Maybe it was because I had, for the first time in my life, experienced what life would be like if it were me on my own: no family or friends to influence my decisions or provide the support that I required before, but no longer need.

Finally, when I reached the bus station in Fort Wayne, I had decided to call Ray's house first. I knew that he had to be back in Fort Wayne by ten because he was working third shift. Since it was almost six-thirty, I thought he might have made it back. He had and he answered

I had no idea where Ray stood at this point, but I knew that in a strange way, he owed me, so I asked, "I'm glad you're home. I need for you to come and get me at the bus station."

Where Ray stood was angry, "I'm pissed at you. You made me drive all the way from Wisconsin alone. So why should I help you?"

"No problem. Just thought that I would ask."

I was about to hang up when he blurted, "Okay, Okay! I'll be there in about twenty minutes."

As I waited in the station, I wished that I still had room in the notebook. There was an elderly couple sitting across from me. Holding hands, they supported each other in the anticipation of their destination which caused them to speak loudly and excitedly. "We haven't seen the baby since he was just little." "Five years old isn't a baby!" "My grandson will always be my baby no matter how old he gets." At this point I could do no more than make a mental note.

I had become so engrossed in their banter, I had not seen Ray pull up. He blared the horn and entreated me to move my rear end.

I threw my suitcase in the back seat and sat in the front with Ray. I kept the notebook with me. Ray looked intently into my eyes, searching for an answer to a question he needed to ask. "Diane didn't really go into much detail about what you did the rest of the week. I have to admit that I didn't really try to find out either." Before he questioned my week, he added, "I owe you an apology. I was not a good friend in Lacrosse. No, that isn't all. I haven't really been a good friend for a long time. I'm sorry."

My response opened the door for us to be friends again, "When the bus left Lacrosse, I fully intended to go home, but when I got out in Chicago, it just felt right to stay for a while, so I did." Then I explained what I had done. I stayed primarily on the activities and not the writing because I wasn't sure that Ray would be interested.

On the way home, Ray got me up to date on his relationship with Diane. I wasn't surprised to find out that they set the date for next year in August. As we pulled in the driveway at my home, Ray asked, "Will you be my best man?"

I told him I would, and when I got out of his car, Ray came around and hugged me. "Diane told me to do that." He smiled, punched me in the shoulder, and then made his way to his side of the car.

I wanted to ask if he had told Diane about Julie. I didn't then. Actually, I never brought it up again.

Mom was at the door, arms wide open. The anticipated question came immediately, and I had rehearsed the answer, "I had a great time all week. I have had experiences that I will remember all my life."

She was more pointed with the next question, "But what about this girl, Alicia?"

I had prepared this answer as well, "She is great. We got along very well and had a good time together. But there is just too much that will keep us apart that we parted friends."

Mom smiled the knowing smile of a mother, "You never know what will happen in the future." With that she led me in the house glad to have me home. The questions lingered with each family member after that, but no one wanted depth, and I didn't offer. They never knew about the Chicago expedition and its effect on me. All they ever mentioned was that I seemed more mature when I returned

A week later I was on my way back to Manchester. This time I had some regrets about leaving my family, but the expectations for my future outweighed melancholy. I was now on a mission to live a life that would make my past proud.

Chapter 46
<u>The First Time Ever I Saw Your Face</u>

When I pulled into the driveway at my home, I noticed that Julie had just pulled up as well. It was always great to see her. She jumped out of her car and came back to mine, "Sorry, I blocked the garage. I thought that you would be home by now." She gave me a hug and a peck on the cheek.

As I got my briefcase out, I explained, "The bypass was backed up with a wreck and you know how people just have to see what happened." As we reached the front door, I added, "I called ahead to let Sarah know that I would be a little late. Is Sam going to be able to make it."

She wrinkled up her nose, "Court case went long today. He'll be here as soon as he can. That's what I get for marrying a lawyer." Before I could ask, I saw Julie and Sam's two girls come bounding out of the house with my son David and daughter Meg. David was two years younger than the rest, but at five he did pretty well at keeping up.

Julie had become my closest friend gradually from college to my early years as a teacher. We went to movies together, went for walks, and always spent a lot of time finding the perfect person for the other. Occasionally, we actually set up blind dates for the other. I found Sam for her. She had almost given up. She actually felt that guys could sense her past and didn't want what she called "damaged goods."

Sam had gone to Manchester with me and had recently relocated in Fort Wayne and knew no one. From the moment he came to town, I was relentless. Julie and Sam had to meet.

At nearly the same time, Sarah had been relocated to the bank where Julie worked. They became instant friends and shared notes on everything, but specifically about men. The more Julie learned about Sarah, the more she was not only sure that I should go out with her, but Julie said from the beginning that I would marry Sarah.

It was a double blind date. I knew Sam and Julie. Julie knew Sarah and me. Just one problem, Sarah had a picture of the kind of guy who drove a van in the seventies. I guess she thought that I was some kind of creep. So initially, we didn't get together. But Sam and Julie did.

Two months later they were planning their wedding and invited me over to Sam's to talk over their plans. I had the kind of relationship with them at this time that I just let myself in. I turned the corner to the living room sofa, there was a brown haired girl. The brown haired girl! Sarah!

I do know that wedding plans were made that night. I most certainly don't remember them. What I do remember is that all the people whom I have known over the last few years had provided me with the vision of the person with whom I would spend the rest of my life. I especially saw what had attracted me to Linda and Alicia in Sarah. It was like with Julie's help they all guided me in the right direction.

"Hey, Mark, where are you?" Sarah was face to face with me. Her knowing laugh so often reminds me of my mother's. "Your son wants to start the party. Do you want to get the grill going?" With that she pulled me to her and kissed my lips, "You know the best part of my day is when you come home?"

With a thankful tear in my eye, I agreed with her.

Epilogue
<u>The Road</u>

Ray and Diane did get married the next year. I was best man. Alicia was to be maid of honor, but she and Nick had just moved to Minneapolis and couldn't make it. The last time that I asked Diane about Alicia, she and Nick were happily married with two children. I never asked again after meeting Sarah.

I have often gone back to Chicago. The first few years I took students to the theater and museums. My brother, Sam, and I took in some concerts and Cubs games over the years. Later, Sarah and I visited a couple of times before we had the kids. Recently, David and I have recreated the pilgrimage yearly to pay homage to the ritual losing seasons of the Cubs that my father and I had started long ago. Each time that I have been there, for just a few seconds, I remember that in 1968 Linda and Alicia's memories were put in safe keeping in that old building, on the shores of Lake Michigan, and at the bus station that eventually showed me the way home.

Chapter by Chapter List of Songs

These are the chapter headings in this book. My intention for you is to listen to the soundtrack as you read the book. All songs can be downloaded from Amazon.Com.

I'd Like to Get to Know You
    Spanky and Our Gang
Shapes of Things
    The Yardbirds
How Can I Be Sure
    The Rascals
The Letter
    The Box Tops
Ain't Too Proud to Beg
    The Temptations
A Man Has to Go Back to the Crossroads
    James Brown
I Had Too Much to Dream
    The Electric Prunes
It's Raining
    Glenn Yarborough

Why Do Fools Fall in Love?
    Frankie Lymon & the Teenagers
I Just Wasn't Made for These Times
    The Beach Boys
The Joker Went Wild
    Brian Hyland
Cry Baby
    Janis Joplin
I Didn't Get to Sleep at All
    The Fifth Dimension
Bend Me, Shape Me
    The American Breed
Love is Here, And Now You're Gone
    The Supremes
Don't You Care
    The Buckinghams
Tell It Like It Is
    Aaron Neville
For What It's Worth
    Buffalo Springfield
Silence is Golden
    The Four Seasons
Brown Eyed Girl
    Van Morrison

Think
        Aretha Franklin
Baby, Now That I Found You
        The Foundations
On a Carousel
        The Hollies
Goin' Out of My Head
        Little Anthony & the Imperials
This Guy's in Love with You
        Herb Alpert
But You Know I Love You
        Kenny Rogers & the First Edition
Oh, What a Night!
        The Dells
The Word Before Goodbye
        Glenn Yarborough
The End of Our Road
        Gladys Knight & the Pips
Traces
        The Classics IV
The Tracks of My Tears
        Smokey Robinson & the Miracles
What Becomes of the Brokenhearted
        Jimmy Ruffin

Something Stupid
        Frank and Nancy Sinatra
Only the Strong Survive
        Jerry Butler
Hair
        The Cowsills
First of May
        The Bee Gees
Hello, Goodbye
        The Beatles
Can I Change My Mind?
        Tyrone Davis
Let's Live for Today
        The Grass Roots
Last Chance to Turn Around
        Gene Pitney
Expressway to Your Heart
        Soul Survivors
Both Sides Now
        Judy Collins
Summer Rain
        Johnny Rivers
Sure Gonna Miss Her
        Gary Lewis & the Playboys

The First Time Ever I Saw Your Face
     Roberta Flack
The Road
     Jackson Browne

22086674R00232

Made in the USA
Charleston, SC
10 September 2013